MW01004449

PILLS AND STARSHIPS

PILLS AND STARSHIPS

BY LYDIA MILLET

Published by Akashic Books
©2014 Lydia Millet

Hardcover ISBN-13: 978-1-61775-275-9
Paperback ISBN-13: 978-1-61775-276-6
Library of Congress Control Number: 2013956781

James Everett Stuart cover artwork courtesy of Spanierman Gallery LLC, New York, New York.

Black Sheep/Akashic Books
PO Box 1456
New York, NY 10009
info@akashicbooks.com
www.akashicbooks.com

More books for young readers from Black Sheep:
Game World, by C.J. Farley
Changers Book One: Drew, by T Cooper and Allison Glock-Cooper

Gray whale
Now that we are sinding you to The End
That great god
Tell him
That we who follow you invented forgiveness
And forgive nothing

. . .

When you will not see again
The whale calves trying the light
Consider what you will find in the black garden
And its court
The sea cows the Great Auks the gorillas
The irreplaceable hosts ranged countless
And fore-ordaining as stars
Our sacrifices
Join your work to theirs
Tell him
That it is we who are important

—W.S. Merwin, "For a Coming Extinction"

DAY ONE

THE BOUNTIFUL ARRIVING
Theme of the Day: Listening

There was a time, not long ago, when it was illegal to kill people. I almost remember normal life back then.

Almost. But not really. I *tell* myself that I remember it, but to be honest it's a mix of made-up and autolearned things.

I was a little kid when the last tipping point came, but part of me ignores that fact sometimes and wants to believe Back Then is my true home. So I invent the world I want to have lived in and curl up in that lost world like a mouse in a burrow. Soft edges and gentle lighting are all around me as I fall asleep, my legs and arms dropping into delicious numbness.

It's safe in the lost world and always the same. Water flows right out of the taps—the kind you can drink, I mean. There are never new bugs, and the airtox alerts are a harmless yellow, never crimson or black. There are woods and a babbling stream on the edge of a peaceful, treelined neighborhood, and I can wander there with no one stopping me.

The vanished world settles inside eternal dusk: here it's always the hour before sunset, my favorite time. On the quiet, dimming street the warmth of living rooms shines from ancient, separate houses—orangey table lamps glow from the windows with the comforting light of old-time incandescent bulbs, while outside the purple dusk deepens, insects called crickets make a chirping song, and dew springs up on velvety green lawns.

No barriers, no nets—you could just walk freely down the street, among the lovely gardens with flowers and bushes. You could step anywhere, practically. I've seen it in old movievids.

Sometimes I get to it by imagining: I set it up carefully, piece by piece, and then sail into it on a dream airship.

Or sometimes I just take the easy way to bliss, like everyone else, and get there with pharma.

Compared to that olden world, the new one's like a vision brought by one of the flatter and speedier pharms. And going back to the vanished place relaxes me, usually, but every now and then it also gives me a strange feeling of homesickness.

Strange because, like I said, that world has never in fact been my home.

I never knew it at all.

Ψ

If you're reading this, I like to think, you got out a long time ago, while the going was good. You're in the far future or in the starry reaches of space—maybe both—watching me from a safe distance. Circling the planet, say, watching over me, a living satellite.

That distance should be safe enough.

Out there the dark of airless space lies beyond the silver capsule you're floating in. Through the thick glass of a round window—I get to design this spaceship so I'm going to make it cool—I can see your face, shining with honeyed light. Because I need the picture in my head to have details, I'll throw in the fact that you're young and attractive. (Like me, or at least I like to think so.) You might be a girl or you might be a boy, I change my mind on that between imaginings.

And with you in the capsule there's even a pet. I always wanted a dog—I always *longed* to have a dog, ever since I saw vids of them from when they were legal—so I'm just going to give you one. Maybe it's Laika, the famous dog from the 20th c. who was shot into space on a rocket called *Sputnik 2*. I browsed about her a lot in a history tutorial I've watched a bunch of times ("Carbon Excesses Vol. 244: The Era of the Pet"). Sometimes I think of her intelligent eyes, about how terribly confused she must have been. Because at first her life was thousands of hours of love and attention, but then it was a sudden blastoff into the freezing cold of space.

The cold that went on forever. Because they never planned to bring her back.

Her dog heart probably broke before she died.

So I bring Laika the Space Dog back to life. I put her in that warm, safe capsule with you—you and your nice family. She deserves it and so do you.

Because of *course* you have a family. I would never make you alone out there.

The capsule is a throwback to the world and style that used to be—like one of those curve-cornered, silver homes with wheels the blue-collars lived in, back in the days of the moon missions. I love the look from back then. These days a lot of kids go retro to the 20th c. stylewise, since that's when most of the vids were made. Back then people could make a livelihood from stuff like that—their own creations. They got to make stuff that was unique, stuff people wanted but didn't need at all. *Way* past what people needed to live.

Not food or energy but words and sounds, scenes and stories. Back then people could take their inner, personal desire and make it into something outside of them, something they loved and were proud of. It was art or music or movievids, it was anything they wanted.

Seeing the swirl of blue-green planet while cut off from all communication, you cosmonauts have a kind of innocence, I guess. You're purified of the contamination of the rest of the human race, all our sadness and the chaos down here. When you read my words they fill your capsule like a song, a song surrounded by the stars and constellations, the streaming cosmic dust.

Maybe you're on your way to colonize a new planet, even, like in the olden stories and vids where alien civilizations turned out to live close by, or we went out with kits and supplies and grew jungles on Mars—lived there in pretty domes, made an oasis on the red planet. In the meantime, hovering here before you say goodbye, you're my beacon. You gaze down from a warm round of welcome in the blackness of space—the universe beyond our haze-gray sky, not cast beneath the pall of the future.

I hope that, from out there in the solar system, you'll just ignore the cheesy names of the different sections in this journal. I know any reader of mine would need to have good taste and so, like me, you won't be into them.

They're in corpspeak, not my own words.

I couldn't bring my face—that's short for "interface," in case you don't know that word—because contracts forbid all personal devices. We're just supposed to "focus on healing." Without my face I have to go old-school and use a pen.

And all I have to write in is the journal they gave us, for writing our emotions in.

They put those titles on the pages. The "Bountiful Arriving," etc. Not me.

I wouldn't be caught dead.

Ψ

It's not that olden people lived in the Garden of Eden, back in the golden times. That is, they didn't *think* they lived in it. They acted like life was hard. Or on the other hand they acted like they had so little to do that they could talk about nothing forever.

I laugh when I watch old screenshows, because half the time you can't tell which were meant to be serious and which were supposed to be funny.

To me the old world looks like paradise. My parents

used to tell me stories of where they grew up, and no, it wasn't perfect, bad things could happen if you had bad luck, but for a lot of people their problems were small in the background. Their problems weren't chaos pouring down, just regular-size problems you could work around. Problems that were more or less the size of a person.

As far as I can tell from the tutorials—we have to log a *lot* of hours on faceschool till we turn eighteen and get our work matches—the human race has always been trouble. We've never been happy with what we had. I've done some browsing in Ancient Myths tutorials and it seems to me we've been like Icarus, that Greek dude with the glued-on wings who flew up toward the sun. The wax on his wings melted—wax acting like glue, I guess—so he plunged to his death.

Or maybe we're more like his father, who made the wings for him in the first place. Who puts their kid in a set of waxed-on wings and sends them flying over the sea? That dad was practically a child molest.

Point is, the two of them had orchards to stroll around in—a blue ocean, green fields, and rolling farmlands. I saw a painting about it: a ship with white sails, a hillside overlooking a harbor, and in the background, so you could hardly notice him, Icarus plunging into the ocean. The wings were gone by then, completely melted off, vanished. All you could see were his legs, sticking out of the water foolishly.

Those farms and fields seem like a vast landscape to me, next to, for instance, the complex where my family lived. But those two guys probably didn't think so. They wanted to conquer the heavens.

That's how it was back then—once, in the past, we thought bigger was better. As far as I can tell, that was our main idea. More, bigger, higher. Of course the tutorials don't put it that way. They're mostly corpspeak about "our human achievements" in "America the Beautiful" over grainy old vids of national parks with pine trees and large brown animals, all furry. Every kid has to take that class. It's called "One Great Nation."

There are vids of herds moving across tall-grass prairies and tree branches with birds flitting about in them; cities of sparkling glass, white buildings with columns. Those sites tell all about how big we were, how high we flew, but not so much what it did to us. (Wax melting. Body plunging. Legs kicking in the air during a drowning activity.) In fact they talk like the system collapse was kind of a tragic accident, like a random asteroid strike.

To see anything but corpspeak veneer you have to look past the pop-up ads and chirpy theme songs; you have to fish around on rogue sites. It's not hard, really, because even though the corps shut them down as fast as they can, new rogue sites keep popping up, and there's lots of juicy stuff on them.

I browse the rogues now and then, but my little brother Sam does it constantly. He knows the hidden places to get to, how to find out corp secrets, even. He's a hackerkid. And while I fish around too from time to time—in the traces of the world's *true* history, where I can see pieces of beauty and sadness in old pictures like Icarus and spectacular olden music—I'm not into codes and puzzles like Sam is. I'm more into beautiful stuff, the history of what we've made, how we wanted to think of ourselves and of the world.

And when I fish around in that history—the shredded patchwork I can make of it, with holes big enough to see through—I find out things. It's started to seem to me like there were moments and places—sometimes in little villages in the mountains with snow on their peaks or sunlit river valleys; sometimes in those clumps of skyscrapers that held ten million people at a time—when some of our ancestors had peace and were happy.

There were moments.

Ψ

We still have laws. It's not chaos in the parts Sam and I know. You get a glimpse of the disorder sometimes, even of a kind of split-second panic, but it's almost like a technical glitch—like a video feed that freezes for just a moment and then moves normally again.

Where my family has lived there's still the rule of law, we have our regular routines. Not far away the cliffs are falling into the sea and the last carbon-sequest forests are turning brown because some beetles from another continent are eating them. Closer to home people are lining up for medicines to cure bugs brought by the new mosquitoes.

All types of mosquitoes and flies have recently moved in from Africa and other continents, following the warmer air and changing conditions. They brought some gifts with them: malaria, dengue fever, yellow fever, West Nile. The flies brought a human strain of parvo, sleeping sickness, the filoviruses they never used to be vectors for. There are vaccines for some of it, but plenty of days, if you're going outside the complex, you have to wear netsuits.

Anyway, in our building there were still burn-free barbeques once a month—the neighbors were up to date on their vaccines and had the codes to prove it. So we would meet new people every now and then, meet them in flesh, not over the bands. We'd meet them on the roof garden or ground-level terraces, or sometimes, when air or bug warnings rolled in on the same day a realmeet was happening, in one of the lobbies, with wallscreen scenes pretending we were all outside. They'd throw up views of the cityscape that tried to replicate the vistas from the roof garden.

That always had a pathetic feel to it and Sam and I always wished they'd just do something else with the screens—we'd rather have had fairylands, animé. Even still photos or old-fashioned movievids. Hell, we'd rather have had just actual, you know, *walls*. It's better to either (1) do nothing, or (2) full-on pretend, than try to imitate something that's already halfway lame in the first place.

Frankly the real views aren't that great.

Sam's a sleuth and a sneak. He likes to look through spyholes; he has a thirst for knowledge and the patience to slake that thirst. Sam looks through spyholes on the face and he sees pieces of the hidden rest of the world. Sometimes it's numbers he's downloading, sometimes it's vids, sometimes it's GIS data.

Once I came up behind him when he was watching a live feed of a complex not far from ours where someone had come up contagious. Sam knew another kid there and the kid had some kind of spycam set up; we watched a scene where corporates came teeming into a condo, zipped up the kid's father, and hustled him away.

I see pieces too, but like I said before, I don't have Sam's craving for facts. What I crave, after a long day, what I look for when I'm browsing, is one beautiful thing. I'm like the small gray fish we used to have, the last legal pet in our building. I bury my nose in gravel, hoping to find a nugget to sustain me. It can be a minuscule nugget, as long as it's pleasing. A flash, a spark. Something to fix on and admire.

When I find one of these things, I add it to my collection.

But Sam reminds me more of that little gray fish during the times when it *wasn't* looking for food. The rest of the time it was just desperate to escape the tank, swimming at the corner edge of the aquarium, its tail and fins constantly fluttering quickly like it was trying to get out. Back and forth, back and forth, corner to corner, from the filter to the air pump, from the fake plant to the fake rock, then up the corner seam and down again.

It's Sam, in our family, who's the rebel. My parents were also rebels once, back in the day—treehugs, at least. They got thrown in jail for saying their opinions about keeping nature around. Not crimes, exactly, but free speech shit—protests about loving animals, chaining themselves to oil derricks to stop drilling, that kind of stuff. My mother lost three fingers that way. On one of her hands she only has a thumb and forefinger, but she can get along fine with them, hold stuff and type, most things she needs to do. The other fingers got in the way of a saw, when she and my dad were treehugging.

She doesn't like to go into detail. My father was with her, and other people too, and she was lucky in the end—they got to a clinic before she lost too much blood.

But they had to leave the fingers behind, Dad says.

That was before I was born. For the past sixteen years, they've been regular parents making a living and taking care of us. My mother's the practical one, my dad's dreamy and has a head full of facts and old memorized quotations. Of the four of us, it's Sam who gets mad at the world these days. Don't get me wrong—it's not that I think things are golden. It's just that, if there's an angry gene, I don't think I inherited it.

Ψ

I don't know how much of a history lesson to give; it depends on when your spaceship blasted off, right?

Sam's hacked some corporate sites and he says it went down like so: The service corporations started as spinoffs from even bigger corps. They got their services made legal

19

bit by bit, because those parent corps were megapowerful. Like there would be a major law passed to help farmers grow food, say, and then a government guy who was paid by a service corp would tack on some fine print saying that some action the corps wanted to do would just be legal from then on.

And when it got more out in the open, they started running ads saying how we needed the service because life spans are so long and old people suffer from terrible sadness. Those ads had powerful music written by famous musicians and were what my mom calls tearjerkers. Eventually it seemed most people figured the service must be a medical mercy. I guess it gradually turned normal.

Nowadays service corps, along with the energy and food and water corps, are either instead of government or just run it themselves. We still have democracy, I mean we pick from corporate leaders whose pics and styles and soundbites post on face. It's voting made easy because you choose the brand that fits you best. You can see vids of the different choices playing with their virtual pets, talking to friends and family. And you can link to a list of leaders' general opinions at the end—stuff like what models they prefer, whether they have a godbelief and if so what it is.

If you look really hard you find the boring stuff, like whether Plan A or Plan B is a better way to spend the corps' money, or whether X or Y should be allowed. Most people are more interested in the homepages though, the look of their wives or hubbies, the musicvids that go with them.

Anyway, the service corps' products get fancier all the time. There are whole catalogs of options you can order in face shops now: personal or couple contracts, home or away, urban or country, private or open, basic or luxury. Each of those categories has hundreds, maybe thousands of different opportunities.

This might sound pretty weird to you, floating above the stratosphere. Like, number one, why do so many people pay serious money to have themselves made dead? And number two, even if beaucoups of them want to die, why don't they just go DIY?

Re: number one, I don't totally get it either. But then I'm young. No one who's sixteen wants to buy a contract or is allowed to—not where I live, anyway. We still have our emo types and cutters and all that, but they do most of it on face. It's style gestures, not actual flesh-injuring. Poses are serious but they're still poses. Young people don't have as many mood problems as older people do, is how the corporates explain the deal to us. I don't know why, exactly, except this is the world we were born into so it's what we've always known. I mean, we're not completely overjoyed or anything, you won't see us leaping up in jubilation constantly at the chaos reports we see on face or even the quieter scene through our windows. I'd say we go from glum to bitchy to outright hostile, on the whole attitude spectrum.

But still, compared to the older ones we're cheerful, so in some ways we must be used to it.

The old people get sad because the world's falling apart,

the world they used to know, and it turns out they loved that world, they loved it more than they ever knew until it was way too late. So now they miss all the parts of it that are going or gone; they miss those parts of the world the way you'd miss a limb or a major organ. Like me they have their soft green lawns and treelined neighborhoods to think of when they want to escape and dream, but for them those neighborhoods were real when they were young.

And now they're only memories.

I should mention, I learned from 20th c. stories and vids that "old" used to mean in your sixties or seventies, for humans. Well, that's like middle-aged now. Due to the GE that boosted immune systems against cancer and heart trouble in the mid 21st c., people who live in the comfort zones make it to a hundred and ten easily. If they choose to.

I hope that answers number one. Re: number two, I hear it's not that simple to off yourself if you're not naturally gifted in that department. I wouldn't know, I've never tried, but I know a kid on face whose parents did. It didn't work out that well. Most older folks who go the DIY route are singles, not people with families, because it's harder on survivors with no official support. People like to be able to depend on a system that's there outside of them, with set rules and schedules and convenience.

Back in the days when death was unmanaged, before the sunset pharms, people already had plenty of death businesses, from what I've read on corp facesites. Even Sam says it's true. It's not like people keeled over and just lay there where they fell.

People need organized ways of dealing with hard things. Therefore, service contracts.

Of course, you can't take out a contract on someone else. That'd be murder. You can only buy a contract on yourself. It made me feel queasy when I found out how death works. Even though I wasn't born in free death times—free death is what Sam and the other hackerkids call it, instead of "unmanaged"—I think about it now and almost feel like making it part of my old-world dreams. I mean as soon as I was old enough to understand that people die, I knew it was managed by the corps. It wasn't surprising, but I did enough browsing to know it wasn't the way things had been down through human history.

That made me feel a little off-kilter, when I didn't push away the thought of it.

Though newsflash, legal killing isn't exactly a recent invention. In old-time wars millions of people were killed and plenty of them never picked up a weapon in their whole life or wanted to hurt anyone.

Ψ

Sam claims the corporates are still out there making war. He says they just don't tell us anymore, since they bought all the news outlets, and that you have to hack around to find out about it. Maybe he's right, or maybe he's paranoid. With Sam it's hard to tell sometimes.

My point is, though: as far as I can tell, the corps are nothing new under the sun. They're just a more obvious form of an old machine, bigger and shinier and with tons of information. They don't have to hide; they run their business in plain sight.

Once we saw a car accident that was apparently a contract—or Sam said it was, at least. We were walking along the street to the vaccine update clinic, we hadn't been out of the complex for nine weeks so we felt like even going two blocks outside the complex gate was an expedition to the Gobi Desert. We were laughing and goofing off and not paying enough attention and then the crash happened, from one second to the next, making us scream and jump back against a building in a rush of fear and adrenalin.

It looked like an accident, but really it was a contract. You could tell, Sam said, because one vehicle was a car, a heavy vintage polluting thing that only the megarich and corps could ever hope to afford, with gigantic carbon fines. And the service guy driving the ancient car—which sped up out of nowhere and rammed a bamboo e-buggy into a concrete wall so that it instantly splintered into a pile of sticks—was wearing bulky protective headgear.

Sam and I wrote about in on face for months, because you hardly ever see that stuff. We got thousands of hits from other kids when we reported the crash. Because a scene like that is super rare.

So when I say the corps operate in plain sight I mean it's the same as with most other businesses—you see the results more often than what went into them. With electricity you see the light come on, not the brooding nuclear plant that squats outside the city in some no-man's-land. If you're rich, and get to eat animal protein, you see thin cold cuts on your plate, not the tubes full of bloody in vitro meat masses at the tissue farms.

Ψ

So my family has come to Hawaii.

Hawaii, like an aging fashionista, is almost as gorgeous as in the olden pics—just in a more fragile, wasted way.

My parents had been here long ago; they came here on their honeymoon more than fifty years back. They bought a hotel and airplane package to Oahu and they loved it. They went scuba diving in the coral reefs and touched real rays and even one dolphin, they said. They took surfing lessons and my father broke his wrist. (But, he told me, it was worth it.)

Of course scuba and surfing aren't options anymore, but we're going to snorkel in polymer reefs stocked with colorful farmed parrot fish and now and then a robot shark. I've seen the vids. I love the parrotfish's bulgy, fat lips.

Back on their honeymoon they ate at restaurants with views of sparkling turquoise bays, they went to luaus and drank fancy drinks with tiny umbrellas made of pulped-up trees. (We still have two of the umbrellas; they're a faded pink and a faded green and have my parents' names printed on them, from a honeymoon party that was held for them. *Robert & Sara,* says the ancient writing, *Hawaii.*) They took small trips to the other islands, even the one that used to be a leper colony.

These days Honolulu and most of Oahu is seawall and salty aquifers and long blocks of abandoned buildings, so the overall feel isn't too festive.

But even so, they still wanted Hawaii. They were both nostalgic. So we came to the Big Island, where we're staying in a hotel with a view of Mauna Kea. I've seen pictures of it from way back when, white at the top and majestic. Well, there's never snow anymore, even at 14,000 feet; snow's legendary now. (I collect pictures of it and even have a 20th c. snow globe I shake sometimes to fall asleep. I brought it with me, along with my other most precious collected items. It's from Japan, snow falling on pink-blooming cherry trees.)

Even without snow, though, the volcano's pretty cool.

It's just the four of us, my mother and my father, Sam and me, the four of us here for our last week.

A week is the period the corps outline, once you pick your dates. I tried to browse on why it's a week, but I couldn't find much; Sam says it's just about control. He claims that when it's longer than a week contract buyers get morbid or even, if they decide to refuse their pharms, hysterical, and then the whole thing collapses.

If it's shorter than a week there's not enough time for goodbyes—at least that's the official line, he says.

My parents aren't that old. My mother's only in her eighties—she had me around the average time back then, in her sixties, and two years later she had Sam—and my father's in his nineties. And though they're pretty healthy physically, they're tired of being sad and they've decided that they're done.

So it's our last week with the four of us together.

Ψ

It would be way harder without the training we did at home, without the pharma regimen they have us on. Even with those tools it's still intense and everything seems to vibrate with meaning. Be cursed with meaning, almost. Meaning's attached to everyday objects—combs, swimsuits, dangling earrings. I'll find my mother's earrings, say, lying on the counter, and I'll pick them up and stare at them—small crescent moons—and that'll make me think how my mother will never see a crescent moon again, because right now the moon is almost full.

I'll stand there looking at jewelry, thinking, *Never again a crescent moon. She'll never look up at that again.*

It's not exactly *meaning*, I guess, since I don't know what the meaning would be. It's more like associations—small things pointing to bigger ones.

Or, uh, *one* bigger one. That being death.

A/k/a Happiness.

Here in the hotel suite, I see these normal items and they're not trivial anymore. A toothbrush looks like it *portends the end.*

This is only the first day and already we're on the brink of tears sometimes, or at least I am and my father is. My mother and Sam are generally acting stoic, though now and then I catch one of their hands or bottom lips trembling. Meanwhile the edges of objects glow, blur, and fade as I look at them. I don't know if that's a pharma effect. Sam and I aren't even on a solid diet of moodpharms yet.

Day Four, I see when I consult the schedule, we have the option of a powerful tranquilizing blend because that's our Goodbye Day.

Day Five is Happiness, but you always do goodbyes the day before, while memory's still intact. The pharma that makes you so happy to go—the diet my parents have already started on, which doesn't build up to a critical mass in your system till Day Five—causes forgetfulness, a particular kind of long-term memory loss that wipes the memories associated with trauma.

Which these days, for old people, is most of them.

So goodbyes are slated for Day Four, the day before the major memory loss happens.

Now I look around my bedroom, in the suite, and I see fresh flowers in too many colors. Cut flowers are almost never real because the crop's so water-intensive, the carbon footprint's through the roof, but these ones are actual plants with cut-off stems and that's such a crazy luxury it seems wrong. Plus the fact that the stems have been cut off means they've only got a few days. The metaphor's creepily perfect. The flowers are in a brief limbo, already doomed but having the appearance of life. Like olden-time dead people, made up like dolls and then displayed in long boxes.

I see chocolates on end tables and when I slide open the thick panel door of the food unit there's pharmawine chilling. All primo luxury items, most of which I've browsed about but never seen before.

And of course there are these flowery bamboo write-fiber journals they gave us, one in each of our Coping Kits, where we're supposed to jot down emotions.

They want us to unload, download, offload, we're supposed to use these notebooks like garbage cans for our feelings, suddenly drop the feelings like they're a pair of dirty pants.

Leaving ourselves looking like naked idiots.

I found it hard to write longhand just a couple of hours ago, since most of my life I've typed. But I'm getting used to it: I even kind of like it, because the feeling of forming words with a pen is cool and weird.

Each day has a preprinted title and a cute little theme that follows the schedule. It's manipulative and pathetic, as though we're not so smart. But they're going to make us take Personal Time every day—alone time without media or face, of course, because they're *verboten*—so I figure I might as well use it.

The flowers are dazzling my eyes as I write this—they're deep throats, they're wounds, they're pandemonium. The purple and red and orange hues of their petals are jangly and overwhelming. I wonder if maybe they don't tell us all the pharms we're taking. It could be that our vitamins are loaded; maybe there are moodpharms in our drinks or food. Sam says the "potential delivery vehicles are multifold." The same corporates own food and pharmafranchises, of course.

Whether I'm seeing with my own mind or through the drugs, either way, the tropical flowers are too much and I wish for the simplicity of fake daisies.

They warned us to prepare for heightening effects—
for the "charged, hypersensitive nature of the parting
experience," as the brochure reads—but still.

Ψ

Right now it's early afternoon. My parents and Sam have
gone out for a walk and from the balcony of our suite I can
see them strolling, their light clothes flapping in the breeze
off the ocean, along a trail above the high, jagged bluffs.

They carry parasols, which protect them from the sun
but also hide their heads from me.

So I guess they could be anyone.

The bluffs were well engineered and have been planted
to look like nature, in a fake garden way. There are scrubby
bushes from the desert, "Peruvian paperthorn cactus" and
"Chinese beach roses" (according to the brochure) and
even, now and then, dune grasses and crests of sand. They
hide the concrete seawall beneath the artificial bluffs so
that you don't have to remember where you are or when—
so that you can almost forget you're not in Old Hawaii.

Forget, in other words, that you're living at the very
tip of the tail end of the fire-breathing dragon of human
history.

Some people forget that all the time, I guess, and some
people say they welcome it. They're called Hot Earthers—
officially called the Hot Earth Society—a group of strict
godbelievers who claim it's all fine, it's how things were
always supposed to end, and chaos is a God message. (I

guess the message is, *I told you so*.) They don't believe in using face and aren't allowed to read anything but the end of the Christian holy book.

Other people try to act matter-of-fact and scientific about it all—like my parents—and so, to help control the chaos, we have models.

People choose what model to believe in and they move according to what, at any given time, the model's trajectories are predicting.

In media the models are sold to the public by nonscientists, as the scientists call them. To scientists that's the worst thing you can be. To a scientist, "nonscientist" is like a swear word.

Scientists stream live on face and say the nonscientists are irresponsible, they're murderers and demagogues. But that doesn't stop the nonscientists from saying what they say, from signing contracts with location corporates and flogging whatever model they want to. Model ad placement is all over the place. The nonscientists are usually actors or musicians, politicians or motivational speakers or godbelief figureheads—celebrities who hawk a model either for money or, every now and then, because they truly believe in it.

"Move to the Poconos! Rolling green hills of the future," one of the famous Wiithletes will say, with an autumn landscape behind him. Maybe he'll smile, swing his remote. "I'm making my whole-life home in wholesome Wisconsin," an actress will croon, all got up in some weird ancient costume with braids in her hair and nonexistent, fully illegal white-and-black cows munching dumbly on flowers in the background.

It's confusing because not all the scientists are honest. A lot of them work for corporates and are only pretending to be unbiased; the best ones work for universities, but those can be bought and paid for too sometimes, so that their scientists pimp a certain model. The average person doesn't know the difference between the independent scientists and this other kind. Montana is the number-one location right now, one university might say, following the money: Montana is where the data shows "optimal livability." But then another university might say to avoid Montana at all costs, head up to Michigan. Go live with the Finns and Swedes on Michigan's Upper P.

Models, like service corps, are everywhere.

I get so sick of the barrage of models. For that one part of our Final Week—getting away from them—I'm actually grateful.

Ψ

So technically it's a week, not counting the long boat trip here and back of course, but for my parents it's only five days. My brother and I, as survivors, have two days for recovery.

No one pretends that that's enough. The service corp language isn't crude, they're far too slick for that. But Jean said it's the policy: those two days are the minimum needed before reentry. You grieve in your own way after that, she said, *at your own pace of sadness-expressing.*

There's grief guidance at home if you buy a luxury package, but we have a midprice, not a luxury. My parents spent the money that would have gone to service for the luxury deal on practical benefits. They bought vaccine packages for us that stretch out five more years, medic coupons, water prepaids, that kind of lifesaving tech and supplies. My parents' contract has Hawaii and this fancy hotel and one or two daytrips, but all the rest of the money they had budgeted went to cover the travel permit and the ship we took from Seattle.

Our contract's not lux, but it's a few steps up from Vacation Basic.

The corp that my parents chose likes to boast how it hires locals, down to the complex where the contractor lives. Of course its parent corp is huge; it's more a style choice than a structural difference. I mean, no corporates are exactly mom-'n'-pop boutiques.

So our rep, when it came down to it, was a lady my mother had once played smallgolf with.

My mother isn't the sporty type, by the way. Just this one time she did a game for charity—smallgolf's a game they used to play on grass, on huge hills that went on forever, so big they had to ride around them in buggies. Now the courses are set up in rec rooms of complexes with green carpets.

Anyway, because my mother had a good sense of humor, at least till recently, she was basically the comic relief, I think. And that one day of smallgolfing was where she first met Jean, the service rep.

Jean had a low-key way about her. She showed up at our condo a couple of months ago, in the comfortable hour before dinnertime when we usually hang out together and talk about our day, what feeds we've seen and friends we've made on face. The four of us were drinking cocktails in the living room. Being fourteen Sam wasn't drinking intoxicants much yet, but my mother, in a celebratory gesture we didn't understand then, had offered him a mini pharmabeer.

And there was Jean at the door—a compact, middle-aged woman from the tenth floor, frosted hair, braided wedge heels. I'd seen her in the elevator once or twice but I never knew she was a family acquaintance.

"This is Jean," said my mother softly. "Jean, these are our children, Nat and Sam."

Oh yeah, spacefriend: my name is Natalie, but I go by Nat. I should have introduced myself before.

The woman smiled and sat down and looked at us with a friendly but businesslike expression. "Your parents thought it might be good to have me here," is how she started in.

Sam glanced up. He had been reading off his handface. He looked stricken, I noticed immediately. "You're service," he said flatly.

"I *do* work with a service company," said Jean, smiling again. (They call themselves "companies," not "corps," because it's more positive sounding.) Jean didn't miss a beat and didn't seem awkward; she had a forthright attitude, without being domineering.

"You're the counselor, or whatever they call them," said Sam.

"I'm coordinating the personal aspect of outreach," conceded Jean.

"On the contract we purchased recently," added my mother, softer-voiced than usual. "Mine and your father's."

Sam picked up his beer and drank the rest of it down quickly, a flush rising on his skin.

I had been sitting at the bay window, looking out over the garden. Our complex was nice, with trees and water features and squirrels in the courtyard—no, wait, they're not squirrels but rather little striped chipmunks, because chipmunks always poll higher.

Squirrels = vermin. Chipmunks = cute.

I liked to drink and take in the view. It was usually just as relaxing as it was meant to be.

But now, without really noticing my own movement, I had turned so I was facing into the room, my back against the view of the trees. Even the next instant I didn't remember swiveling. In the pit of my stomach was a heavy new stone. And at the same time my arms and legs felt light and liquid, like the bones in them had weakened.

"Why didn't you tell me?" was the thing I said, obviously stupid.

"We're telling you now, sweetheart," replied my mother, and came to sit beside me on the ledge. She put one arm around my shoulder—her left arm with the two-finger hand. She calls it her claw sometimes.

I've never been grossed out by it, but on the couple of

occasions when I've introduced other kids to her in flesh, I've seen them do a double-take and try to hide their pukiness. After the second time that happened I made sure I warned them so they could plan their smooth reaction. Their being disgusted made me feel bad for my mom—though she *herself* always seems pretty cool about people's reactions.

My father says it's a badge of honor to her, "and so it should be," he adds.

"I know it's difficult to hear," my mother said. "But it's all according to schedule. The timing is what they recommend."

They don't encourage the parents to get emotive when they're disclosing. (Sam and I had heard about the protocols on listserves and from facefriends as well—facefriends whose parents have been contracts in the past. It makes things worse for the kids, the corps say, if parents get feely at that moment.) And sure enough I noticed she wasn't applying a squeeze of consoling pressure with her arm; she wasn't looking deep into my eyes. She was being careful, walking a tightrope of proper behavior.

Corps always stress to contract buyers that following the rules is what allows survivors to emerge with psych intact. They even have ads like that: *Let your survivors thrive* . . . I can't recall the rest of it, but basically the message is, *Do what the service tells you to, or we'll make you feel hella guilty.*

My mother was just sitting there next to me, her arm lightly applied, keeping a quasi-professional attitude that seemed to mirror Jean's. After a moment she shook the cooling cubes in her cup with her other hand and raised the cup to drink.

I looked at her then and I couldn't help thinking she was only half there.

My father, standing gazing at us with his pharmawine in hand, had a kind, bemused expression that reminded me of how he'd looked when we were younger, when Sam or I would cry and he had no idea how to stop it.

"You can still take it back," said Sam, with a kind of hurt urgency. "Please, Mom—Dad! Take it back!"

"Honey," said my mother, "we don't *want* to. Or maybe a better way to say it is that we . . . we can't. We've lived for you two ever since the tipping point, sweetheart. You've been everything that kept us going. We try to hide the side of us that feels so desp . . . that feels it's time to go. But we can't live with it forever."

The tipping point was when it got out that the globe was in this runaway warming cycle with these feedback loops of heat and there was nothing we could do to stop the sea from rising or get back the melted ice that used to cover the top and the bottom of the world.

So anyhow.

"Now both of you are practically grown up," said my mother. "Nat's so mature for her age. Sam, you are too. You're both very intelligent, you're both *so* much more capable than we are *already!*"

Under normal conditions we would have snarked at that, but it wasn't normal conditions.

"We know that when it comes right down to it you don't

really need us—not in the day-to-day sense. You *think* you do right now. But we know deep down that you can take care of yourselves. We trust you. At first you'll miss us and that's perfectly natural. It'll be tough. We understand. But then you'll pull yourselves out of that mourning process and be stronger than ever. We know you will."

"You can't say what we're feeling," said Sam, shaking his head. "Or *will* feel when you're dead. Sorry."

"It helps, for peace of mind," said Jean to Sam, "if you keep any argumentation for later. During this encounter, this time of disclosure, we've found that what allows for peacefulness is a *listening*."

"Fuck listening!" said Sam. He was bright red by then—like someone had dealt him two slaps, one on each cheek.

"And really," went on Jean calmly, as though he hadn't said anything, "there's no rush here. There's plenty of time. Remember, all contracts are voidable right up until the end. So there's absolutely nothing to make you nervous."

She didn't mention what we all knew: that there's a stiff financial penalty for last-minute cancellations. She didn't *need* to mention it. My parents had a friend who canceled just five hours before, paid through the nose because at that point it was like 90 percent of the full price, then ended up buying a new contract a couple of months later. Meaning less money for the survivors—a tainted legacy.

Also, embarrassing.

It happens.

"But you're doing so *well*," begged Sam, turning to my mother.

Myself, I felt frozen.

"You're doing really well, you've got your moods well stabilized, lately," he argued, in a firmer tone.

"No, yeah, son," said my father. "Well . . . we're not too badly off. We're not complaining about our, you know, our *personal* situation. Relative to . . . we feel so lucky. Look, in terms of our particular, individual lives, we *are* lucky. No question there, no question there at all. And you know— there's no specific event catalyst here. But we agreed . . ."

"We made an agreement that we would go when you two were ready," put in my mother. "And we feel that time has come."

"We made an agreement," my father echoed.

Sam was staring at him stonily and my father looked like that stare was making him nervous—and I guess it was.

"We need to quit while we're still ahead—leave while you can remember us the way we *want* to be remembered. With our real personalities. You saw how Mamie got after she passed a hundred. We need to leave when we can do it right."

There was a minute of silence, because although we'd seen my grandmother stop making sense we knew it wasn't about her. For starters, they were both more than twenty years younger than Mamie had been and nowhere near the demented zone.

"Quit while you're still *ahead?*" I asked.

I didn't know whether to call bullshit on him. What stopped me was a sudden suspicion he really believed what he was saying.

"Darlings," added my mother, "you were born so *recently*—it's only been the blink of an eye. You're great at just living in the now, you roll with everything. You have resilience. Both of us admire you for it. We so *admire* that quality. We wish we were that way ourselves. But we're not."

"Oh, *please*," countered Sam.

"Try to see it from our point of view!" said my father. "When we were young, there were still big animals swimming all over the oceans! The rivers and the forests had all this life in them, not just the rats and pigeons. They barely cared about carbon footprints then, they were still trying to grow bigger and bigger instead of downsize. You could go anywhere in the world—we drove a gas-burning car when we were young! We flew on real airplanes! Sara—our honeymoon flight emitted *two hundred tons* of CO_2, didn't it, honey?"

"It did," nodded our mother, musing. "For maybe three hundred passengers. A five-hour flight, children! Insane to think about now."

"The only people who agitated were treehugs like us, and everyone ignored us. And even though both of us *were* treehugs, we still flew. I mean, it was the opposite of illegal—it was *encouraged*. There were desserts made out of ice. And cities lasted for *centuries*."

"We know this already, Dad," said Sam. "It's ancient history."

"But it wasn't the luxuries we had," continued my mother, clearing her throat. "We couldn't care *less* about those. What we miss was the feeling that we were supposed to *be* here. When this world was truly our home we didn't have to keep changing gated communities every couple of years just for access to high-rated drinking water that didn't have to be tested daily. Can you believe, we used to use drinking water to wash away our personal *waste*? We didn't *have* to stand in lines whenever an alert came out to wait for nearly useless shots that would maybe possibly keep our children alive through the newest strain of a bug-borne disease. We could choose our own food, not have it rationed out and delivered. Look—we could go out on the street whenever we felt like it. We'd meet new people whenever we wanted!"

We'd heard it all before, frankly. My parents keep thinking, somehow, that one day we'll hear about how different history was and for the first time light will shine down like godrays from up there in the cumulus and we'll get it.

But we're like, there's nothing *to* understand. I mean, yeah, it's different now from how it used to be. We know that. Isn't that pretty much the *definition* of history? We *do* get it. Time passes. A bunch of stuff changes. I bet it's always been that way, with parents lecturing kids about the olden and golden.

Sometimes we get restless about our parents being stick-in-the-muds. In one sense it's like, get used to it! This is the *actual world!*

I used to feel that way fully: impatient with them for whining about past excellence. But recently, I have to admit, I'm not quite so sure anymore. Sometimes I feel unsteady on my feet all of a sudden—mostly when I get a peek at something disturbing on face.

In flesh we don't get much of a chance at being shocked, or not often. Mostly, Sam says and I agree, that's just because we can't get out of the complex much.

"For old world people like us, you know," said my mother in a realer tone, "it's like we're watching a tragedy. You see? The play was long and really painful to watch, and it stretched across the entire horizon. But finally it ended and now we want to leave our seats. We're desperate to leave our seats! We're aching from watching this!" She was getting agitated and I watched her stop it and bring her expression under control again. "But the actors just keep taking bows, again and again . . ."

"Damn those actors," said my father, and he and my mother suddenly smiled at each other, two smiles of sympathy that vanished quickly when they seemed to remember what was going on.

"What's a play?" asked Sam, with slight and grudging interest.

He doesn't go in for 20th c. vids the way I do. There are plenty of plays to browse, I've found old performances called *Shakespeared* or *Broadsway*. I watched one once. Plays were like movievids, but for the mentally challenged and also deaf people: their actors spoke very, very slowly, pronouncing their words extremely loud and exaggerated.

"So, uh, then *we're* the ones taking too many bows?" I interrupted. "That you don't want to watch anymore?"

"I didn't actually mean that, sweetie," said my mother. "Bad simile, I admit. You have kept us here because we *want* to be with you. And we still do. We'd stay with the two of you forever, if we could. But . . ." She looked queasy all of a sudden and turned away for a second.

"Our point is," my father said, "we don't think we can bear to observe—what happens if the trajectory—if it keeps going how we think it will. Of course, we hope and pray it won't," he added, tossing back the last of his whiskey.

"We hope we're in the wrong. We hope our model is deeply flawed," my mother nodded.

Their model is one of the most popular, mainstream ones. It's kind of on the pessimistic side of average, maybe, but not far from the middle. Its macropredict is a global population crash a few decades from now, then disintegration of the species into small, isolated outposts in clusters around the last freshwater aquifers in temperate zones, surviving hand to mouth.

I'll be in my sixties.

"We figure, go early, while everything's—while there's still hope, you know," said my father. "For you . . . and . . ."

But somehow he had confused himself.

He looked for a place to put down his empty tumbler, rotating as he held it out, as though there should be a table beside him. But there was nothing, so he strode backward toward the counter that divided the living room from the kitchen.

What they weren't saying, but obviously were, was they

couldn't stand to see *our* future. They could stand their own misery but not the prospect of us biting the dust too.

It's widespread. Along with the carbon footprint of new humans, it's why there are no babies anymore.

But most people don't talk about it.

"Your model is pure fantasy," said Sam.

Sam doesn't have a model. When it comes to models, he's an atheist. I'm more like agnostic.

"Let's all be kind, shall we?" said Jean, more purring than rebuking.

"Honey," said my mother to Sam, "don't be angry. Or," and she shot a look at Jean here like she was doing something she'd been taught to do—"I mean, I know it's hard, and I understand your anger, I really do, honey. But please *try* to understand our needs as well. We've been thinking about this for years. You are the *only* things that kept us here. I promise you, Sammy, we don't take it lightly. It's very painful for us too."

"It's never an easy decision," put in Jean.

Not too helpful, I thought.

But then, they put the counselors there partly to deflect family members' fear, rage, and resentment from the contract buyers. Once you see it, it's transparent.

"Your mother has always taken care of things, Sam," said my father, in profile. He was fiddling with a pile of black olives on a tray. The olives were stacked in a pyramid, like in a picture I'd once seen of ancient cannonballs. They should have been a tipoff that this was a special occasion, so to speak, because they're not the kind of food we get every day. Yet I hadn't even noticed them till now.

My dad poked at the top olive with a red-flagged toothpick. He didn't seem to have an appetite.

"She's worked hard to keep you kids safe and healthy," he went on. "But she's so *tired*. Bone-tired. We both are, if I'm perfectly honest. Not in our bodies, in our minds. We don't want to go downhill mood-wise and then have you always remember us that way. But it's what will happen. If we don't just get out soon."

We sat there for a while, not knowing what to say— nothing to say at all. We had objections but it felt like there was something large and breakable in the room.

Eventually Jean suggested we take a walk outside, through the courtyards of the complex. Walks are quite popular with the service corps. *Low-cost momentum and a natural mood boost!* The corps believe in forward motion; they don't approve of standing still.

So we prepared ourselves fresh drinks, mostly in awkward silence, and took them with us into the elevator. Sam stood next to me, behind our parents and behind Jean, hunched and pale with his back to them. We gazed outside as the car descended.

The elevators in our complex are external and made of shaded plexi (salvage from an olden shopping center, my mother says) so you can see the sky and then the buildings below it and then, as you drop, the changing levels of the courtyard gardens. Above the tops of the trees swoop hills and valleys of Invisinet, a mesh you can't see till you're up close to it. It used to be used in zoo exhibits, when those existed in the flesh as well as on face. Now it keeps the approved wildlife in and banned wildlife out.

The management doesn't want random unknown starlings or doves—they could have parasites, could bring in one of the flus or malarial spinoffs, migrating just like people do, with the heat waves and microclimates and changing ecologies.

There are also, in these courtyard gardens, more exotic birds, beyond the sparrows and pigeons: some peacocks and peahens, a moody emu, a bevy of fat quail. The groundskeepers bring in new animals now and then to mix it up a little. They're my favorite part of where we live, and I go out for my sun time to the maximum allowed because I love to follow them around whenever I spot them.

After a couple of floors with a sky view you drop into the canopy, the trees opening themselves to you with their complex curving architecture and green hollows. There are squirrel nests there—or sorry, chipmunk nests—and elaborate, well-populated birdhouses, even the odd raccoon. Sam claims he saw a porcupine once that sat right on a branch, huddled like a spiky ball. Looking too wide to balance there.

Down through the green canopy, down along the tree trunks, and finally we landed facing the landscaped rock gardens, the fountains and splashing waterfalls of perfectly reclaimed sewage. At ground level the courtyard suffers from a minor mouse problem, and stepping off the elevator onto the patio we saw little beige mice skitter away from our feet.

They sneak in for the birdseed.

"What a nice evening," said my mother, and we looked up dutifully at the fading bands of red and yellow in the western sky.

One thing we do have, in the new world, is beautiful sunsets.

Ψ

They're on their way back from the cliffwalk now. I see them coming up the path again, so close they're almost beneath me—I see the three circles of their shiny white umbrellas.

We have our first counseling session next, then spa treatments, then drinks and dinner in the Twilight Lounge. It's the flagship room of the resort, which calls itself the Twilight Island Acropolis.

And that's another thing you wouldn't know from outer space, o astronaut reader. This kind of resort hotel is partitioned. It's not a contract-only venue, although there are some like that, only for contracts and survivors. No, parts of this resort are multipurpose and others are only for us. Don't get me wrong, all resort guests have been carefully vetted for their codes—no one has to carry their handface here to transmit them. We're all preapproved for socializing with each other, just in case, but service likes things organized. They don't want a chaotic mingling; they don't like humans milling around loosely.

The Twilight Lounge is a contract-only area.

We have a map of the hotel—it came inside the Coping Kit—and all the colors just for us are shaded in pale lavender. We can go into the other parts too, but people who don't have contracts can't come into the lavender areas. So you won't see newlyweds in the lounge, or casual vacationers. Of course, vacationers are only the superrich these days or people with high connex. But some extremely affluent newlyweds buy travel permits, and Hawaii's Big Island is still popular with them.

Anyway, I haven't been to the Twilight Lounge yet. I've only been to the lobby, the waste room down the hall, and this suite.

Half the time I feel like throwing my arms around both of my parents and not letting go, the other half of the time I feel pretty distant. Even a little bit repelled.

The handbook in the Coping Kit has whole sections on the psych of Final Weeks. They claim that repulsion is caused by resentment, along with some "feeling-detaching mechanics."

I can believe it. The worst I've felt so far was when Sam and I picked them up at the condo to leave for the Port of Seattle. They'd helped us to move out by then, to this group home for survivors who aren't quite old enough to live alone. It's where we're going to live starting when we get back, after the boat trip home. We'll be there for a year and a half, until I turn eighteen. If I've got certified by then for work phase, I'll get matched with a corporate and take on Sam's guardianship as a wage earner. I'm fairly cool with that part of things, because we'll meet new people in the transition home—new people our own age. It's not terrible to contemplate.

We have to be in big rooms of bunkbeds, separated by sex, and it's nothing fancy, there are plenty of chores and obligations, but my only real friend in our old building had to move out not long ago and I miss having flesh friends. The ones on face are good, I'm glad to chat and vidconf with them and everything, but still it's not the same.

Our former condo was completely bare—nothing was left of where we'd all lived for several years. The only things my parents were bringing with them, besides clothes and mementos we needed for Final Week, were bedrolls, tooth-cleaning equipment, and some instant caffbev. Their luggage stood in a neat row against the wall, small cases packed with lightweight toiletries and clothing.

The sight of that luggage made me feel like the stomach was falling out of me. Like gravity was sucking me into a hole in the floor.

We already knew rationally that they'd gotten rid of everything they owned—we'd helped them to sell some of it and donate other stuff, and then the older and more precious things they'd carefully given to us; they even classified the items and filed them. But it was still a shock to see the sterile emptiness of those rooms.

Another family was moving in later that day. A family, I thought while I looked at the luggage, that was staying alive.

At least for the moment.

"Well," said my mother perkily, turning back to cast a glance at the clean and bare living room as we were filing out the front door, "goodbye, everything."

Ψ

One thing that's a relief for adults is, we don't have babies around anymore. Brand-new humans are something you never see these days, not in our country anyway, or at least not in the rich parts, which we call the First—no one would wish this spinning-out world on them.

It's not even legal to have them, now.

The no-baby thing started when the last tipping point came, right after Sam was born. That means you won't find anyone around here any younger than Sam. Sam and I are what some people call the last generation. There are these labs—*banks* they call them—where they keep eggs and sperm frozen, in case things get better but by then it turns out we're all too old or can't have kids anymore. I know, it's kind of grisly. I browsed that they keep the eggs and sperm in huge rooms, active refrigerators with a major footprint, not the low-end, passive wall-set fridges people use for food at home.

In the poor parts of the world (like I said, we call the rich parts the First, and the rest is where the poors live) the facenews says they keep on having babies. Some of the countries try not to, but still the babies are arriving. We send those countries charity shipments of pills and stuff—the corporates and houses of godbelief both brag on doing it—but it doesn't always get where it's going, often it's sold or stolen.

Ψ

On the sailboat out here, Sam kept to his bunk a lot, seasick and also still angry. My mother and father spent their time holding hands, lying beside each other on deck chairs, and reading or watching the ocean. I did a little of that, but more often I wandered the boat and talked to the other passengers.

It was exciting to have so many brand-new peeps around, all of them with different styles, ways of talking, even smells. The last time I'd met so many new people at once was when we moved, under the last traject, to our new complex. It was kind of awesome. Some mornings I would wake up basically swelling with excitement at all the faces I was going to see, the mannerisms they would be using, the funny little habits people had that I hadn't seen before. Habits you only notice in the flesh, like one guy pulls on his earlobe when he talks and there's a woman who laughs whenever she says an opinion.

There were a couple of people I liked best: a crewman named Firth who was funny and rude and made remarks about the other crewmembers behind their backs; a pretty Asian-Am woman named Xing. Xing was always nice to me, and very interested in hearing about my family. I wasn't used to people being interested.

When I got tired of talking to new peeps—because

it really took it out of me, even though I loved it; my cheeks and mouth would ache sometimes from smiling and talking—I used the publicface in the passenger rec room to keep informed on news and facefriends. And at mealtimes we met together to eat (even Sam, once he got over the seasickness) in the boat's cafeteria.

The captain had a twisted humorsense and always kept the wallscreens tuned to weather as we sat there and ate our meals. Usually that's thought to be in pretty bad taste—in the complex at home it was practically *verboten*. Screens would always play vids or scenes, never news or weather.

So in the background, as we ate, scrolled daily lists of updates on sea rise, tsunamis, hurricanes, heat waves and droughts, crop deaths, methane and carbon eruptions, famine fatality totals, bug vectors and paths, certified plant and animal extinctions.

Sam and I weren't that bothered by it, it's just the weather to us, but to my parents it's not. My mother says weather is something else, weather means how warm or cold it will be, whether it's going to rain or be clear all day, windspeed, humidity. (When she says that, Sam and I kind of roll our eyes, like: *Weird. Boring.*) She says that's what "the weather" used to mean, that what we have now isn't weather, it's chaos description.

Anyway, we often ate in silence, with my parents depressed by the screens and trying not to look and the passengers at the other tables making small talk or arguing about celebrity model spokesmen or popular new trajects.

Trajectories—*trajects* for short—are subsets of models. They tell how things are supposed to go down in particular locations or for certain groups or commodities—for instance, the eastern seaboard has a traject, or Toronto, or corn crops, or bird flu. Trajects are the "applied specifics of a model," as my mother puts it. Phew.

It was at mealtimes, when they put all of us together, that I noticed the different groups on the boat. There were the smooth-looking people from the First, contracts mostly and a few *megarich* newlyweds; the crew and the cooking and cleaning staff, more hardscrabble in appearance; and then some obviously-not-rich passengers, almost an underclass, who reminded me of facefriends I had in Indonesia and Singapore. Indonesians have had it hard, ever since this big tsunami killed a quarter-million people about two hundred years ago. I heard about it from my friends and browsed about it too, mostly on disasterpage, which keeps a tally that's updated every few minutes.

The Indonesians are the opposite of the chosen people. Or maybe they *are* the chosen—chosen for suffering. I browsed that's even *part* of being chosen, in some godbeliefs anyway. You have to suffer to be special! The Indonesians must be superspecial, then, because they get one mass-death event, then another. The waves, quakes, and bugs just keep coming. It's gotten so bad that, like with Bangladesh, people make mean jokes about the whole country.

I know, wise cosmonaut: flat lame.

I made friends with some of the passengers but the

Indonesian-looking men, most of whom wore the same outfit—some kind of uniform, I guess, like police or medics—would never talk to me, even when I tried to tell them about my cohort of facefriends from that area. They shook their heads and claimed not to speak American.

My dad said maybe they were strangerhates.

We're a melting-pot poster family: part white people, part slave-trade African, part extinct Seminole. Sam's lighter-skinned than I am; he looks more white, where I look like nothing or everything. Whatev. People don't judge each other based on colors or sex orients that much these days, which used to be a major bad habit. That part's pretty prominent in the tutorials, because the corps are proud to boast how we got over it.

But what we have is strangerhate, which is just people who are so afraid of anyone they don't already know that they won't talk to them, period. People migrate so much, and everything is up in the air, and sometimes people's handfaces can't read each other's vaccine codes, and then people get scared and even violent, keeping strangers from touching or breathing them. So now we have xenos. Some of them don't ever want you to come close. To show that they feel that way, to stop any approach, they wear these creepy sunglasses that turn their whole faces dark. No one but xenos wears those things, so it's always a sign to stay away.

Anyway, the trip felt long because it was always the same routine: all you saw was the boat and the sea and the sky. Clouds and airtox gave us a whole sky full of purple and pink glamour, so at sunset we'd gather on the deck with drinks and spectate boringly.

I say "boringly" because we'd do nothing but look, but actually I liked those times. They were like no times I'd ever had before.

I'd never been to a place with so much water and so much air. I loved the colors of both of them, and the sense of eternity.

Ψ

One day there was a brief alarm when the crew thought a tsunami was coming, but that obviously never panned out since I'm here writing this. Way out to sea, tsunamis aren't tall like they are when they finally hit the coasts.

The only different thing was passing through the Great Pacific Trash Vortex, where the eternal oil plastics swirl in the middle of the sea. It was so huge it took us three days to sail past a small edge of it. Sam actually came out of bed for the first day of passing the Vortex and stood with me at the rail and looked at the garbage through a scope. You could see individual pieces of it, some of them really old—things that aren't made these days because of carbon and poisonous dyes. It was a field of primary colors, bright yellows and reds and royal electric blues and stark white.

Milk jugs, my dad showed us, from when they drank cow's milk before raising cows was criminal; bicycles you wouldn't think would float, huge fishing nets cast over the jumbles of smaller debris from when they sent huge trawlers out to catch schools of wild ocean fish to eat.

And once we saw a brown inflatable pony wearing a purple saddle with flowers printed on it.

They say the Vortex is bigger than South America.

Ψ

I think what put my parents over the edge was another trip they'd taken, a light-rail weekender to the place where my father grew up. One place for all his childhood! His family lived there, in the same house, for twenty years, he told me. Amazing.

It wasn't a coastal town in the strict sense—it wasn't right on the beach—but it was on a river delta, maybe twenty miles from where the true coast used to be. And so, when the first storm surges came that seawalls couldn't stop, the town got a wave of coastal refugees. Wave after wave came after that, though most of the people didn't stay. Back then they were migrating to places like Ogallala, with fertile land or thick forests. If you look at an old map-animation morph you can see the masses moving away from the coasts, inward and upward from New York and Florida, from Southern California and the ruined cities of the desert—Las Vegas and Phoenix, say. The animations look like storms or vast, sky-darkening flocks of birds.

If there were any such flocks.

But we're the only birds that darken those skies now.

Sometimes, at home, I take a mood softener, sit at my screen, and gaze at the map morphs dreamily. You can customize them to show whatever details you want—the continent shrinking as the oceans rise, plus the massive migrations, say. And you can filter the migrations by category, a game I like to play when I have nothing else to do. Where did Latinos go? you can ask the morph, and choose a color for the migrating Latinos. Where did the women go? and you can make the women pink. Where did the whites end up, the blacks, the Jewish, or the Catholics?

Then you can sit back and watch the swirling trails of color.

They can't keep such good records anymore, because of the chaos. So what you're looking at is pretty much historical stuff. But still, it gives you a sense.

I also like to watch the building of the seawalls. You see the swamping of Cape Cod, which happened too fast for walls, and the swallowing up of the Florida Keys: ditto. Islands all over the oceans get smaller and smaller, contracting to the size of pinheads and then vanishing— the famous canaries in the coal mine, the super-early casualties like Micronesia and Tuvalu. Or you can zoom way out and watch the planet rotate, see the surges of ocean that followed the melting of the ice on Greenland and Antarctica.

There's something lovely about it, lovely like Eno or Mozart, yet—especially if I haven't had my pharms—it can be pretty sad. I didn't know those places, but once, after I watched a morph, I browsed some pics of them the way they used to be and I got way teary.

Anyway, my father's hometown had been leveled by all

the waves of refugee camps. Nothing was left of the playgrounds he swung and climbed in when he was little or the leafy cemetery where his parents were buried. All that was gone—even the precious trees, cut down uselessly for fuelwood it was a major crime to burn anyway. The grassy meadows had been trampled down into dirt and the whole town had turned to tent cities.

His baby brother, my uncle Den, died awhile back in a DIY. He didn't have his own kids and hated the service corps.

Sam and I were sad when Den went, we barely knew him but we both had this one memory of a visit: Den took us out of our complex for a walk through the code zone—a safe zone made mostly of sidewalks, between the complexes, where everyone's updated on vaccines—and showed us pictures on his handface as we strolled. Where there were just regular parts of other complexes butting up against ours—mostly parts of condo buildings or sometimes a small veg-garden—he called up an olden-time city map on his handface. It was a sat map showing real photographs, from both the air and ground, of the olden-time city.

"Here there was a museum," he would say. "See? It looked like this. Yes: stone elephants! And they had a whole huge room with scenes from an Egyptian tomb—I once came here on a school trip and saw a real mummy. Even a mummified cat. It was creepy but I loved it. And over here, right where the outdoor waste room is, there used to be beautiful trees and in the middle of them was a library." He went on and on like that, showing us where things used to be before the tipping point, when people didn't need codes—before the new bugs and the new regime when people mingled freely.

But Den was too sad, and when I was about ten and Sam was eight he wrote some fond messages on face to all of us and went for a DIY.

So other than us, my dad has no family left.

After the trip he and my mother seemed hollowed out.

Ψ

I browsed that the final dinosaurs, before they went extinct around sixty-five million years ago, were duck-billed creatures that walked around eating plants. Hadrosaurs. They had these big bony crests on their heads. They lived in North America, not too far from here.

Those dudes were some weird animals. You kind of look at pictures of animals like that, with giant head crests, and you think: *Fail.* They look so outlandish, those critters. Impossible. It's really not too surprising that they're gone.

Still, it'd be way more awesome if they weren't.

Actually, that was the last *nonavian* dinosaur. The real last dinosaurs are the birds.

And maybe us.

DAY TWO

ORIENTATION & RELAXATION
Theme of the Day: Loving

I don't recommend family therapy.

At least, not if you're in a Final Week. It might be okay if your family was in a regular frame of mind and all you had to argue about was something like who was on the face too much playing what my dad calls "frivolous games" like *Serial Murder 6*. Or if you had words about who was shirking their turn to empty the human-waste compost.

But what happened with us wasn't pretty.

We went into the hearing room feeling low—not Mom and Dad whose pharma is already giving them a lift, but Sam and I. The hearing room is where you do the *listening*. Our service corp is really into its jargon—all the corps pretty much are, they call the trademarked words their "language technology" because they're into owning every detail of the styles that they've branded—so rather than *therapy* they like to use these words that end with *-ing*. They say that makes the process more about *being and nowness*.

Right before we left, Jean said to me and Sam: "Life is a gift that's wonderful and yet oh so fleeting. Does a butterfly complain about having to pass into nothing?"

"A butterfly doesn't say squat," interrupted Sam. "A butterfly's a retard."

Jean patted his shoulder. "A butterfly spends all its time *living*—flitting between the fragrant and colorful flowers. Experience your parents' time with you not as an automatic entitlement that everyone has, oh *my* no. That's really obsolete thinking. Think of it as an act of bountiful giving, leading to a bountiful letting go."

Our service corps can't get enough of "bountiful."

So there we are, in the hearing room in our nubbly beige hotel robes, all sitting on these tatami mats around a burbling water feature full of rounded rocks, with wave lightforms rippling on the fabric draperies and some kind of quiet hippie flute music tinkling from invisible speakers.

Tall bamboo plants in water, liberally placed.

In comes the therapist, a/k/a the Vessel for Receiving.

I swear, that's what they call them. *Vessels for Receiving.* Sounds like a toilet, huh.

So then our personal VR, a whiter-than-white lady with flowing blond hair and a long, light-blue robe that gives her a kind of princess aspect, sits herself down in our circle, smiles serenely, and purrs, "Welcome, all. Let us hold hands. *Be* in the *gathering.*"

The water burbled, the flute warbled.

But Sam has a knee-jerk reaction to corp jargon. "I'm not even doing this for five minutes if you're going to use those full-of-shit, empty expressions," he said. "We're not sheep and we're not brainwashed. At least, not *all* of us are."

"An angriness," said the VR, and smiled again in a saintly way as though the "angriness" was a special treat.

"Sam is your name, I know. Sam, please allow me to be your vessel for feeling-receiving. My name is LaTessa. You may offer your angriness to me. That's what I'm here for, Sam. I will receive the anger you're so abundantly giving."

She had him for a minute with that one. His jaw unhinged and his mouth hung open, à la moron.

"Please, honey," added my mother, who had a decent tranquility vibe going due to her Day One pharma regime. "An open mind, okay? Remember what we discussed. Anger is fine, anger is absolutely what happens. But also—try openness. Try being open, if you can."

"Open yourself to possibility," said LaTessa.

That snapped him out of his gape-mouth deal. "There's open, and there's gullible."

"All the expressing is welcome," said LaTessa, lilting and silvery. "The angriness is so *natural*, Sam. And we are not here for a judging; we are here for a *listening* and a *loving*. Offer the angriness to me and I will be happy to hold it for you. Nestling the angriness *next* to me, Sam, I will take *care* of it."

So this went on for a while, with Sam saying the whole thing was crap and LaTessa saying nothing except that she *welcomed* his *angriness* and she was there for *receiving*.

Personally, I was wondering when she would get tired of all the gerunds they were making her use and call someone in to give Sam a quick shot of trankpharms and keep the session moving.

But she never did.

I won't say that she wore Sam down—that would be

a definite exaggeration. Still, after a few minutes of acting out he settled into a kind of slump and stopped looking at her when she talked. He wasn't going to walk out, because he didn't want to hurt the 'rents' feelings that badly. He wasn't willing to go that far, I figure. So all he could really do was sulk.

There was mandatory hand-holding after that and my mom and dad said how painful it was to leave us. They said it was the hardest thing they ever had to do and they didn't mind dying at all, they only minded having to leave the two of us. They said why couldn't it be a better world, why did the world and our ultimate history break their hearts like this? My dad said he was angry with the dead people a long time ago who didn't stop the warming before the feedback loops started. He talked louder and louder and said they were energy hogs and food hogs and overall hogs for a super-easy life. He kept saying "hogs." Just hogs hogs hogs.

LaTessa said calmly that she received his anger, *and* the world was *yet only the world*, it was a *sunset-time glorious nowness of being*.

Very insightful, thanks for that, I thought.

She never said "but," she always said "and." I don't think there are any *buts* in language technology.

At that point I was suspecting maybe she was actually a member of the Hot Earth Society, who welcomed the chaos as an end to sin. But I didn't ask, because the session wasn't about her and who cared what she thought anyway.

My parents had made peace with leaving the friends

and acquaintances they still had, they told LaTessa.

"Some of our friends are already thinking along contract lines themselves," my mother added.

My father nodded and said they had an understanding, their generation. They felt for each other, but they also knew what time it was. (Whatever that fossil expression meant. My dad's the worst when it comes to using fossilized expressions.) So they didn't worry so much about their adult friends.

Then my mom looked over at Sam and me and averted her eyes. "But my—I mean—it's a cliché, I know, but it's so *real* to me: it seems like yesterday they were babies. I held them and wanted to protect them forever."

Then she started crying; she was sobbing even though the pharma was making her smile while tears ran from her eyes. But I have to say, that smile made it worse, not better. My father's eyes were wet and he got choked up, but in his case the tears didn't actually come out.

I started blinking rapidly.

I was wishing my own pharms were more powerful, at that point. I mean I know maybe it's weak—Sam thinks it's weak to use pharma every day, lately he's been suggesting pharma should be for special occasions. I don't know where he gets this stuff—a rebel listserve or somewhere like that. Sometimes, even though it's weird, I can almost see his point of view, but other times I feel like, *Come on, small angry-dude brother, live a little. Everyone can't be wrong. Can they?*

Plus there have been times I was on pharma when I

saw things I'd never have a chance of seeing flat. Pharma can turn the ugly into the beautiful.

Of course, it can also work the other way around.

Sometimes a visionpharm helps me work on my collection. I don't need it, but I can definitely use it to good effect. Once or twice I've found things whose loveliness I wouldn't have seen without the pills I was on. But, see, that loveliness is real, because later, after the pills wear off, I can still see it in the collected thing.

For instance, this one day I took a visionpharm because I was sad—a facefriend had caught a bug called Marburg and she died. I'd really liked her, we'd been gaming for over a year and vidconfing for just the last month or two; she had freckles and a sweet smile. I didn't want moodpharm, for some reason, I wanted visionpharm instead.

And after I took it I was wandering in the complex thinking of her and I found a plain rock. Somehow the rock became lovely to me, like I could see pieces of stars in it, pieces of primordial matter. In that plain rock I can still see the beginning of everything.

Even when I was flat again, I still loved that rock.

Mostly what Sam objects to is the controlling attitude that pharma has, their ads and slogans that make it seem like if you're not on mood-management pills 24-7 then you're callously "playing mood roulette." They try to make it seem like you're an irresponsible person if you're not a max-dose regular. Selfish and flaky—even a little bit insane.

It used to be they just hard-sold the pharma to grown-ups, but now they figure they have to capture the youth population too. We're getting older and sooner or later, they figure, we're going to get hella depressed.

So they're already grooming us to have an eventual death wish. I mean it's obvious, we're not stupid. And in a way I guess it's creepy, yes, as Sam has said to me more than once. But then it's also nature. Is it more creepy or more natural? I can't decide. I mean, it's always been natural to die. And wise to accept death since it's the biggest fact of life. Blah blah.

And yet.

Sam says he has nothing against death, in and of itself. What he doesn't like is management, which he refers to as "pharmacontrol." He and his hackerfriends on face like to get mad and they have their own lexicon of angry words. Among the hackerkids there are a bunch of different factions; some say they don't believe in pharms at all—though most of their parents make them stay on their daily doses anyway, of course—while other ones only believe in fastpharms because they don't think being sped up is bad. They think it helps their rebel cause.

Some of them wear their hair in old-time punk styles to show us all what big rebels they are. That always makes me laugh—the mohawks and silly drawings shaved into the stubble and all that—but not in front of Sam.

"He's fourteen," is what my mother's said to me about Sam and hacking. She smiles and sighs.

Anyway, the session was carnage. The blinking didn't contain my tears and soon I was pitiful, I had the runny nose going on, and I even started to hiccup at one point from the crying jag. So I promised myself I'd take a stronger cocktail as soon as we got back to the suite. There are different levels you can opt for at any point, if you're not doing great at the so-called coping.

I was thinking: I just want the sadness to go away. Or at least be a lot less so I can stay relatively calm and stop blubbering. I don't want me falling apart to be my parents' last sight; I want to get through this with a bit of grace.

I decided to try to collect something really soon, because that always makes me feel better. Collecting focuses me.

This isn't exactly a feel-good diary, is it? But don't worry, I promise it'll get better. So if anyone's out there, please keep reading: it'll be roses soon because I'm dialing up my pharma.

Before long it'll be one big, long love-in.

Ψ

It's morning now, the morning of Day Two, and this is our Personal Time. Mom and Dad are walking along the cliffs again and looking out at the ocean; they're kind of obsessed with it. They keep thinking they're going to see surprising life jump out and flash in exuberance—that suddenly some great ancient creature is going to surface from beneath the waves.

They know, rationally, that it's impossible. But there's this part of them that doesn't quite believe that, either. After all, the ocean is deep.

But the ocean is also turning anoxic, the scientists say.

It's happened before. It happened, for instance, 250 million years ago in the Great Dying, otherwise known as the P-T extinction event—the biggest mass-death event in Earth's history. Before this one, that is. So now it's happening again. The seawater got more acid from all the carbon it was storing, which we pumped into the atmosphere and sank into the water. And so the ocean food web has mostly collapsed, from the bottom to the top in a ripple effect, first the corals and mollusks and other animals with shell-like coverings, when the more-acid seawater stopped them from growing those shells. Next it was the animals that ate them, sea otters for instance, and then the animals that ate *them*, etc., all the way up to marine mammals like whales and dolphins.

And these big burps of methane are bubbling out of the seas along the continental shelves and causing even more heating up—along with the methane burps from melting permafrost, which brought about the tipping point. So now we've got the feedback loops.

And doom, and end of planetary life, and shit.

Unless the scientists are completely wrong.

It sounds flat negative, I know, but I'm actually in a good mood this morning. There are hummingbirds here!

I've seen them before in zoos and parks, but never just buzzing around wild. They can flap their wings ninety times in a single second! And fly backward. They're like jewels. They have shimmers, green and purple and golden.

I wish I could collect the sight of them, like on my handface vidcam, but I don't have it with me. And you can't collect them for real, of course. People used to collect animals by killing them, though, back in the clonal period, when white people were going around killing the other kinds and taking over their countries.

Back then collecting *meant* killing.

But I found something cool. It sits in my favorites box with the other things I couldn't stand not to bring. It was half a broken egg, just fallen on our balcony here. I have no idea where it came from; I haven't found a nest and there aren't any trees up here. But there was the half-eggshell, when I stepped out this morning, delicate and white. I'd never touched an eggshell before. We get synth-chicken eggwhite in bottles, once a year.

The eggshell is so fragile and thin I can hardly believe it would keep anything alive. *It's preposterous!* I feel like saying. And yet I'm pretty sure that's just what eggshells do. What I found was closer to two-thirds of an egg than half, I think—you can see how the top would be shaped, the slightly pointed top that separated from the rest.

I look at it and I don't know if the bird inside it died or hatched and flew away.

So as I was saying, the ocean—which used to contain oysters and orcas and who knows what all, even these bizarre creatures called seahorses—mostly has bacteria now and amoeba things and schools of mutated jellyfish.

Plus of course the garbage vortex and mile-wide chemical streams.

But still Mom and Dad stand at the edge of the bluffs, their arms around each other's waists, and look out over the faraway waves like anything could be there—like those waves might still be the glittering roof over a marvelous underwater kingdom.

Sam's lying on his bed reading. He brought an antique book that was a gift from my father. *Lord of the Flies*. My dad split his collection between us, but I haven't read any of mine yet.

Me, I'm sitting here on the balcony watching the palm trees swaying in the breeze, listening to the fronds rustling, looking at my eggshell, and thinking about the Twilight Lounge. We went there after the nightmare therapy session and our massages, to eat dinner and relax. At first I'd been creeped out by the parts of the hotel that were set apart for contract people, but it turned out to be okay.

Though maybe a bit hardcore.

It's kind of this skydeck setup, this restaurant, bar, and pool platform that juts out over the cliffs and looks like a big transparent bulb. You have a 360-degree view, there's one of those pools with a waterfall at the end that makes it look like it's just disappearing into the sky or ocean, depending on your angle. We sat at a poolside table and had our drinks in hand—my parents' were custom-made pharmabevs since it's a delicate balance; as far as I know ours were just generic—and were waiting for food when suddenly soft music started and this water show slowly began.

Out of the pool, where luckily no one was swimming at the time, rose these mermaid creatures on a platform, with long green hair and silver-green tails. It happened kind of gradually: their heads came first, from the water, and then their curled bodies on these fake rocks with fake seaweed and white round things sticking to them, some kind of extinct mollusk, I think, from when we still had them.

The mermaids had seals at their feet, not real ones obviously but pretty good robotics. And they were singing a beautiful song. It was ethereal, if that's the right word. Like it was both coming from them and not coming from them at once.

And when I say *them* I mean not only the mermaids but the seals too. The seals had mouths and they opened and closed along with the music. From where I was sitting I could even see the eyes of those robot seals, these big, black eyes, and they looked deep and wet and sparkling.

I've never seen a live music show before—that kind of crowdscene has been against the law my whole life—only virtual shows on face. I mean the animals were robots but the mermaids looked like real people, beautiful women wearing tails. So I was really excited and so was Sam. We were under a spell right away.

While they sang, the sun outside was sinking down over the sea. As the sky turned indigo, darkness descended on the dome over our heads and out of the darkness these flowing images appeared. There were these scenes, maybe from old movies—scenes of the ocean world that used to exist right around here, in Hawaii. Crossing the dome overhead were whales, big ones with their babies swimming right next to them, close to the mother whales' bodies. When they appeared these haunting whale songs also began, mixing with the live voices of the mermaids and the seal robots.

And then the whales faded and schools of fish swam past us where the whales had been, moving and flashing with the light of their thousands of tiny bodies. And all in a row, like a parade, dozens of other creatures passed before our eyes—these lit-up creatures that looked like alien spaceships, things with tentacles, strangely shaped sharks, big rays and small rays, dolphins or porpoises, otters and these seals with tusks, and a bunch of other things I don't know the names for. In one scene there was a boat and dolphins following behind it, leaping and playing alongside, jumping out of the water again and again, and this went on for a while until they went under again, and then the ship faded.

The whole time some sad music played; parts of it had no words and other parts did. One song the mermaids and seals sang went, *Heaven, heaven is a place—a place where nothing, nothing ever happens.*

After the ship was gone the dome became scenes of beaches—these pure, flat sand beaches they used to have with no seawalls at all. You could see waves crashing right on the gently sloping skirts of sand, and nothing but sand meeting water for miles and miles. They showed these natural pools between outcroppings of rock, and in them small creatures walked or swam—some that looked like insects, almost, with lots of legs, and tiny octopi and darting fish like minnows. There were some long-gone people on the beaches—whole families, happily playing together right in the open and wearing only small swimsuits.

They had no hats to shade against the sun, only those skimpy suits and bare heads. A family ran in the shallow waves, including a chubby midget kid with nothing on but puffy white underwear, smiling persistently. They showed two handsome men with their arms around each other, girls making a fort out of sand with spades and buckets.

And then we left the beach behind and were underwater again—an ancient reef, fish swimming everywhere and the dark silhouettes of people snorkeling above them with rays of sunlight beaming through. Spiky bright-colored anemone—I've seen them in the fake reefs—and red urchins and orange-and-white clown fish and even those things that look like insects again, big insects wearing body armor.

And then the last thing was the whales returning: a pod of them, you call it, swimming toward the underwater camera. A whole family of whales, singing their mournful songs. And then they swam away from us again, getting smaller and smaller until they disappeared into the dark.

The lights went up a little after the whales were gone, though it was still pretty dim, and the mermaids and seals silently sank back beneath the water of the pool. Sam and I saw that our mom was crying, and then we saw that this time our dad was too—not making any noise, just silent, big tears running down his cheeks and into his mouth. Of course, because of the pharma both of them were also still *beaming*. They smiled and smiled and tears ran down their cheeks and dripped right off their chins.

I was—well, I'd never felt that way before. Overwhelmed. I'd seen some of the old footage on face, but it's so different on that scale—it's personalized and miniature, it's cutely enclosed in the colorful frames you've chosen for your browse experience—and somehow you feel superior to it, like it's a snapshot or a fairy story.

But this was huge and real.

And then, of course, it's not real after all, being just ancient history, with nothing left. Ghosts filling the room, a world of amazing and mysterious ghosts.

So Sam and I were blown away, just sitting there blasted and in a daze. At the same time I was thinking—for Mom and Dad, and the pain of their memories—what are these corps doing? Are they, like, *torturing* them?

Because it was bittersweet and shit, I got that, no kidding. But it also seemed like a knife twist in a wound.

Ψ

We have a family field trip in the afternoon. Before that, a few minutes from now, Sam and I have our Survivor Orient, where we go to a special session with some other future survivors of this week's contracts.

I've got my beige robe on already and am just waiting to go. Like with the family therapy, they make us all dress the same; no makeup or other decorations. *We are survivors and loved ones, joined in togetherness of being,* says the handbook in my Coping Kit. *Dressing for impressing is not how we are striving, in this together-time. We are simply being, deeply authentic and without appearance divisions.*

Sam just went back into his room to dress in his own robe, but before that he was in the living room for a while, talking to me. He decided not to take any moodpharms this morning. He says he wants to be "perfectly lucid," is how he put it.

"But you're supposed to take the minimum *dose*, at least," I protested. "You know you are. Mom and Dad need you to."

"Nat. It's *my* decision. I'm not gonna be spaced out while this is happening," he said, standing in my doorway.

Our parents had finished their daily cliffwalk by this time and were in a couples prep session titled "Bountiful Passing."

"Okay," I said. "So yeah, it's up to you. But I have a right to say what I think about it. Are you going to give Mom and Dad a harder time, if you don't take a basic dose? Because this is, like, *their* time. It's *their* last week, not ours. It has to be about *them*."

"I have to be honest, Nat. I can't make any promises."

"But Sam," I replied, more and more annoyed, "they're *already* doing something so hard! And you're going to make it even harder on them?"

"Don't be a brainwash, Nat. They're taking the easy way out. *Something so hard?* Bullshit. They're doing exactly what the corps want them to do."

"That doesn't mean it isn't hard for them."

"It *should* be hard. Because it's wrong, and it's cowardly, and it's completely fucked."

We were looking at each other right in the eye, which we don't do that much since, I don't know—maybe since Sam hit puberty. He started getting all shifty around when he turned twelve. But now he's direct again, suddenly.

It kind of made me nervous, in fact, because he can be intense.

"Well," I said, "that may be true or it may not be. But even if it is, we can't *stop* them! They're 100 percent certain. And we don't know how it is, Sam—we don't know what it's like to be them!"

"Sure we do. They're human. And so are we."

I was looking at him, shaking my head.

Everyone old buys a contract, sooner or later. It's their choice when. It has to be.

"They're sure what they want," I argued. "The contract is already in. So why not give them some peace of mind now that they're definitely going? Why not let them have their last days the way they want them?"

I was thinking of my collection, and how my parents must want their last days to be like one of my items— perfect despite its tragic imperfections.

Beautiful even when broken.

Sam stared at me for a second, blinking. Then he ran a hand through his nappy brown hair. "Because it's not right, Nat," he said slowly. "None of it is."

But he's still going to the survivor session. For one thing, he has to. And for another, he says he wants to keep alert and pay attention to everything.

Ψ

Here's how it was at Survivor Orient: they put us in a different hearing room this time, a larger one with a kind of open space in the middle that had a cactus garden and quasi-artificial breezes and little hanging bells. There were twelve of us there, they keep the sessions small, and most of the survivors were in their twenties; Sam and I were the two youngest.

And Xing was there! Xing from the ship. She smiled at me although she didn't wave or say anything—we're not supposed to talk before the session gets started. I was so happy to see her, though.

The VR was LaTessa again. I guess we're just assigned to her, and so are those other families. For this whole week she's going to be our designated headshrinker.

We started with five minutes of silent meditation, during which the fake breezes breezed and the real bells swung on their threads and rang tinnily. But then nearing the end of it some of the future survivors started to sniffle and cry, already.

Strangers crying is embarrassing in a way I'm not quite used to yet. I mean, it's embarrassing to cry in general, who wouldn't feel that way? Even if you don't get self-conscious easily it's raw to be seen like that. But crying in public yourself is a different kind of embarrassment from watching other people do it. I have to admit I felt a bit stronger than them, since I wasn't—right off the bat before anyone even said anything—showing my sniveling side.

So then these masseurs and masseuses filed in. I don't know if they're corp or hotel employees, they all wore robes a lot like ours and they looked Hawaiian—a little dark-skinned, about like me, and fit and robust, like they don't do much traveling but spend their time in one place in the sun. They went behind us and started to give us these massages.

I don't really like that. It's too groovy.

Sam shrugged his masseur off right away and said, "No thanks, man. Nothing personal but it's not for me."

This was disruptive so I looked at the masseur guy Sam was blowing off. He was young too, maybe around my age, I thought, and I saw humor in his eyes, which, at this place, seems to be rare. There's not that many people here who are big on laughing, they're trained to focus on serenity and the solemn vibe of parting.

"If you be gratefully welcoming," said LaTessa gently to Sam, "you'll find a forgiving space opening."

"That's really rad," said Sam. "Still, though. I'll go ahead and pass."

This time LaTessa gave up easily—maybe because the other survivors were staring at Sam and getting distracted. My own masseuse was really digging into the shoulder area so I had to stop looking at Sam's guy, who stood back patiently with this funny kind of sympathy in his brown eyes, and keep my gaze straight ahead.

He must have had to wait for permission to leave from LaTessa, because he just stood there patiently without moving, until all the masseurs finished their work and withdrew from the people they were massaging. He didn't seem offended or awkward but just graceful and sort of self-contained.

Eventually they all filed out again quietly.

By this time the snifflers had stopped sniffling and LaTessa made us hold hands and name the emotions that we felt. As we went around the circle saying our feelings, it struck me that everyone was zomboid. I wondered if the others were taking more pharms than us; but then, a second ago they'd been crying. So they weren't mood-leveled. Who knows.

They mostly said variations of the same thing—they felt abandoned, they loved their parents and/or they were pissed off at them, the dying was selfish; one with a hardcore godbelief said contracts were against God's plan.

It was all about them, was what I noticed—survivors, not the people who had to die in three days. But I guess that's the point of therapy.

Then Xing spoke up. She asked how she was supposed to go on with her life, knowing the last generation had already been born, which meant that she would never be a parent herself and neither would anyone she knew.

Not that she wanted to; she didn't, not at all.

"But," she said, "these are the last parents, you know? The parents that are choosing to go now, they're some of the last parents around. Sooner or later, and probably sooner, in the First, there won't be any parents left. Not only no babies and no little kids, but no parents. Doesn't that seem kind of *weird*?"

"Hella weird," said Sam abruptly. He really looked at her. "And hella dangerous."

"Dangerous?" asked someone else.

"Dangerous," said Sam firmly. "A world full of people who don't have kids and never will. It's kind of a huge psychotic experiment, isn't it? I mean it's never happened in the history of the world. Even the corporates talk about it. Not loudly but they do. A world of people who may be the last generation. No consequences to what they do. A massive social experiment."

I glanced quickly at LaTessa then to see if that had pissed her off. But she had her usual serene smile on, smooth and unwavering.

"So now we've got, in the First World and corporate leadership, this old population that's getting more and more decrepit," Sam went on. "And then we've got the poor parts where they're still having kids, which is making them even poorer plus emitting huge amounts of carbon we're totally unable to put a lid on. We've got actual armies guarding our farms and water. If it weren't bad enough that the global biome's collapsing, now it's two kinds of people against each other too? Ancient and rich against young and scrabbling to survive?"

"But it's already divided like that, isn't it?" said Xing. "It's *already* the First against the rest . . ."

"Why don't we just, like, kidnap the poor kids if we need them so badly," suggested a meathead-type guy.

Xing and Sam both shot him a look of disgust. Even LaTessa cleared her throat.

"We're headed for the next tipping point," said Sam, looking around. "We've had the planetary one. Pretty soon now we're going to have the human one."

"A social tipping point?" asked Xing.

"The corps have already launched it," said Sam, peering at the meathead. "*Total war*."

There was a shocked silence. Xing looked a bit alarmed. It didn't seem like anyone knew what Sam was talking about.

I didn't, anyway.

"I am feeling," said LaTessa after a few seconds, with a little head incline, a clos*ing* of the eyes and a reach*ing* out of her slim, graceful arms to the future survivors sitting on either side of her, "a gently bountiful healing is calling to us all. A lovely call for *inward* focusing. This is a *personal* listening. Let us *be* in the *gathering*."

Ψ

My parents are out of it today—no doubt the sunset pharms are kicking in more. Not that they're actually forgetting stuff yet, but they do have a kind of blissed-out quality.

I suppose maybe it's okay, if it's what they have to do. But it's also a bit alien.

After we got back from our separate sessions, ate lunch, and took a little relaxation time, we had a field trip on the schedule. We get two field trips total, one on Day Two and another on Day Three. My parents picked them out beforehand from a menu of options.

This one was to a snorkeltank.

It was like a guided tour, and other people went with us—other people in what I gather is LaTessa's official group, because a bunch of survivors were there, including Xing. Luckily, LaTessa herself didn't come with us. A little LaTessa goes a long way.

She may even know this.

When early afternoon rolled around we put on our swimsuits underneath our clothes and trooped out to the front of the hotel, where they loaded us into an all-terrain e-buggy—this open-air, mostly bamboo bus contraption that runs off a solar battery. It's got a really wide roof that hangs pretty far off the sides to give a lot of shade and has solar collectors on top. And it goes really slow.

We went uphill then, away from the ocean and toward the volcano. We passed some lava, all black and curved and crinkly. The guide announced that the volcano still erupts now and then so there are cracks and holes, some places with hot, orange-red magma showing through, and if you're on foot you have to be careful where you step.

Sam was beside me on the seat. He leaned over and whispered in my ear that he wished LaTessa were with us after all, so he could push her in.

"That's not very *forgiving*, Sam," I whispered back after a minute. "How can she hold your abundant *angriness* if she's *being* all *shrieking* and *screaming* in a *limb-removing burning?*"

Sam guffawed.

I was glad, maybe a little proud of myself, because he

hardly ever laughs. Or even smiles. He's Mister Serious.

Mostly though we were quiet and watched the scenery, keeping our childish *venting* to ourselves. Sam pointed out that his masseur was along for the ride, still wearing his same beige robe. He and two others sat next to the tour guide, up at the front with the bus driver.

"They don't wear name tags, did you notice?" Sam whispered to me. "That's because they're local support staff. Like, contractors, not corp employees. So the corps don't like to *individuate* them. That's what they call it. They're supposed to remain *anonymous*. Basically so the corps can easily change them out and no one will notice."

"How do you know this stuff?" I asked.

"I did my homework. Before we left. I needed to know the details."

A bit paranoid, maybe, I thought, but I didn't say it. I'm leery of Sam's conclusions sometimes but I trust him for the raw data. He knows things, and I for one am glad he does. Even if my browsing mostly goes in different ways from his.

After the best part of an hour we got to the tank location. It's sunk into the ground, so when you come up to it—after you get off the bus and walk through some jungly vegetation—it just looks like a big natural pond, except there are a few small decks built into the sides and stairs made out of rock. They handed out snorkel masks and tubes and fins and we messed around for a while making sure we had the right sizes of everything. You didn't need a wet suit, they keep the water a nice warm temperature, so we just slipped our regular clothes off and our gear on and we were ready. My parents and Sam and I lined up along the deck for our turn.

Xing was standing right behind us, looking like some kind of elegant little duck with those big black flippers on her feet. Two cute old people, who I assumed were her parents, waited quietly at her side; the mother was tiny, the father was very tall. I noticed they were way older than my own parents, probably past the century mark.

While we were waiting there, watching other families slip into the water ahead of us and seeing their snorkel tubes spread out like miniature periscopes on the surface of the water, my father pointed up into the waxy green tree canopy. There were bright-colored birds there, parrots or something. But one thing struck me, and I could barely believe it hadn't struck me before.

"Where's the Invisinet?" I asked, squinting. "I just realized! It hasn't been on any of the gardens. Ever since we got here!"

"Maybe it's too high up to see," suggested Sam.

"Oh no, dears," said my mother. "They don't use the Invisinet here. Because the islands are so far out in the middle of the ocean, you see."

"No need," nodded my father, smiling beatifically. "The invasions they're most afraid of have already happened. Damage already done—in terms of wildlife that flies through the air, anyway. There aren't too many long-distance migrant birds left, so the residual risk is pretty low. Most of the invasive parasites that still show up are insects, and they actually come off passenger boats just like the one we sailed in on. After all, we're thousands of miles from nowhere."

It was bizarre—animals walking around, or flying, whatever they were doing, just on the loose, completely open to the sky.

When we finally went in it was great, better than the tank I'd once been in back home, which was strictly an indoor setup. They had real saltwater plants growing, and you could touch them. And there were the usual fake corals, but they looked really real, and along with the robot fish they had some live ones—you could tell because when you swam close to them they flitted away faster than the robots were able to. You're not supposed to touch robot wildlife because it can wreck them, but their sensors aren't always perfect and they tend to move sluggishly.

It was wild down there, the light shining through the water, the creatures swimming beneath, and my parents seemed happier than they'd been in a long time.

When we got out after our half-hour ended, and were sitting stretched out on one of the decks drying off while my mother went to use the outdoor "convenience station," Sam took my dad aside. The masseur dude with no name tag was standing nearby, handing out drywipes and putting away people's masks and fins.

"You could have more of this," he said. "Isn't it great? You could have more of all the things you love. Dad, *really*. Come on. You don't have to do it."

My father just patted him softly on the shoulder.

"Son," he responded, smiling his blissed-out pharmasmile, "much as we might like to, we can't go out snorkeling."

Ψ

My parents don't know it yet, but my brother's gone AWOL.

That stands for Away Without Leave, in case you didn't know. It's an old army term they use when soldiers run off to get a break from the killing.

Sam's may or may not be temporary. I'm worried.

And my parents don't know about his disappearing act yet because we're in the middle of Personal Time—they're off at some kind of healing session—and meanwhile he took off and left me a note. It said he needed more Personal Time than the slots we were given; it said he'd try to be back by evening. But it didn't promise.

You're really, really not supposed to go off-plan. They make that clear in the training, and then they state it again and again inside the Coping Kit—how it's all about a certain *pharmaflow*, a certain *time-shape of being*.

It's weird to think I don't know where he is. In all of our lives, it's been incredibly rare that I didn't know exactly what he was doing and his activity location. We always had our personal faces, with GPS trackers and all that, and we were good about updating so our parents wouldn't worry.

Plus there was the fact that we were barely allowed outside the complex. Except for special occasions.

But here there's no face, not for contracts, and so he's just gone. He's just somewhere out there.

He's like the birds with no Invisinet.

When I woke up from my catnap the note was right there on my bed beside me, scrawled hastily on a page torn out of Sam's own journal—the one they gave him that's identical to this one I'm writing in. The first thing I did was beat a path to his room to make sure he wasn't pranking. His journal was there on his bedside table, the opening Day Two page ripped out. Otherwise the notebook was completely blank.

But I did find, tucked into the back of it, a piece of write-fiber I didn't recognize, which he'd probably brought from home. At first I ignored it; then, since I found absolutely nothing else in his room that would give me a single clue, I pored over it for a minute or two.

It contained neatly written lists of numbers—numbers and places. They were big numbers, and the places were countries or cities or regions. I'll copy a piece of it here:

Guizhou Province	*500,000*	*3/3*
Mali	*1,300,000*	*8/12*
Uttar Pradesh	*8,000,000*	*9/10*

Okay, so I have no earthly idea what this all means. But it goes on like that, a list of places—all somewhere in the poor parts—with big numbers for each, and then fractions, which also might be dates.

I just tucked it in an inside pocket of my skirt, in case it's something private or important—in case my parents end up in here, looking to find out what Sam is up to.

I don't know why I took it, actually. But I did.

And now they're coming back in from their session.

Ψ

Tonight it's just the three of us at dinner.

My parents didn't take Sam running off as hard as I thought they would—they didn't freak out, didn't cry or pace around or anything. Probably the pharma mood-level.

But what they *did* do was call the corp.

I asked them not to, I said Sam would be back soon, later tonight, probably, and could we just keep it in the family? I showed them the note he left me; I told a white lie and said he'd meant it for "all of us." But they didn't even consider my request to keep the whole thing quiet. I mean, not for a single second. They said smoothly that this kind of thing happens, the signs were all there in Sam's *angriness* and his *rebelling feeling*—they actually quoted LaTessa to me.

And the key way to respond is, my dad said, "We just don't panic, okay, honey? That's what service is for. *Guiding, receiving, and streamlining.* We just need to keep them informed of all developments."

His face looked plastic when he said that.

And then they called it in.

For some reason, this pissed me off more than other things have. Usually I'm not pissed off, I'm pretty chill most of the time even without the slow-down pharms. But this got to me. More than the decision to buy the contract in the first place, because, I mean, sooner or later their generation always does. But this was something else—it was going too far, I thought, going too far in sneaky increments, it was a piecemeal betrayal of us that had turned a corner, because now, undeniably, they were showing more loyalty to the corporation than to Sam and me.

It was like: *Are you guys corp robots?*

I've been thinking about why, and it seems to me it's plain old fear. They're afraid of not doing everything the corp says to do in Final Weeks. They're afraid if they don't then something will go terribly wrong.

So here we are waiting for our dinner in the Twilight Lounge, and as my parents drink their cocktails and hold hands and smile, for once I'm the one sulking.

Sulking and writing in my journal.

Tonight's show was called "To the Stars," and it featured madeup vids of outer space and the life cycle of a star, from birth to supernova. They had facts rolling overhead: the number of stars in the galaxy, the number of galaxies in the universe, the number of years since the Big Bang. How even energy fades and dies—not really disappearing, the narrator said, but merely changing forms.

It was okay, but nothing like "Ancient Oceans." The ancient oceans kicked way more ass.

One upside, though, was that tonight's show didn't make my parents cry. Not a bit.

The menu tonight is vegetable protein steaks and pan-fried root veggies.

I'm not too psyched, frankly.

Ψ

Wow.

After dinner, around ten p.m., there was a knock at the door of our suite. Mom and Dad were already in their sleep garments, and their cool-down pharms were making them practically nod off on the couch where they were reading, so I went and opened it.

First I was relieved, and then I was alarmed.

Because there was Sam (relief) with a corp worker on each side of him (alarm). These ones had name tags—uniforms and name tags, and faces like the side of our concrete-reinforced cliffs.

Big guys. Between them Sam looked very small.

He wore a facial expression that was trying for apology or obedience or something, but behind that I could see another emotion—I don't know, triumph or pleasure or excitement. His eyes sparkled.

"We found him on the grounds," said one of the craggy uniforms. His name tag read, *Rory*.

"Sorry, Mom. Sorry, Dad," muttered Sam.

"Samson," said my father, rising belatedly from the sofa.

"Oh, good," said my mother, and she stood up too.

Their response time was long, and I noticed my mom's brown eye makeup was a bit smeared. I wondered if she'd get all doddering and bleary as the sunset pharms took over. I really hope not.

"Have you seen the smallgolf course they have?" asked Sam, with childish glee. "It's so totally cool and awesome!"

Clearly he was dialing up the kid thing for the benefit of Rory and his colleague. These days not all adults know how kids are supposed to act at different ages; they just don't have enough experience with the last gen to know what's normal for age nine compared to, say, age fourteen.

Of course, Sam hasn't seemed much like a kid since before he was ten. I'm pretty sure I'd never heard him say *cool and awesome* anyway, even before then. That's more the kind of gush I do.

LaTessa would never have fallen for the idiot disguise since she'd already seen him function at his real mental age. But maybe, I figured, these rock-faced guard types didn't communicate with the feeling-believing VRs.

"I didn't know you liked smallgolf," said my dad. Instead of instantly seeing through Sam's kindergartner act, as he would have even *days* ago, he seemed befuddled by the situation.

"Are you kidding?" replied Sam, and walked over to the sideboard to pour himself some electrolytes. "This course is rad! They have hologram olden-time players, you can play against them. Like famous golfers from the big-course days. There's a robot man named Tiger!"

"Let's make sure there's no more going off-plan, okay, Samson?" Rory interjected sternly. "It causes inefficiencies. It's hurtful to your parents and it's extremely disruptive."

"Sorry, guys," said Sam, but at the same time he shrugged like he was too clueless to fully get the problem.

"We'll keep him on a short leash from now on," said my dad, half-jokingly.

Then Rory and his colleague did these little head bows and retreated. There was silence after the door clicked closed, with Sam glugging his drink down as though he was dying of thirst.

"Sam, dear," said my mother, "we may be on heavier pharma doses than you are, but we're not *completely* out of it. Are you really expecting us to believe you took off just to look at a golf course?"

"I'm sorry," said Sam again, dropping the little kid façade. "And Nat, sorry to you too. Felt suffocated. I had to get some space."

"But you *have* space," said my dad. "It's built into the system! Your own room—even your own balcony! We went over this in training, Sam. The importance of the schedule."

"I'm sorry to disappoint," answered Sam, a new stiffness in his voice. "What can I say? My bedroom didn't feel like space to me. But you know what? Right this minute it's not looking so bad. Tell you what: I'll go in there now."

And he went. And shut his door behind him.

My parents looked at each other, my mom sighed, and then they gave me their goodnight hugs and went into the master bedroom to sleep.

I headed to my own room, but I didn't go to sleep. I waited. And sure enough, a few minutes later Sam slipped in. No knock. He closed my door softly behind him.

"The corp mikes the main room," he whispered. "But

not the bedrooms, they don't have the manpower to listen in everywhere."

"Mikes?" I blurted.

"Shh! They're sensitive, though. Keep it to a whisper."

"Are you saying they—they listen to our family? They listen in to what we say privately? In the suite?"

"They monitor the microphones if someone goes off-plan," he whispered, sitting down next to me on the bed. "They don't bother otherwise. But if you go off-plan you get flagged."

"Really," I said, probably a bit coldly. "Thanks a bunch, then. And how did you find *that* out?"

"Keahi told me."

"Keahi?"

"The dude from the massage pool. His name means *flames*. In Hawaiian."

"So you get your top-secret info from a masseur."

"He's not just a masseur," said Sam, shaking his head. "But listen. My list is gone. You have it, right?"

I thought about denying it, because I was annoyed at him. But that would be too mean.

"I have it," I said, and went to the closet to get it out of the pocket I'd stuffed it in. "I couldn't make head or tail of it."

"Something I'm researching," he said evasively, and tucked it away. "I'll tell you if it pans out. Meantime, I need your help. I really do, Nat. This is so important."

"My help with what?"

"First I have to swear you to secrecy."

"Are you kidding?"

"I mean it, Nat. I've never been more serious in my life."

He was so close to me I could see the white ends of his eyelashes in the candlelight and a faint orange trace of 'lyte juice on his upper lip. It made me think: *He's still just a kid!*

But I could see how big a deal this was to him. Whatever *this* was.

"I don't know," I said slowly.

"We have three hours of Personal Time tomorrow morning. Three whole hours—it's their final healing session. That's why it's so long. It's the biggest chunk of free time this whole week, and the last one before Goodbye Day. So I want you to come with me. But the rule is, no questions. Not till we're out of range."

"Range?"

"Away from the hotel. Please, Nat. I've never cared about *any single thing* in my life as much as I care about you coming with me."

"But you'll bring me back here in three hours? You promise? Because I don't want to upset them. I don't want to do anything like what you did today, Sam."

"We'll be back," he nodded.

So that's the plan.

Ψ

After he left my room I went out onto the balcony. I stood looking up at the constellations and thinking how lame

"To the Stars" was compared to the real thing. Then I thought about last night's show, "Ancient Oceans." And it occurred to me that, as great as that show was, the real thing was probably a million times greater.

For a second that scared me. For a split-second I was on the edge of a terrible cliff. I think maybe I got a glimpse of the world how Mom and Dad may see it—this landscape of beauty that's been lost.

Then I grabbed hold of the balcony's railing and I was back in a normal mode again. I concentrated on the solid, familiar feel of the railing against the palms of my hands. I said to myself, there's history, sure—there's always going to be history. There always has been, there always will be. Things are always changing. And sure, a lot of that old world is gone. But leaving is what alive things do.

Out there among the stars there are probably a million worlds being born and dying. Just like people used to be—just like the animals were. Before the being-born part stopped.

This is just *one* world, I thought. It's not all of them. It's not all that there is.

I thought of the butterfly Jean wanted us to be, all flitting between the flowers on its light feathery wings, blah blah. Okay, the way she said it to us was corpspeak and weak. But still, I can't deny she has a point. Things die, things go extinct, that much is true, it's just the price of living. Only a rock stays the same.

And who would want to be a rock?

Boring.

It's normal, I said to myself. If you're not a rock you're lucky. But if you're not a rock you also have to pay for it.

Day Three
Remembering & Appreciating
Theme of the Day: Lasting Togetherness

'm up early today, so early the others are still sleeping. I brought this journal with me to a bench on the cliffwalk.

Some of the benches have awnings and I chose one of them. You can only see the ocean from where I'm sitting—I mean if you look straight ahead there's nothing but blue over the line of tufty grass at the edge of the cliff—but if you walk closer to the edge and peer down you can make out the concrete and metal architecture of the seawall. I wish I hadn't looked over; I wish I still had the illusion that the bluffs were natural. Because it's nice: hummingbirds buzz around, diving into the red flowers and feeders.

The sun's just come up and I can see boats sailing in. Passenger-boats are powered by wind and sun, but not the corp and military transport boats—some of those use massive batteries and have no sails at all. They're big and stay far off the coasts, mostly, dispatching pontoon boats to bring in batches of supplies. On the way over, my dad told me about big luxury ships they used to have for people to vacate in—giant and white and towering like miniature cities. They had really bad carbon footprints, them and the jet planes and the fossil-fuel cars.

I will admit it: I can't decide what you, my spacegirl

reader, already know and what you have no idea about. So sometimes I probably tell more than you need to hear, and sometimes I probably tell less. Sorry.

I'm rocking some moodpharms today, nothing too strong. It's not the absolute min dose, but it's the second-least you can take. I was going to dial it up further and then something about Mom's blurry eye makeup last night turned me off.

Personally, I don't want to take the risk of becoming some kind of tottering wreck.

But there's another risk too, because this afternoon's going to be heavy. Before our field trip we have a session for all four of us, cheesily called "Togetherness Memories." The hardcore emoting session comes tomorrow on so-called Goodbye Day, but we're supposed to prepare for it today by watching old homevids. My dad helped a corp worker run a bunch of family footage together, pick music to set it to and all that, and we're going to spend an hour watching them in one of the hearing rooms, after our Day Three excursion is over.

Talk about tearjerkers.

And later this morning, of course, in Personal Time, Sam's making me hang with him.

People are up and passing by my bench now, walking along the clifftop with their parasols. There's a lady with a curly white dog—a robodog obviously—and a group of cottontops jerkily race-walking, the goofiest sport ever invented.

And I just saw Keali or Keahi or whatever his name is,

the worker Sam's apparently made friends with, pushing a cart loaded with drywipes toward one of the pool areas. He smiled at me and half-saluted.

So he's cute. No biggie.

The bells are ringing in the clocktowers —they have those kinds of quaint touches here, nice chiming bells to call out every hour from these tall, thin white towers with bulbs on top that jut out of the hotel buildings—which means I have to go in.

Fruit smoothies and corn toast for breakfast.

$$\Psi$$

I don't know what to write first. Let's see.

Well, my parents went off to their healing. And the first surprising thing that happened after that was, Sam came into my bedroom and gave me boots.

Yep. Boots.

They didn't fit exactly right, they were a little big and rubbed along the heels, but he said I had to wear them anyway. They're these solid, heavy boots of a type I've never seen before—really thick soles and a lot of ankle support. He said he almost ruined his sneaks yesterday, and that if he hadn't been able to borrow someone else's at the last minute he would have tracked mud and ash into the hotel suite.

And that would really have raised his buddy Rory's eyebrows. Because you sure as hell don't get much ash or mud here on the grounds of the resort.

So that's when I knew we were going off-campus.

He's my brother, what can I say. I had more doubts, yes, when I saw the boots, because I'm a good girl, a/k/a wuss. Always have been.

But I wrestled with the doubts and after a while I won. I don't need to detail my wrestling match here. You get it. Anyway, I put the boots in a shoulder bag, along with some water Sam told me to bring. I slathered on the sunscreen. And we left.

First he made me go out with him to the common area, where he says the microphones are, and have a fake conversation about how we were going for a marathon swim, in case someone was listening in. Sam says they don't monitor guest activity in all the pools. And then there was some sneakiness getting off the grounds. First we went toward the pools, through a couple of places they apparently have cameras in. But then we ducked down a hallway where they don't.

Sam had it planned.

He led me through this small staff exit near one of the kitchens, past a field of perfumed food compost they keep nicely hidden and surrounded by bushy fragrant herb plants like lavender and sage and mint and rosemary. We hunched down into the cover of some hedges and changed into the aforementioned boots, tucking our clean shoes away in our bags. He showed me a hose where we could wash off when we came back; he took me past a huge solar-panel array, a gravel lot full of parked e-buggies and buses, and then some satellite dishes all pointed in the same direction.

And suddenly we were in a jungle. At least, that's what it seemed like to me. The trees and vines and shrubs were thick around us, there were beetles and ants on the ground and birds on tree limbs, and the only place to slip through it all was a narrow dirt pathway, barely a shoulder's width across, with protruding roots that constantly bumped against the toes of my boots and made me stumble. It was shady and, except for a few birdcalls and the sounds of the ocean breeze in the high-up foliage, very quiet.

It was uncomfortable and irritating.

And also strange—mostly in a good way.

I've never been in a park before where there weren't paved walkways; I've never been in one where you didn't know for sure that hundreds of other people had already walked there that same day. Sam said it wasn't even a park we were going through. He said it wasn't planted on purpose but had just grown that way.

"This is nothing," he boasted. "Wait a bit."

He showed me where some trees were marked, a triangular notch you had to know about to tell it was out of place, so you could find your way. We bent over and half-crawled through a big metal pipe under a gravel road, full of dead leaves and some garbage, and then it got even wilder; the narrow path was gone and we had to push our way through branches that snapped back at us, making me a little testy. I got a branch in the eye once and swore loudly. It hurt.

But there was a wild smell in the air, a smell I didn't recognize, that lifted my spirits. I couldn't decide what it reminded me of—something long ago or from another life.

Then suddenly there was lava.

It was dried up, it wasn't hot—I didn't see any orange-lit holes where Sam could murder LaTessa. It was just these big, gray tongues lapping at the jungle.

We jumped onto one and walked up it for a while.

But by this time I was getting nervous, because it was neat and all, I had to admit that, but it was taking forever.

"It's not that far now," said Sam.

We were walking up a lava slope and then we stopped to look around. You could see the canopy of trees beneath, the jungle we'd just come through, and stretched out in the distance beyond it the resort, all these white buildings. Beyond the blobs of white you could faintly see the ocean shining.

"Pretty good, huh," said Sam.

I nodded. It was breathtaking.

And we were all alone. No tour guide or anything.

And no parents.

The wind picked up our hair and cooled the skin on my arms so it rose into goosebumps.

I felt a stab of—well, I would have to call it grief.

Mixed with longing.

Because it was beautiful. And lonely.

There was all this air around us, and there was the big blue sky above. Beneath us there was a huge lake of emerald green, the specks of white, the shine of water on the horizon. And above it all just the two of us, in our thin, fragile bodies of skin and bone.

We were alone, standing on the lava slope, feeling the wind, and waiting for time to pass.

And I thought: *So this is how it's going to be.*

It almost flipped my stomach. But I didn't want to pass the sadness along.

"It was totally worth it," I said, and smiled at Sam.

"Oh," he replied, after a second. "Oh—you mean the *view?* Yeah, cool. But this isn't where we're going."

Ψ

When we finally did get to our destination it was through these tunnels in the lava—tunnels Sam said the corp didn't know about, which were actually called lava tubes. They were spooky like a Halloween scene, all gray and black inside, with wrinkled walls and cavernous rounded ceilings. I half-expected bats to flap out at us like in an old horrorvid. But of course that didn't happen, since bats all died out from a white fungus on their noses in the 21st c.

And when we came out of the lava tube we were in a caldera, Sam said, which is like a dent on the side of a volcano where the ground once collapsed inward after an eruption. It was surrounded on all sides by lava sloping up, so that it was like a bowl-shaped valley, protected on all sides.

It was full of fruit trees and greenery and life. We wandered through a grove going in, and I looked up and saw avocados and mangoes and bananas and I don't know what else, all growing right in front of me and just hanging off branches to be picked—stuff I'd only seen pictures of on face, mostly, that we only get to eat in powdered form or sometimes, on special occasions, dried and sweetened.

People lived there. Mostly Hawaiian looking but there were some whites and blacks and Asians and mixed people like us too, and they were all wearing beachy style clothes, ragged shorts, and bare chests, in the case of the guys, or halter tops or shirts for the girls and women, with patterned sarong-type skirts that wrapped around their waists and tied.

All the colors were pretty muted though—no reds or yellows.

"It's camouflage in case of flyovers," said Sam. "They're rare. But they can still happen."

And the whole encampment was hidden that way, I saw. There were these pavilion tents with big cloths strung up overhead, whose green was exactly the green of the trees—even patterned with leaves and branches, or some of them had actual leaves and branches positioned on top. Some were mud brown and some were green and gray, in splotches. In the middle of these tent structures there was something Sam told me was called a Quonset hut—long and low and rounded on top like a half-cylinder, a house-sized tube laid on its side and sunk into the ground.

It was painted green too, and palm fronds decorated the top.

"But wait," I said, getting alarmed. "These people, Sam. What about their codes? I mean we were vetted so we don't *need* to show them. We don't need our handfaces.

But what about these people? How can their vaccines possibly be up to date?"

"I know," said Sam, nodding. "That's why I haven't introduced you yet. First off, they don't get too many new bugs here. It's pretty rare. Because it's an island. But remote or not, there's always a chance. There could be a bug here we don't know, and they could be immune to it, and we might not be. Or also, you and I could carry a bug *we* don't notice, that doesn't hurt us but could hurt them. It's a risk we all take. But you need to choose for yourself before I expose you."

"So, I mean—you've already dealt with them!" I was suddenly scared. "You met them in the flesh without your protection!"

"And they met me," said Sam solemnly. "They took the same risk. In fact, theirs is the greater risk. They said it's a risk they have to take—that now and then they have to take a risk like this one."

I gazed at him for a minute. It was against what we'd been taught. It was the first rule of safety we'd grown up with. And here was Sam, breaking it.

Like it was nothing.

"I don't know, Sam!" I burst out. I was pretty much panicking.

Sam was already exposed, though. That's what I thought next. He was exposed and I wasn't. And where would I be without him?

He said they'd give me a general shot they had, if I agreed to come in, but there'd still be some risks on both sides. They didn't have our same vaccines and we didn't have theirs.

Long and short, I agonized for a few minutes and went back and forth on it. Finally I gave in. I'm not going to lie—I was afraid. But more than anything, I think I submitted to what Sam wanted because I felt I couldn't go back. I felt I had to be there, I had to go forward, I had to stay with him.

It probably wasn't the smartest decision. But I made it.

And we walked forward into the clearing.

"That's where they keep their tech," he explained, pointing to the Quonset as he led me through an open area in the middle of the tents. There was a little shelter there with a hole that went down into the ground. "That's well water. And in the Quonset there are power hookups and weather systems on the wallscreens and face and all that. But we don't have clearance to go inside it yet."

"What *is* all this?" I asked, though I was barely listening to his monologue, since some kids around his age were waving at him from a far tent, where they were kicking some kind of ball around on the dirt.

"You know: a settlement." Sam lifted a hand at them and then stopped walking to turn to me. "It's what you might call a rebel camp."

"Rebels against what?" I glanced around to see if I could spot any men holding clunky black weapons who could possibly want to shoot me. But all I saw was a couple of ladies in not too much clothing, busy cooking pancake-like items on a hooded portable stove.

"Against the system," said Sam. "Against the service corps and their partners and the armies. Against the whole power structure of how things have come to be."

I looked around and it seemed like a kind of picturesque place, but it didn't seem like they were doing anything *super* illegal.

I mean, there's no law against tents. Is there?

"Are you sure you're not being overdramatic, Sam? I mean, aren't they more like back-to-the-land, off-the-grid people? That's not illegal, it's just hippie."

"Come here," said Sam.

We went behind a tent and past the kids playing ball and through a gate.

And that's when I saw them.

These weird, massive creatures almost as long as I am tall. These hard-looking, big brown humps on their backs, white and brown spots on their legs.

I almost screamed. But didn't. But I did freeze and stare.

"Sea turtles!" Sam exclaimed proudly.

They were clustered around a pond. Instead of mud around it there were piles of sand. And in the sand there were some big oval objects I realized had to be eggs— though they were *so* much larger than the broken eggshell I'd collected. They were way bigger than that, and one of the turtles was flipping sand over them.

The turtles raised their heavy-looking heads slowly as we walked nearer to them, and their huge brown-black eyes didn't blink. It was so cool how different their eyes were from ours—there didn't seem to be any whites at all.

I was rooted to the spot, but then—the way their stiff heads moved so slowly on those thick, stalklike necks as if maybe they needed some lube in the joints or something—it came to me: *Of course.*

I got it. They had to be turtle robots.

"Way impressive," I said. "They look so real!"

"They *are*," said Sam. "I mean, think about it. These people don't have the money for robots."

I stepped a little closer, my boots sinking into the sand. The turtles didn't move; they were completely inert.

Faulty sensors, I thought. "Come on. Classic robot defects—look how sluggish their reactions are! See how their heads move so slowly? I'm serious, they're pet robots that are defective."

"Seriously," said Sam, "turtles are just *like* that. See, Nat, they breed them here. They have to keep the sand and water a particular temperature and everything, because most turtles went extinct from temperature change. If it's too hot the eggs all come out one sex. I'm not clear on the different species yet, but that's what happened with the loggerheads and the hawksbills, maybe, I think."

I stared at the turtles. They moved with this intense, almost insane deliberateness. Like for them there was really no hurry. They were chill.

It was very hard to believe they weren't robots, to tell you the truth. I mean, I've never seen a so-called wild animal that's longer from head to tail than my arm. The closest I'd come before today was probably turkey vultures eating carrion on the road—those buzzards can get pretty big, and the poor things have wrinkled red faces that hang down like an old man's butt. Or maybe the raccoons that lived in the gardens of our complex, but they're not really wild, since they get fed garbage and live under Invisinet.

And even zoos don't have sea turtles.

Sea turtles are supposed to be all gone.

"So why us?" I asked. I couldn't tear my eyes away from the turtles. "How come they let *us* in here, if it's so secret?"

"I have an inside source," he said.

And finally I looked up, and there, standing a couple of feet away, was Keahi. He had his arms crossed and was just looking at me and smiling slightly with his mouth closed.

I almost didn't recognize him without the beige robe. Instead he was wearing this dull, sage-green outfit that matched the Quonset hut and the tents.

"He's been close to us the whole time," said Sam.

"You were never out of my sight," said Keahi.

I realized I'd never heard him say anything, up till then. He had a deep gravelly voice.

"Okay, so that's creepy," I said.

He was attractive though and it made me feel abnormal. I should have been more creeped out than I was, if you want to know the truth; I already have corporate watching me, I don't need any more spies.

"It seems like we just walked in here," said Sam, "but there were people surveilling us all the way. They have to."

"We do have a lot of surveillance," said Keahi, almost apologetically. "We have to."

"But—is it illegal for you to live here? I mean, where do the corporates you work for think you live? They know you have to live *somewhere*."

"Well, there's onsite rooms for contractors," answered Keahi. "In the resort. But as for our families, they think they all live in a poor coastal complex a couple miles down the cliff from where the Twilight is. That's where they get most of their local employees."

"Then—why would they even care if you guys have a camp here? How would it hurt them?"

Sam and Keahi glanced at each other sidelong, like maybe I was a mental challenge.

"First off, harboring wildlife is illegal . . ." said Keahi.

"But that's not the service corps' focus, that's up to the army police," I said.

"One and the same, actually. And in the second place, they look at this island as their own. They don't care that we lived here for centuries before they bought up the coastal real estate."

"They hardly let anyone in, Nat. We're lucky," put in Sam.

"So then," I said stubbornly, "why us?" I still wasn't quite believing all the hush-hush stuff. It seemed like little boys playing pretend, to me.

And then this older woman stepped out of the trees, an older woman with silver-gray hair, which was a new one on me—I thought they got rid of the gray-hair gene a long time ago. I was staring at that weird silver hair as she spoke.

"Because your brother reached out to us and we can

use more people," she said softly. "Hi, Nat. Hi, Sam. My name is Kate."

"She's one of our leaders," said Keahi. "And also, my mother."

"Oh. Hi," I said.

"We need young people, Nat. So we did some monitoring, which I hope you'll forgive us for when you get to know us and why we do what we do. We did some background checks and held one of our councils. It's not a democracy here—at least not the kind you're used to—we vote on real stuff more. Beliefs. Actions. And here's the situation: we think this place might be the best opportunity for you."

"Need young people for *what?*" I asked. The whole trip was starting to make me nervous. Plus it was getting late, and I worried we'd keep my parents waiting.

"Why don't you follow me," she said.

We went back out the turtle gate, behind a row of tents at one edge of the encampment, and down a flagstone path in the dirt to a low building—not a Quonset but a bamboo shack with a pointy thatch roof. There were flower boxes in the windows (open, no plexi) and a mat in front of the door.

Before we went in Kate handed us these white fibrous masks and told us to wear them over our mouths.

"They're more vulnerable than we are," she said, mysteriously. She knocked on the door, and it opened. She turned to us and raised a finger to her lips, then stood back to let us in. Sam went first, and then me, and then Keahi.

It was just natural light inside, light streaming in from those big windows, and there was a soft colorful carpet on the floor. And then there was a row of miniature bamboo beds with odd vertical bars on the sides.

And in the beds were very small people with heads that were way too big for their bodies. It looked like almost a deformity. They had barely any noses either, just tiny flat nubs. They had round, soft faces and bald heads.

In other words, babies.

"They breed those too," whispered Sam, while I stood there staring.

There were four of them, and they were asleep and not moving, but then one of their small, fattish feet would jerk a little, or an arm would move.

I mean, since Sam was born, when I was only two myself so I don't really remember it, I've never seen one. Except on face, of course.

Then one of them woke up. The only way you could tell was that the eyes opened. They were deep blue and the white part was completely clear, like I've never seen—no bloodshot veins or anything.

And he or she looked at me, just gazing.

It was surprisingly cool. The thing had a kind of inner glow, or something.

"Well, not breed, technically," said Keahi's mother, laughing. "Of course, we agree with the corps that there are too many unwanted babies out there already. But here they're not unwanted. We just started this part of our work recently, when babies began coming to us from the poor parts. They're smuggled out of where they're born and brought to us; we take them in and raise them. And there will be more. If we have more people, like you, to help us nurture them. You're older, of course, but you're not Old Worlders, as we are. You're New Worlders. Children *like* other children. And failing that, other young people. They're happiest when they can play with, and learn from, their peers."

"I can't believe it," I said, and stepped closer.

The woken-up baby did a kind of almost-smile deal.

"Are we—am I allowed to touch it?" I asked.

"Her," said Kate, still smiling. "Sure. Here, why don't you give her this," and she handed me a bottle with white stuff in it.

I took the bottle and leaned over the bed, which, with the bars on it, seemed like an infant prison. The baby reached out and grabbed the bottle and started sucking on it.

It was too weird. The fat-cheeked little human really got a serious mouthhold on that thing. I couldn't have torn it away if I'd wanted to.

I touched her arm-skin. It was unbelievably soft.

"Why don't we go outside again and let the little ones sleep," said Kate. "We'll leave you to it, Aviva."

Aviva was the nurse person, the one guarding the babies. She smiled at us as we left.

Long story short, Kate sat us down and talked to us in her soft, level voice, with Keahi watching the clock to make sure Sam and I could still get back on time and not raise more corp-worker eyebrows. Meanwhile, an old Japanese-looking gardener guy in a straw hat brought fresh fruit on a platter—slices of mango for each of us.

It was far and away the best-tasting thing that ever touched my tongue. I'm not kidding. Kind of distracting, because as I was eating this wild, amazing food unlike anything I'd ever tasted before, and freaking out a little, she was talking to us about some heavy issues.

I can't write all of it down. I thought about not writing down any of it. Because what if a corp rep found it?

So I wear this journal everywhere I go now. I keep it in a bag I never put down, even while I'm sleeping. It never leaves my body. I keep a candle and matches in the pouch too, so I can burn it, if need be.

For now I'll just say this: they want us to come live with them. They want us to never get on that boat again.

And it's crazy, I know. But there's this one thing that they have that no other people do—at least no *adults* I've ever met.

A future.

Ψ

We made it back to the hotel just in time, and only because Keahi led us out again and it went a lot faster downhill, with him in front, than it had uphill with Sam.

Our parents didn't notice anything weird, at least not as far as I could tell. When we got back to the room they'd left us a message on the board: they were in the shower rooms down the hall, freshening up for lunch. That meant they'd be back any second, since the luxury showers here take up to four minutes, so we used our sinks—the only plumbing we have in the actual suite—to wipe down a little more carefully. We'd already wet our hair at the hose when we stopped off to clean and put away our boots; we had to look like we'd been swimming. Now we lathered up with scented soap in my room too, in case we still had any eau-de-jungle about us.

We checked each other over and agreed to talk again during Personal Time tonight, then went out and sat all docile on the living room couches waiting for them, me with my journal and Sam with his old book about flies.

Next was lunch in the Waterfall Room, where we ate spicy gluten wraps at a small table surrounded by these water features planted with spider plants and flowers. There were red-and-blue tropical birds squawking and flapping around near the ceiling. The Waterfall Room's not lavender so there were tourists there too—couples on honeymoon holding hands over the tables, probably ignoring the unromantic signs on the artificial rocks that said, *Reclaimed Sewage Grade C Do Not Drink.*

Like anyone would drink from a fake waterfall anyway. Did they think that, without the signs, people would just lean over and suck it up?

The pools are reclaimed sewage too, of course, but at least it's Grade B. Also, they keep it pretty clean in there, like in the rest of the resort, though I did notice the odd splash of parrot crap on those hollow rocks.

Anyway, the mood was pleasant, more or less. I liked watching the noncontract people, living their regular lives. And I hadn't taken any new pharms because I was still thrilled and excited from the morning; I felt jangly, but in a good way. Everything was in flux suddenly—as though, for the very first time in my life, not everything had been decided for me.

And then lunch was over and it was time to watch our homevids.

They put us in this pitch-black room, which I sleuthed was supposed to be an imitation of an old theater from the mid-20th c., though quite a bit smaller. It was the custom back then to watch movievids in big strangergroups, before crowds of random people were a bug danger. I think there must have been a godbelief temple aspect to those cineplexes, because their rooms were dark and you weren't allowed to speak, and all the attention was focused on a massive screen up at the front, where images of beautiful people were blown up all perfect and a couple stories tall. The cineplexes had supercooled air, my father says, and everyone sat respectfully, like for a godbelief worship, and listened without speaking to the booming sound systems.

We didn't look at each other because it was so dark. But now and then if I glanced sideways I could see the light from the screen flickering on Sam or my dad or my mom, see them in profile as they gazed.

The vids themselves were your standard family stuff, nothing shocking, except I'd never seen most of them before. My dad and the corp tech had done a good job—

the music was up-tempo for most of the hour, and there were scenes of us from different stages of life. The twist on it was, it started with the most recent memories and then it went backward from there. So the first scenes we saw were from this year and last, me and Sam talking over the dinner table as Dad held the camera, the two of us decorating a birthday present for my mom, and then we got younger and younger, till we were little kids again.

There were the usual occasions—parties and holidays, guests who I didn't know from Adam anymore. Scenes of little kids filing into our condo, each showing his or her codes at the camera and smiling goofily. There were family trips—we never took a big one like this before but we would go, once a year, a couple of hours away on a bus or something, or do an overnight on a boat. My father was something called an insurance manager they used to have, I guess there used to be corps that ensured other corps didn't lose all their money. But on his own time he played music and stuff like that. After insurance ended he went into model marketing, selling models to large entities— basically promoting them.

My mother was good at all kinds of applied *and* brainy things, she studied risk and science and then went to work as a chemist for a pharmacorp, before she got depressed and quit. Yep, ironic. My father used to tell me privately that she quit everything then. The only thing that kept her okay was deciding to look at things a simple way, "focusing on a single point," as my dad said. So she accepted a simple model instead of using her brain anymore and tried hard

117

not to think of the large, only the small and what was right in front of her.

It was one day at a time after that, he said, always one day at a time.

We also had a small family legacy from generations ago when, believe it or not, one of our ancestors was a rap-music dude. I'm not kidding. He had a gangsta rap album that sold zillions of copies but he was mostly a businessman. When my parents were prepping me to deal with money stuff last month, they told me that. He left us actual *gold*. I never knew before.

There's not that much left anymore from the rap guy, Rakim somebody, but it's what let them afford Hawaii, for instance. Their careers were regular-paying jobs, more or less—regular jobs for white-collar Firsts, anyway. So we're the lucky ones, which is part of how Sam and I have stayed healthy. We've always lived in that one-millionth of 1 percent of the population of the First that isn't constantly moving, that has gated communities and security.

Anyway, so we were kids in the homevids, and then we watched ourselves as babies. We'd never seen those vids before, since my parents couldn't stand to dwell on the past—they *made* the vids back then, but couldn't ever bear to actually watch them. So all this time the footage had sat in a storage pod, waiting.

When I saw those movies all I could think of was the baby I'd met at the camp. Actually the baby version of Sam looked a lot like the camp baby. Even *I* did. We both have brown eyes, but other than that it was surprising how much we looked like that baby . . . maybe that's normal, maybe a lot of babies look the same. I wouldn't know. There was Sam, with me, a little bigger, standing over him smiling, and then Sam wasn't born yet and I wasn't yet walking, I was still crawling, and then I was just lying there in the baby bed like those small humans were today. And then I was a misshapen red lump lying on my mother's chest two minutes after being extracted.

More tearjerking than the vids of Sam and me, though, were the ones of our parents before we even existed. Because time kept unspooling backward as the memories kept playing, and so my parents got younger and younger. The quality of the footage of them was good—sharp and full of color.

In front of my very eyes they turned into kids again. And I don't know, somehow it broke my heart to look at them.

In one scene they played a game sort of like smallgolf, hitting balls through these little bridges on some green, green grass. I've always longed for grass, and for the big old trees that shimmered in the light with a million fluttering leaves moved by the wind. Watching them smile and laugh as they hit a red ball through the arches, I felt this strange yearning—I wanted to *be* them, back in that other time. I wished they could have stayed there, lived on forever in that happy moment. I wished they'd never had to see what came next.

Another scene was of my mother laughing and talking with her friends, then putting her arms around the neck of this really happy-looking shaggy dog. The large pets were outlawed first for their footprint, so she must have been in her twenties. Because by the time she was thirty you couldn't keep anything bigger than a hamster.

Watching that scene, I suddenly agreed with Sam.

I knew it was against what I was supposed to think, against what my parents wanted, against the service corps and everything.

But I didn't want to let them go.

Ψ

The Day Three field trip was called "Jungle Hike," but after this morning and the homevids it was a total let-down, with the exception of three howler monkeys they brought in that Sam said were probably tame anyway. There were never monkeys in Hawaii, back in the day, so that was fully bogus.

Still I liked watching them, they made odd calls and swung around, these fuzzy black shapes with long arms swooping and leaping in the vines.

I was completely distracted the whole time, in a mood turbulence—a tingly confusion, a sense of thrill. I didn't mind, I really dug the sensation, but I also didn't pay much attention to the hike. It was actually just a guided walk along brick pathways in the gardens, with a youngish corp worker named Chad walking backward in front of us and making the odd hokey joke as he pointed out extremely uninteresting plants.

So I'm going to skip right over that to what happened tonight. Because tonight turned out to be a fancy surprise party. They called it the "Eve of Goodbye Gala." It wasn't a surprise to the contracts themselves, but to Sam and me it was.

What they do is, they invite all the week's contract families—and there are hundreds of us—to a big bash, with fancy food and drinks (and custom pharmabevvies for the contracts). They had a live orchestra playing old standards in the main ballroom and big audio systems doing music for the "young people" in a smaller dancehall next door. Personally I love all music, especially loud, which is a rare thing to hear, so I was into both rooms. They even had professional dancers to lead the ballroom dances when that was the kind of music playing.

We all had to dress up. *Black tie* is what they called it. My parents had ordered special outfits for the occasion for all of us—a long, shiny silver dress rental for me and a tuxedo for Sam—and they busted those out like special gifts.

I felt half-guilty then, because Sam and I were both unpsyched by it—we had more urgent things to do, and we were thinking about that when our parents sprung the news on us like it was the best thing since sliced pita. I got that service was trying to imitate the golden days, when people had realmeet parties all the time, but still: a big party seemed beside the point.

Because it was a crowd event we had to have booster shots first—we were up to date on all vaccines, of course, but since the gathering was large the corp wanted extra protection. Sam was paranoid, like maybe there were some sneaky controlpharms in the needle along with the vaccines, but if that was the case it didn't do anything to him. So we did the boosters before we got dressed up, and then we all headed down to the party—my father, in his tuxedo, looking pretty swank for an old guy and my mother looking picturesque in a white ball gown.

My own dress was tight and uncomfortable but I told my mother it fit perfectly.

The main ballroom for the gala was the Twilight Lounge, all changed around so there was lots of open space, and then the smaller studio next to it, with the so-called youth music, had mirrors on the walls and sparkling balls that hung from the ceiling and turned. In the main room were long tables of food and servants going around with silver trays of fancy drinks; they'd tricked-out the little alcoves around the room with screens where clips from everybody's homevids played, and some of those images were also projected on the ballroom walls, with happy images when the music was fast and more poignant images (I noticed a lot of babies and old people in those segments) when the slower songs were playing.

So from time to time I would look up and see a faint image of my mom or dad floating across the wall. Trippy.

The only people we recognized were the ones from our survivor group. I talked to Xing for a while; I liked her more and more. She comes from a community not too far from ours back home, about twenty minutes away, so there were a few things we had in common—a game club we'd both belonged to at different times, a food center we both knew. All I could think about, while we were talking, was the camp, the turtles, and those wild babies. I found myself wondering what Xing would think of the whole thing and wanting to tell her about it, but I knew I couldn't, no way, so instead I led her into the disco room and we tried dancing around a bit.

Our parents had put in some song requests for us, knowing my taste for old stuff, so we heard "Backwater" by Eno on the big audio, one of my favorites, and a song called "Ghosts of American Astronauts" by some ancient obscure punk band that Xing was a fan of. (It made me think of you, spacefriend.) Neither were dance numbers but they were still amazing to hear. With the lights and the rhythm and all the crowds everywhere, and the slight buzz of my wheat beers, there were a couple of times I felt like I was flying.

I looked around for Keahi sometimes, I admit, and would catch a glimpse of his dark, elegant head as he passed by in his beige robe with a tray of drinks held up, and every time my stomach would do a small weird flip. Like I had something to look forward to. I didn't know why, it didn't make sense. And then the flip would go away and I'd feel sheepish.

At a certain point Sam came in and got me, on a parental pretext. We traipsed out of the room and through a couple of doors and into a back passageway, where Keahi was hovering. I was suddenly nervous to talk to him, but he only smiled and said in a soft voice that he needed to find out where Sam and I were on the whole fleeing-society-and-joining-the-rebels thing.

"I'm still thinking about it," I said. "It's only been a few hours!"

"The problem is . . ." began Keahi, and he was looking at me in a way that made me feel like I should find something to do with my hands, or my feet. I don't know. My limbs. "You see, we need a decision. I'm sorry to put pressure, but plans have to be made soon."

"I'm in," said Sam.

I wheeled around and stared at him. "Even if I don't come?" I asked after an uncertain pause, and even before I said it I started to feel queasy.

Because Sam, after this week, will be all I have.

"I'm sorry, Nat. You're my sister. But I can't—I just can't stand to live in that world anymore."

We stood there for another few seconds, me confused and trembly, Sam biting his lip and staring at his feet, and finally I told Keahi I'd decide by midnight. Sam had a way of contacting him.

When we went back into the main ballroom we were walking a few feet apart. I felt alone and there was nothing I could say to Sam in public anyway.

Ψ

Xing found me again at the dessert table a little while later, where I was halfheartedly spearing a rice pastry off a tray with a colored toothpick.

"What was that all about?" she asked. "He said your parents needed you for some emoting, and then you went away in the opposite direction from them."

I stared at her, alarmed. I was thinking, if she noticed something fishy, anyone could have.

Anyone—like service.

"I'm a psych counselor back home," she went on, a little apologetic. "I pick up on things."

"He just—you know, he's having a hard time," I bluffed. "He has some problems. With this whole thing."

"Hmm." Xing nodded slightly, but I could tell she wasn't quite buying into my vagueness.

But the party went on, and we did the things there were to do—drinking, eating, dancing. It would have been a blast if my thoughts and feelings hadn't been going in at least twenty directions, including death and rebels. I went to check up on my parents a few times, who seemed to be talking with other contract couples, making the rounds, enjoying themselves. I looked at them once, chatting and lifting their goblets to their lips, and I thought: *What's in your heads? Aren't you frightened?*

But it passed. And there they were, still laughing and talking.

As the night wore on I got a little more buzzed, so by the time the climax of the evening came I was definitely pharmatipsy. A service guy, some kind of exec or manager or something, stood up in front of the orchestra and gave a little speech about how special it was to share this historic and bountiful night with all of us. He said it was a privilege to be near us in this intense and lovely parting. Then he said it was his honor to introduce an operatic recital, just one song. After the song we would have the very last dance and then the party would be over.

"And so, before the goodnight waltz, I give you this evening's pièce de résistance, the lovely Greek diva Maria Callas in hologram from the mid-20th c. with a command performance of—from Giuseppe Verdi's 19th c. master-work *The Force of Destiny*—'Peace, Peace, My God.' Ms. Callas will sing in the original language of Italian."

He left the stage while people clapped and the lights dimmed and then an elegant woman appeared where he had been, fading in slowly. She had black hair wound up on top of her head and wore a long dark-red dress. She bowed her head slightly and then peered up again sadly and began to sing, though of course her voice was coming from the sound system. But I have to say it was perfectly synced.

I'd never listened to opera before, I thought it would be high and screechy and flat boring, but this was—it was beautiful. I didn't understand a word.

We stood there rapt. And when the last note faded, well, there wasn't a dry eye in the house, as the old folks used to say.

I thought: *I am collecting this moment. It's invisible, it's intangible, it's nothing solid, and yet it's perfect and it will always be.* I closed my eyes and concentrated as hard as I ever had before, trying to remember it exactly and minutely.

I'd never collected something before that wasn't an object.

I thought, this is a whole new kind of collecting for me. *I can collect pieces of time.*

Even Sam, standing a few feet away from me—who had shot me a cynical look when the corporate guy said the name of the song—had tears in his eyes. He wiped them right away, though, when I noticed.

There was complete silence in the ballroom and then a wave of quiet and worshipful applause. The name of the last waltz scrolled over the orchestra and they started to play something called "The Tennessee Waltz." It had vocals to it, playing over the sound system along with the live instruments.

I was going to sit down, because I have no clue about waltzes, but then I felt a tap on my shoulder and Keahi was standing there.

"May I?" he asked, and I was too surprised to say anything. I let him take my hand and lead me onto the floor where the contracts were gathering and slowly starting to dance. I saw my parents in their black-and-white costumes, smiling at each other with shining eyes in a kind of predeath, pharmadaze, and felt my throat constrict.

Somehow Keahi knew how to do that kind of dancing. Maybe it was part of his job, I was thinking, maybe he trained in that field along with massage and drink serving;

maybe he was supposed to step in and dance with the survivors who didn't have anyone else to dance with.

But whatever the reason, he was good at it.

"Just follow what my feet do with your feet and you'll be fine," he told me.

And so there was this song, and this sad music, and I let him float me around and I wasn't even crunching his toes. Plus he smelled good. Okay, I'm coming off idiotic, I know. I may as well admit, I've never had a boyfriend. It's hard to meet people, with crowd rules. Once there was a guy at my game club that I liked a bit, and maybe he liked me and we kissed once, but then his family moved to Illinois. They had to go. They had to eke out a living. They'd stopped being in the one-millionth of 1 percent.

We danced past and through the crowd, with that song in our ears. A woman's gravelly but sweet voice sang, "*I remember the night, and the Tennessee Waltz, and I know just how much I have lost . . .*" and I was crying.

And I knew Keahi could tell, even though my face was over his shoulder and he couldn't see it straight on, but he didn't pull back to look at me or make me feel embarrassed about crying. Instead he danced us out from under the Twilight dome onto the balcony, which jutted away from the ballroom, and you could hear the crash of the waves far beneath and see the stars spangling the skies.

"There aren't any mikes out here," he whispered.

This great starry blackness was over us, and the lights from inside fell across the balcony floor. To one side stretched the endless ocean, the ocean that once contained a world.

And then as we danced, taking just small steps, out there on the balcony over that ancient sea that was invisible in the dark, he whispered again into my ear: "Nat. Don't stay where there's no hope."

I was still crying like a wuss and staring over his shoulder through the blur at the people inside, looking so fine and even proud in their suits and fancy gowns; most of them were prepared to die. I thought of my mother and my father when they were babies. Now that I'd seen babies personally—those chubby, clear-eyed creatures that seemed like they'd be so ridiculously easy to hurt—I felt confused. Once even my parents had been these completely helpless creatures, utterly dependent on other people to protect them.

Maybe now they were helpless again.

"I don't want to see you live your life as a drone," he said. "No one's promising we can win. But the point is we have to fight for it. Life is for *trying*. Don't you see?"

It was exciting to be out there over the sea, with the volcano rising massively into the sky behind me, though I couldn't see it. I felt warmer knowing there were those ancient turtles sheltered beneath that mountain, lifting their feet off the warm sand with that ponderous slowness.

And the babies, and the fruit trees, and the other living things I'd heard about but not yet seen. I thought of the not-so-green-green grass of home, and it seemed like someplace I'd lived a long, long time ago.

Even though there were only a few weeks and one ocean between us.

There was the transition housing or the jungle. The babies and turtles or the place I'd grown up in.

I whispered: "Okay. I'll come with you. But I don't want to come alone."

Keahi pulled back, so we were at arm's length, and looked down at me.

We just stood there quietly, but I felt like the universe was rushing and tumbling around us.

Day Four
Commitment & Communion
Theme of the Day: Goodbye

They don't even trust us to say goodbye. Not entirely. And that's inconvenient for Sam and me.

Because Happiness, a/k/a Death, is scheduled for tomorrow, Day Five. Which means that if we're going to have a chance of saving my parents, most of the time we have is today. At least, that's the way it seems to me. But they've scheduled a group healing session this morning. To guide us in our process of "Commitment & Communion." To give us tips and techniques, etc.

And then, early this afternoon, a one-hour session with just our family and the VR.

LaTessa has a full slate too. Xing mentioned that her own family's one-hour session was planned for first thing this morning, so LaT. must have those private meetings back-to-back all day. That's a whole lotta goodbye for one Vessel to Receive, don't you think?

Even knowing how much pharma they're on, I'm surprised my parents aren't more bummed. Or scared. The inside of their heads, at this point, is pretty much a mystery to me. But then again, this morning it's more obvious than it was yesterday that they're not all here anymore. The pills are taking them to Happyland already.

I didn't notice it so much last night, with the party and the new things we'd just found out about and all that. Maybe that's why the service corp throws that party that particular night: to distract survivors from the personality changes in the contracts.

Because right away this morning, when we came out of our separate bedrooms, I looked at my dad, who was pouring himself some caffbev in the kitchenette, and I got a strange feeling.

My father's always been a details guy. A dreamer, sure, but he's always read a lot and loved to know things and tell us stuff about the world—he's like a clearinghouse of information about books and history and animals and bug vectors and what have you. But when he glanced up at me from that caffbev, he didn't look like a guy who would know any details at all. He smiled, but it was a loose, almost impersonal sort of smile. His mouth had a slackness to it.

Also, the pupils of his eyes were dilated really huge and black.

Which made me feel chilled.

"So, um, Dad," I asked, a little nervously, "how're you feeling?"

"It's going really well," he said, but he looked past me, not at me directly.

"Yeah? Have you already . . . like, forgotten things?"

"Forgotten . . . ?"

"You know, because today is supposed to be the day when the forgetting begins," I said. "It was in the training."

"We're going to forget things," he nodded.

I was like, *Ummm. Yeah.*

"But you haven't yet, right?" I nudged. "You still know who I am, and all that."

"I know who you are." He lifted his mug to drink. "You're my little girl."

"Good job. A-plus," I said, trying to make a light joke out of it.

"You were born in a hospital with beds of tulips," he went on, musing. But as he said this, he still wasn't looking at me. He went over to a vase of purple flowers and touched one of the petals gently. "You were born in the night."

Now, there was nothing wrong with saying that. He said it in a nice way, on the fond side. It just didn't sound like *him*, exactly.

"When you were just a few months old," he started again, "I said to her, *Now, did you ever think we'd have such a lovely daughter? Such an amazing little kid . . .* because when we were young, before you had to get the permits and all that, we never even thought about it. We didn't want to have children, for a long time, because our spirits were broken. But then we changed our minds, you see. Your mother decided. She thought we could still have something of our own. Something to love and be loved by, in all the chaos descending. She said, *Whatever the world is to us, maybe they'll see it differently. There is the sky, after all. There's always the sky. And they have a right to see it. The world deserves new eyes to behold it.* That's what she said to me, when we decided to have you. *The world needs new eyes to behold it.*"

I was staring, because he'd never said that to me before.

"Of course, too many people thought that, didn't they? *Billions* too many . . . because the world didn't need new eyes at all, did it? *No* eyes. No more. But maybe one day . . . the eye evolved more than once, after all. Rebirth is possible! Millions of years from now new creatures will walk these green hills . . . we think of that often, your mother and I. Who knows what new forms may evolve? Maybe there'll even be another wave of mammals . . ."

And then my father put down his mug of caffbev and began to sing.

To *sing*. My dad. I vaguely remembered him singing, back when he made his own music, but not lately. Not since the tipping point.

After the tipping point he'd never sung again.

He sang in this deep, solemn voice.

"And did those feet, in ancient times, walk upon England's mountains green? And was the holy lamb of God . . . on England's pleasant pastures seen? And did the countenance divine shine forth upon our clouded hills? And was Jerusalem builded here, among these dark Satanic mills?"

Sam came out of his room then, rubbing his eyes. But our dad didn't stop.

"Bring me my bow of burning gold; bring me my arrows of desire; bring me my spear, oh clouds unfold! Bring me my chariot of fire!"

I remember practically the whole thing. I wrote it down right away.

"Whoa, Dad," said Sam, after my father stopped and was just standing there.

"Your Uncle Den always loved that hymn," explained my dad, musing. "It was his favorite. The poet William Blake. The sentiment was misplaced, of course . . . crusade mentality . . . but the song is still a fine one, don't you think? Old William Blake himself. By God, sir. Yes. A great genius."

And he reached out for his drink.

After that outburst he kind of settled into a resting cycle, absent-seeming. But that was how we started the morning of our Goodbye Day.

Ψ

I'm not going to write down the dull details of the group session—basically LaTessa telling us how to be nice to each other, how to forgive the effects of the pharma on our parents, how not to resent the changes we see in them because those changes are in aid of a greater good, namely the "peak emotional experience" of their Bountiful Passing.

And her reminding us in no uncertain terms to please self-medicate generously if we found ourselves "creating barriers to loving."

But I'll tell you what happened as we left the room: Keahi handed Sam something. He slipped it into Sam's robe pocket without anyone seeing. I didn't notice it myself till we were back in the suite. And even then I didn't have much time to get what it was or what was happening. I went down the hall to use the waste room, and then when I got there and was actually peeing, who should stick his head into the women's section but Sam. Ick.

Luckily it was just me between the curtains.

"He says be very careful, that we can't tell them *anything* about what we're planning," he hissed. "*Nothing.* Total radio silence. All we can do is follow the group's guidance. There's a Plan A and a Plan B. But no talking. None. Got it?"

"But—"

"And the rest that you need to know is, about Mom and Dad? They'll try. But they can't make promises. Keahi said to make sure you knew: it's way harder with the contracts than with us."

And then before I could say anything he scrunched up the note. Which had been in his hand. And ate it.

That kind of bamboo fiber was only ever good to eat for extinct black-and-white bears.

"Following orders," he said, chewing. And made a pained grimace as he swallowed.

Ψ

So that meant there was zero chance of getting my parents' approval. Not that they would have given it anyway, but I'd been considering trying to sabotage their pharma or something so they might be more receptive.

But no. It was too high-risk for the people in the camp, I got that—especially when I remembered how quickly my mom had ratted Sam out to service. All he'd done was go off-plan for a few measly hours. This was a lot bigger than that.

For now, Sam had told me before he left the waste room, we had to act like everything was on track and keep saying goodbye.

We had a little Personal Time on the plan before lunch, so I settled down in the living room of the suite with this journal while my parents put earbuds in and hooked up to their favorite music. Music's a big part of Final Weeks, as you may have noticed. Normally they would have held hands doing that, they've always been pretty affectionate with each other, but I noticed that this time they just sat side by side on the couch, expressions peaceful and slack.

Like holding hands would be too much work.

We had the sliding doors to the balcony open, and a nice breeze swept in off the ocean and lifted the curtains.

But then, while I was writing the section before this one, there came a knock on the door. I must have been the only one who heard it—Sam had earbuds in too and was listening to his own music in an armchair and jiggling one leg—so I got up to answer, passing Sam on my way. He didn't glance up or take his earbuds off, maybe because he didn't want to seem vigilant. Maybe they've put hidden cameras in the living room now too.

And at the door, when I opened it, was Rory.

He smiled and everything, as much as you can with a face like that. But it wasn't a smile I liked, exactly.

"Good morning, Nat," he said. "Happy Goodbye Day. May I speak with your brother, please?"

It wasn't really a question.

"Sure," I said, casual and friendly. "Come in."

So Rory entered and walked over to Sam, whose chair happened to be facing the other way, toward the balcony looking out, and tapped him on the shoulder.

Well, it was more like he grasped him on the shoulder.

My parents had their eyes closed to the music and didn't open them right away.

Sam turned around, playing it cool, and looked up at Rory and took his earbuds out, one by one, very chill.

"We need to have a little talk, Sam," said Rory. "Just you and me. Man to man."

And then my mother did notice—I guess the sound of Rory's voice filtered through her purple haze—and she sat up and took her own earpieces out, looking disoriented. And my father must have felt her movement on the sofa and opened his eyes and did the same.

"I'll talk to you, dude," said Sam. "But you don't have to be so bossy about it." I guess he figured if he was too friendly that'd be suspicious also. In its own way.

"I'm stealing your son for a minute," said Rory, all smiles directed at Mom and Dad. "I'll bring him right back, I promise."

"Oh, yes," said my mom, but she was also shaking her head, kind of confused.

"Nothing the matter, though," said my dad. He might have meant it as a question but didn't seem to have the energy to say it like that. The opposite of Rory, who said commands like he was asking politely.

"No, no," said Rory. "Just making sure we're all on the same screen here."

"Where are you taking him?" I asked as they headed for the door. "Can I come with? I mean, shouldn't I be on the same screen too?"

"You're fine. Sam and I are just going outside for a real quick powwow."

Powwow?

I don't think my Seminole ancestors would have liked Rory.

The door closed behind the two of them.

I stood there wondering if I should go after them. And then I thought, but why? In a fistfight between Rory and me, it's pretty clear who would prevail. The guy must weigh like 150 kilos.

Plus he had the whole corp on his side.

But that felt gutless so I did run to the door and open it again, and I stuck my head out into the hall in time to see them disappear around a corner.

"Nat! Nat," said my mother, urgent at first and then trailing off. "Are you . . . doing something, honey?"

"I was trying to see where he was taking Sam."

"Taking him out for a real quick powwow," echoed my dad, nodding to himself slowly, bobblehead-style. "That's all."

"Relax," said my mom. "You want to listen? There's extra earbuds there . . ."

And they were already putting their earpieces back in. Just like that. They lay back, rested their heads, and

139

closed their eyes again. In that second, I didn't regret at all deceiving them.

I wanted my real parents back. Or nothing.

And maybe it would turn out that I couldn't have them, I saw then. Maybe I'd end up with nothing. Because it struck me, with a shiver of recognition, that it was more than just this past couple of weeks, more than this trip. It was ever since they bought the contract a couple of months ago. Ever since then, they'd been a little bit different—a little more *generic*. As though someone had flipped a switch in them. And this was the most extreme I'd seen them, but in a way it made me see the subtler changes that had come before.

Like when they told us about buying the contract, in the condo with Jean. I hadn't heard them argue a single time since *weeks* before that. Maybe months. And my parents love each other a lot, but they've always fought now and then. I hadn't heard my father tell an off-color joke, which he always liked to do. I hadn't heard my mom swear. She was kind of a potty mouth, my mom. In bygone days.

And I hadn't heard them laugh, either. Not a real, raucous laugh. Of course, before I'd chalked that up to them being about to die.

But now I'm not so sure.

Whether I would ever see my real parents again or not, I knew—after they let Rory the man-mountain hustle Sam out of there and went right back to their music without so much as lifting an eyebrow—that if all there was left of them was these pale imitations, I'd have to take my chances.

Ψ

As it turned out Rory hadn't been lying: he did bring Sam back, right before we had to go downstairs to eat. And Sam still had the same cocky-kid look he usually cultivated in Rory's presence, so it must not have been too much of a torture session.

Or so I thought till Sam went into his room, while my parents were freshening up at their sinkbowl, and I followed him.

"He shot me up with a trank," he rushed, under his breath. "It hasn't set in yet but it should be about two minutes till that blood gets to my brain. So I'm going to be zoned really soon."

"He can't do that! It's in the rules! It has to be self-administered!"

"Not if you're a minor who goes off-plan," said Sam. He was talking at high speed. "Fine print. What made them suspicious was me sticking my head into the waste room to talk to you—there's cameras in that hall. But they don't have anything solid. So you have to be extra normal this afternoon—and because I'm going to be tranking soon you need to have my back. There may have been some kind of sodium pentothal pharm in the needle—like, truth serum. So if I start talking weird, if I start talking a lot at all, *dose me.* I mean, knock me *out.* Use all the pills in my

Coping Kit. There's not enough to OD. Promise! Any sign of talking too much. Nat, promise me!"

"But that could be dangerous, Sam! You mean over the max dosage?"

"Screw the max. *All the pills*, Nat. Put me to *sleep*."

And he rummaged around in his kit and handed me a trank vial. It was still completely full.

"I'm scared of it, Sam. There's so much *in* it."

"Here's the alternative—we miss our chance. Mom and Dad are gone for sure and who knows what happens to the camp and the animals. And those little kids? We go back home, if you can call it that—*I* don't—and we can never come back."

The door opened and we jumped.

"Nat? Sam? Are you ready for lunch, dears?" My mom stood in the doorway.

Sam was already getting a glazed look in his eyes. "*Promise*," he said, softly.

"Okay," I said reluctantly. "I promise."

"Promise what, honey . . . ?" asked my mother.

But she was turning away already, and we didn't have to answer.

And then we were leaving the suite, and Sam brought up the rear, walking slowly.

Ψ

Lunch was a major drag, with Sam drugged like that. Rory must have given him a megadose, because five minutes after he gave me my instructions he lapsed into a stupor. He was silent and couldn't hold his head upright and when he did say something it was slurred.

It made me angry.

And what was also frustrating was that my parents seemed not to see it. Or maybe they did see and just didn't care, pharmazoned. I don't know. It was strange to be the only one acknowledging that he was completely zomboid.

At least he wasn't talky during lunch. He picked at his food with no interest and stared down at his plate. At a certain point these wandering dudes with black and gold-braid outfits and big hats and pygmy guitars came up to our table; they were going around serenading the diners in a more or less embarrassing fashion and suddenly we were it.

"Mariachis!" said my dad.

"May we play a request, sir and madam?" they asked my parents.

"Mmm, maybe 'El Paso'?" suggested my dad. "The Marty Robbins classic?"

"'Black Diamond Bay'!" said my mother.

So they stood there and strummed this song on their instruments and the main guy also sang—some kind of weird song about a volcano erupting and people gambling before the lava got to them. I would have thought my brother would like it but Sam didn't even look up, just picked apart a circle of soylami into thumbnail-size fragments till it was shredded all over his plate like the aftermath of a bomb. He seemed completely absorbed in this deliberate, painfully slow process. And once I saw a line of drool string down from his lip onto the table edge.

It was yuck. I felt really bad for him, that he was in this state and also that people were seeing him this way. But more than that, it scared me. Because it was hitting me just then, watching him, how serious the service corps must be. To grab a smart, energetic kid by force, stick a syringe into his arm, and make him into a zombie.

They're not kidding, I thought. But why do they need to get so hardcore?

That's what I was wondering as the musicians in the big hats crooned. *"The dealer said, it's too late now/You can take your money but I don't know how/You'll spend it in the tomb . . ."* Meanwhile my parents were swaying and smiling slightly and coming off foolhardy.

I was thinking, well, what if my parents *were* to back out of the contract at the last minute? How would it hurt the corp? I mean, people do it occasionally, and as far as I can tell they sacrifice all the cash they already paid—no refund at all except for funeral expenses—and then they usually go running back to the corps a few months later and pay for the whole deal again. So the corps shouldn't mind at all, it seems to me.

In fact they should practically be *glad* when that happens and they can double their money! I mean, sure, it creates disruptions for the group, when contracts suddenly back out—I've browsed some sites that say it can have a ripple effect among the other contracts doing Happiness that day. They get spooked, then unpsyched, and there's a bit of a stampede. Away from the Bountiful Passing.

But even in that case, the corp's still making all its money, right? It's not like they don't get paid. So why do they care so much? Why do they want to be *so* sure my parents are going to die tomorrow, on schedule, that they decide they have to muscle into our room, shoot Sam up, and leave him there at a lunch table, in a public place with strangers looking at him, with spit hanging out of his mouth?

Maybe contract pullouts look bad for the corporate image. I guess the bottom line comes down to image, for them.

Still, I'd have to say a drooling survivor at a mariachi luncheon looks bad too.

And also, when we've been told those stories in the past—the stories of contracts who reneged at the eleventh hour—they're always told in a way that makes the contracts seem insecure and selfish, like by paying double out of fear they're making things poorer for their survivors, and so they're the ones with the disgrace. Not the corporates.

Because contracts don't come cheap.

I don't fully get it.

Ψ

We had to take Sam to the session like that, our private family session with LaT. He wasn't drooling anymore, after we left the restaurant, but he was tripping over his feet as he walked, muttering under his breath. You couldn't even understand what he was saying—a relief—but I was on high alert, because what if it was secrets he was telling? And what if he got louder and clearer? Pharma can come in waves sometimes, affecting the brain first one way, then another. He'd been quiet till then, but that didn't make me confident.

To spill the secrets in front of LaTessa, I figured, that would be the worst possible situation.

So I kept close to him as we headed to the hearing room. I held one of his limp arms and walked beside him and I listened, through the hotel lobby, into the elevator, then down the twists and turns of lavender corridors, passing other contracts and family members as they navigated their own way through the maze.

All striking me, for the first time, as total sleepwalkers.

But what he was mumbling was all gibberish, as far as I could tell, and my parents, walking ahead of us with their arms around each other's waists, didn't seem to be paying any more attention to him now than they had when he was drooling over his lunchplate.

We got there and sat down in a circle around the water feature, as directed. Sam was like a crazy person or a booze migrant, not looking up, doing little hand gestures to himself, little laughs, shit like that.

LaT. came in, and her gown was even more arresting this time because it was whiter than white, like a bride—and it even had a very small train that wafted in the air behind her and didn't seem to touch the floor. LaT., I have to say, could win an Aryan Princess Beauty Contest. She's like that superthin olden doll with yellow hair, one of the famous toys they used to make from oil. When she sat down the dress settled around her in a filmy cloud.

She must have been briefed by Rory, most likely she was in on the whole thing, because she didn't even blink at Sam's condition.

"I want to wish you a happy, happy Goodbye Day," she said first off. "Let us join hands and *be*."

We held hands, with me grabbing Sam's, which was sweaty and trembling, and my father on his other side taking his other one. This was when we were supposed to bow our heads and close our eyes and meditate, but I just watched the others do it. With LaT.'s eyes closed, I noticed on her lids the weenciest bit of silvery eyeshadow.

So LaT. was breaking the no-makeup-in-sessions rule. Huh.

And Sam was still babbling to himself, but mostly it was silent, his lips moving, his head shaking back and forth, like no, no, no, like he was denying something constantly. I think he was trying to hold himself in check. I wondered how I was supposed to dose him now, in the middle of the session, if he got louder. I started to feel even more anxious.

There was a waste room nearby, a couple of doors down the hall—could I get him there, if I had to? Would LaT. even let me?

I was getting pretty majorly anxious; I was on the edge of my seat, or would have been if I'd had one.

"And now, Robert and Sara," she said to my parents, when the moment was apparently done, "I trust you're feeling loving."

"Very," said my mother—or, rather, the pharmazone impostor who had taken her over.

"Express your perceiving," said LaT. gently.

My parents just looked at her and smiled.

"I know," said LaT. "Words escaping."

"It's just . . . nice," said my mother.

"Nice," echoed my dad.

She wasn't getting much from them, obviously. Pharmadrones. She smiled and nodded sympathetically and then she turned to me.

"And you, Nat," she serened. "Is there a beingness you feel like sharing?"

"I guess so." It seemed to me I should fill as much space as I could right then, so that Sam couldn't fill any. "I guess my problem is, you know, we're supposed to say goodbye today. And we've had all the training. Which I appreciate. And so none of this is unexpected, and I realize that. But still, my problem is I feel like I *can't* really say goodbye. Because I believe they've already left. Before, we didn't say goodbye because there was going to be time later. Now it's later but I'm not sure who's here to say goodbye to."

"You know, Nat," said LaT., a little chiding, "your loving parents are being next to you, *so* closely. You can still be expressing to them."

"But I'm not sure it *is* them. It's more their pharma that's here, their pharms speaking through them. Not them speaking through their pharms. That would be fine, or at least I could take it. I'm used to it. But this is like their pharms have taken over. Don't you know what I mean?"

Of course, I didn't really care if she knew what I meant, and I also already knew that she knew. I was talking emptily, just to hold onto the airwaves.

"The selves of your parents," explained LaT., "are fully whole, only ensconced in Happiness-promoting. A self is not taken, a self is being augmented. Please, Nat, be with us fully in the triumph that is healing. Remember, only contentment is designed. The self is always still there, the self is a noble spark, bountifully persisting."

And that was when Sam spoke up.

"No, no," he said, urgently if still a bit slurry too. "That isn't it at all."

LaT. swiveled her head to look at him. Really swiveled— like a robot. For a second I thought she was one. But no. There aren't robots that high-functioning.

"Sam," she purred. "Wonderful. Sharing a feeling?"

"They're gone. You took them. This isn't them, it's just a memory," said Sam. "It's like, the side that's faceup, floating on the surface when the person has already been drowned."

He was flushed and sweaty-faced and shaking his head.

And he hadn't said anything yet but I knew then, I had to get to him before he did.

"You're taking them for the quotas," said Sam.

I had no clue what he was talking about. But I saw LaT.'s eyes widen in shock.

This was it.

"He's going to throw up," I interrupted, my voice panicked. "He's gagging!"

Sam eyeballed me a little, fear in the whites of his eyes, and a split-second later he *was* gagging, he was hunching forward and making motions of being sick.

"I'll get him to the toilet," I rushed, and I got up, and I grabbed him by the hand and pulled. LaTessa stood up too, but I pushed him past her and out the door, we were basically running, and it was a blur after that. I got him to the door of the waste room, and then we were inside and I took the vial out of my robe pocket and shoved the pills into his mouth, with him half-helping and half-flailing, and then he was swallowing and it looked like he really was gagging, but I didn't have time to watch. I threw the vial into a composting toilet and then even—this is a gross part—shoved it down under the top layer of straw, which thankfully wasn't too shitty, and turned around just in time to see Sam leaning over the sink, where he must have washed down the pills with some Reclaimed Sewage Grade A.

And then the door was flung open. I mean this whole thing took under sixty seconds.

I couldn't wash my hands because that would tip them off, so I stood there with the faint pungency of compost on my fingertips, hoping no one else could smell it coming from me. And Sam stood over the sink, face streaming with sweat and bright red, and it did look like he might have just thrown up.

But he had swallowed the pills.

And water was washing down the sink. So for all they knew, he *had* been sick.

I was afraid. Of the service employee standing in front

of me—not Rory but his friend from before, another man-mountain with a name tag that read, *Olaf.*

"I'm sorry," I said shakily. "I know it's totally disruptive. But he just—he had to throw up. Maybe a reaction to his pharms?"

Olaf jerked his head at me, to say, *Get out.* (It was a men's waste room, by the way.) He didn't bother to make nice. "Wait in the hall," he said. "Don't leave."

So he stayed in the waste room with Sam, and I went out. As I was standing in the hall, following orders and waiting for them, I noticed a door cracked open—it must have been the door to a room just off the healing room, I think, because the healing room door was only a few feet further along the hall. It was open a couple of inches, like it hadn't quite connected and clicked closed when someone quickly went in. I don't know whether it was just boredom and restlessness or whether I was purposeful, but something made me sneak closer until I was near enough to detect the voices leaking out of it.

And then I heard a man's voice say, not loudly but forcefully all the same, with a threatening tone: "That shit can't happen. That's major demerits. I bet you forfeit the whole week's bonus."

And then a woman's voice: "You've got to be fucking kidding me. My whole bonus? It could be nothing. And it went down in two seconds flat. What the fuck was I supposed to do? *You* fucking tell *me*, Rory."

I knew that voice even without the phony serene vibe and careful language technology. And it belonged to LaT.

151

Ψ

Sam and Olaf came out after a minute and I led Sam up to the suite, with Olaf lumbering at our heels. When we got up there he was mumbling about how he was afraid he was going to be sick again. Actually he was just falling asleep, I could tell, and I was worried about all those pills and what they might do to him. I wasn't quite as certain as he was that he wouldn't OD.

But I was also relieved he wasn't saying anything shocking. And that I'd been able to keep my promise. It had been a close call.

Olaf didn't let me stay with Sam though, I had to go back to the session and he escorted me the whole way. When I went in, there was LaTessa, completely returned to her serene self. Like nothing had happened. My parents were holding hands with her, and all three of them had closed eyes and were trancelike.

I was feeling shaken because I guess in some way I'd trusted that LaTessa was who she pretended to be. In some way I wanted her to be a real VR; if she was going to say that jargon I'd wanted her to *mean* it. I didn't want her to be someone who was flat-out pretending. And now I knew she was. She was just like the other thugs, nothing but a regular service employee, and all her language technology was a veneer. She wasn't a shrink, she was a con man.

On one level I'd always thought she was fake, sure, partly because of Sam's cynicism and partly because her way of talking had too many rules for me. But still I must have hoped she wasn't. I must have hoped she did have secrets, somewhere inside those words ending with *-ing*. Good secrets, like a godbelief. And now that hope was dashed.

Who knew what else was fake? This whole thing could be a house of cards. Underneath all the pretty surfaces, it might all be people swearing like LaTessa, people trying to pull something.

In fact now it seemed to me like it almost had to be that way, and I'd always been a sheep, just like Sam said. A sheep and a brainwash.

I bit down so hard on my teeth that they hurt. I didn't want to be a sheep.

I waited politely till LaT. and my parents opened their eyes again and sat down at my place.

"Illness is part of being," said LaT. consolingly. "Sam will be being fine later. For now, Nat, let us continue the loving expressing."

All I could think of was the tone of her normally silvery voice, saying, *My whole bonus? What the fuck was I supposed to do?*

But I tried on a weak smile and pushed myself back into a therapy frame of mind.

$$\Psi$$

When my parents and I got back to the suite Sam was still fast asleep. My parents just stuck their heads in his door quickly and then went out onto the balcony; I took a closer look myself, being worried, but his breathing seemed normal so I told myself he was okay. For the moment, at least.

We had a group cliffwalk scheduled next, which was supposed to end with a guided Goodbye Ceremony. I wasn't sure what to do about Sam.

But as it turned out I didn't get to decide.

Because who should show up while I was writing in my journal but Olaf and Rory. And behind them was Keahi. And one other young Hawaiian guy in a robe without a name tag.

At first I was alarmed, I thought Keahi had been found out, maybe. Then he smiled at me, and it warmed me up. It was that reassuring.

"We've brought two supervisors," said Rory to Mom and Dad. "They have health training and they're going to watch your little guy for you, until he's ready to go back on-plan. You can rely on them absolutely, they've been thoroughly vetted and are 100 percent trustworthy. Sound good?"

He was all fake cheer and business as usual.

Mom and Dad nodded gratefully, like the corp was providing its usual top-notch service.

"What we suggest is you three go on your cliffwalk, and then, if he's still not up to snuff, Sam may have to miss the Goodbye Ceremony. Of course, if he feels better by then, we'll bring him down to join you. We think he'll feel better. We think it'll work out fine."

"Wonderful," said my mother.

"Perfect," said my dad.

And then the man-mountains went out the door and it was just Keahi and his colleague.

I couldn't ask Keahi anything or tell him what had happened because I had no idea if the other Hawaiian dude was loyal to the camp people or the corp. But I felt way safer with Keahi staying there than I would have with Olaf or Rory.

So we got out our parasols and water bottles and the small bag of items they'd told us to bring—some keepsakes and little tokens—and looked at our map to the Goodbye Ceremony, which was being held in a garden a ways along the cliffs. And I said goodbye to Keahi as though he was nothing special to me, casual and polite. And we left.

I felt a tug of regret that Sam couldn't be with us for this part. And then a tug of resentment, because it was service's fault, it was all their fault and if this turned out to be real, all of it—really my parents' Final Week—then the corp would have ruined it for Sam. And he would have missed his only chance to say goodbye properly.

Sure it was partly his responsibility, and I got that, but they didn't have to be so brutal with him.

Some of the other contracts were also out walking—we had the same destination after all—so it wasn't the solitary, windblown experience it could be.

"You are a source of strength, Nattie," my mother said suddenly, as we walked, and reached out to squeeze my hand.

"A source of strength," agreed my father.

"We love you very much," added my mom.

"Our love for you will always be," said my father.

I felt a pang of something then, because they seemed sincere and not as zoned out as they had been. I also felt nervous, I realized, because I had no idea what would happen. That would make *anyone* nervous, wouldn't it? I didn't know what Plan B was, or for that matter Plan A. I didn't have any feel for how good or bad our chances were. I didn't even have the information to take a wild guess.

And it hit me that we could so easily fail, that it was a David and Goliath thing and why had I been acting so confident? Ever since yesterday, the people I'd met and the things I'd seen, I'd actually been going along kind of assuming we *could* save my parents, and so maybe the goodbyes weren't necessarily real. But what if they were, because we couldn't succeed after all? What if service was too polished for us, too big and smooth of a machine?

The smart money would definitely be on the corp, not a couple of kids and some tent-dwellers with turtle pets. What if this really *was* my last day of ever knowing my mother and father? And here I was going through it without thinking so, without believing it—almost casually, because I was stupidly confident?

And here I was, without pharms in my system. As the corps put it, running flat.

And suddenly I missed those pharms. Badly.

I thought, I'll *need* my pharms if these guys actually die. And if I'm lucky enough to be alive, and not locked up somewhere, I'll be out in the jungle too. Pill-less in the palm trees. They probably don't have much pharma in the rebel camp. Not moodpharma, anyway. They probably can't get it. They have to live completely unmanaged. That's their whole deal.

I thought about bringing my Coping Kit with me into the jungle, and wondered how long its small supply of pills would last me, and I realized I was scared.

Then Xing was at my elbow and she said hello brightly and distracted me. Her parents talked to my parents, and she and I walked a little ahead of the four of them.

"Where's Sam?" she asked.

"He got sick to his stomach," I said.

"Really?"

"Maybe it was nerves. Or side effects."

"That's not what I heard," she said, her voice lower.

I looked at her, horror-struck. "What do you mean?"

"I heard you guys are planning on going somewhere," she murmured. "Just like I am."

I almost stopped walking right then, but she put her arm around my shoulders casually and gently pushed me forward.

"No look of surprise, please," she said. "Keep your expression normal and lightly smiling. There we are. Good. Quite nicely done."

"But why—"

"There aren't any cameras now, but in a few feet we're back onscreen. The next one's right there on that bench. So watch out, because we'll soon be surveilled again."

"So—did—they found you too?" I stammered. "You've—you've seen it?"

Then I was instantly frightened that maybe I'd said too much. What if she was a spy from the corp?

"I'm familiar with the camp," she said. "It's why I'm here. And they didn't find me. I *am* them. And *I* found *you*."

Ψ

Joining the Goodbye Ceremony was easier for me after that. I had plenty of questions, believe me, but I felt a lot stronger knowing Xing was in on it—that it wasn't just Sam and me striking out on our own. That somehow, for some reason I didn't understand, she'd brought us in.

The ceremony was supposed to be a celebration of our parents' lives, a kind of funeral before the fact. Because they don't really do funerals *after* the fact, the service corps, that's only for DIYs. No burial or cremation anymore—they passed a law saying burial was a land waste and cremation had too big of a footprint. So what happens to your body after you die is, it gets put in a tank where it's dissolved by these enzymes. And that breeds a bunch of new enzymes they can use for good purposes, like breaking down compost or cleaning water supplies or fertilizing gardens, depending on what kind of enzyme you decide you want to recycle into. You can pick; it's a line item on the contracts.

And instead of funerals after you die, they have these Goodbye Ceremonies beforehand.

Ours was okay. It really wasn't that bad.

It started around sunset, when we'd all finished our walk along the cliffs and had made it into the garden at the clifftop; we sat down in the rows of decorated chairs they'd set out facing the sea. They had a little white ornamental doorway at the front, nearest the cliff, a bit like you might have for a fancy wedding, and there were flowers. There was a VR type who talked about Bountiful Passing and then said antique poetry; there were a couple of musicians who played a keyboard and an old string instrument to accompany him.

Then as it got darker they gave the survivors little balsa boats for each of their parents, or whoever the contract holder was in their family. A couple of people had aunts or uncles under contract, a brother or sister—it wasn't parents for everyone. So I had two boats and Xing also had two. They were delicate but not too lightweight to hold things.

And into the boats we were told to put the small objects we had brought with us from our suites, and before that from home—the objects that symbolized our love for the ones who were leaving. I'd brought things from my collection, because I knew it had to be things I didn't want to part with or else it wouldn't mean anything.

For my mother, I put in a dried leaf off a plant of ours at home, because she really likes plants and this one in particular and she always took care of it and even talked to it, though she also made jokes about people who talk to plants. The leaf was tinged in red, with red along its veins too, and so it reminded me of a person, it was both part of a plant and a kind of copy of a body, so it reminded me of my mother, who'd once been a treehug hippie.

And I put in an old photo of the two of us, when I was little and she was holding me. I thought she would like that. She'd told me, once when she was really sad and having trouble snapping out of it, that since the world died—as she put it—we were all that lived for her, Sam and I. As well as all she lived for.

Into my dad's boat I put a seed, from the bowls of seeds he used to give to the chipmunks in the complex garden, and a drawing I had done for him when I was much younger, five or six I think—a drawing of a bird that I claimed looked like him and labeled, *Daddybird*. He'd kept it all that time. I thought of putting in something musical, because music was always his first love, but I didn't have anything.

Then we held out boats, and the VR guy passed around candles, and we put those in the boats too. He passed out long matches and the parents lit the candles for us—then my mom lit her candle and my dad lit his.

All the contracts stood up there, on the cliff, in a silent crowd just gazing out at the sea. And the rest of us, the survivors, walked down this steep, winding path from the top of the cliffs to the ground beneath, where the ocean stretched out. Down, down we went, walking slowly, carrying our boats carefully with their candles burning and wax dripping onto the things we'd put into them.

Finally we got all the way down, and it was fully dark by that time, though there were also a few tiki torches here and there to guide our way. We stood on a kind of dock they'd built, and we knelt down and placed the boats gently onto the water, where there was a channel. Somehow they'd engineered the waterflow right there, in this little protected cove, so that instead of the waves washing the boats back against the dock, it carried them slowly out to sea. We stood there and watched as our boats floated away from us, a fleet of flickering candle glows dispersing and, in the end, sputtering out.

A song came to us from the cliffs above, a high, sweet song drifting down on the wind. And also, up above, the contracts were watching the boats sail away—my parents standing side by side and gazing, as they always loved to, over the former great wonder that was the Pacific.

We waited and waited until the trail of lights disappeared.

DAY FIVE
HAPPINESS
Theme of the Day: Happiness

It was in our instructions, not from the corp but from the camp: we had to go on illegal pharms.

I'll rewind to explain.

After the Goodbye Ceremony last night, we got back to the room to find Sam wide awake—and of course not feeling sick in the least, since he never had been. My parents went to bed and Keahi and the other guy left. In Sam's room, where they'd double-checked for bugs and cameras and found none, he told me Keahi had given him a wake-up drug and fed him to get his strength up, and then they'd had a long talk session—he, Keahi, and the other guy, who also was on our side, as it turned out.

They'd laid out the plan for him, but he wasn't telling it all to me, only part. And the part was new pharma. Because we had to seem like we were completely with the program, and on Happiness Day it's impossible to fake being cool with it all, they said, without a mood-stabilizing drug at the very least and to be safe also some uppers. But the drugs from service wouldn't let us behave the way we needed to.

Keahi actually gave Sam the drugs we were supposed to take, since the Coping Kit didn't have the right kind. The Coping Kit drugs would have made us *feel* okay but they were also opiates and would have doped us up too much. *Induced passivity* is what Keahi told Sam. So he gave Sam drugs for us that wouldn't stop us from thinking or moving but would mimic some of the other effects—good cheer and giddiness and loving and all that.

That was where our dark-brown eyes would come in handy, according to Sam. Because the one danger with the replacement pills was, they made your pupils shrink. Whereas the corp pharms made them dilate. And it would be important to keep the corp workers from noticing those small pupils.

They could still notice, Keahi'd warned Sam, even though the brown of our eyes made the size of the black pupils harder to notice. So it was key that we didn't get too close. We should still meet their eyes if any of them established eye contact, Keahi had instructed, because if we looked away that would be suspicious too.

So the rule was, stay at least a couple of feet away at all times—three or more feet was best.

We practiced it with each other in Sam's room, before we went to bed. We figured out how far three feet was and practiced walking up to each other and talking normally, not being self-conscious about hiding our eyes. It was surprisingly hard *not* to think about them once we knew that both looking directly at someone *and* evading someone's gaze could put us in danger. We practiced all we could before I went back to my own room.

Also, Keahi had said, the pills we were going to be on would give us more energy than the corp pharms would have, so we would have to be really careful not to act too amped.

Well, then we went to sleep, and when we got up this morning we took the drugs. I have to say, I'm on them now. And *energy* is almost an understatement. This must be what it's like to be crazy.

I want to go and keep going.

Keahi said to funnel the physical feelings into doing normal things, like writing in this journal, for me, or for Sam reading and music-listening. I'm trying, but it's hard. I would prefer to jump up and down and run in circles.

Meanwhile, my parents are—just as the corp brochures promised—what is called pharmahappy. They still know who we are, but they don't seem to know much about the world anymore. It's like the world has reverted, for them, into what it used to be—or maybe they're just living in a different time zone today, like they're back in the middle of the last c., when things could still pass for normal. Here's an example:

The corp sent breakfast to the suite, so we could dine in privacy. Happiness Day isn't a big day for public occasions, really; they serve all the meals in-room, and most people eat them on their balconies. So a cafeteria worker or waitron or something—wearing the usual beige robe but also a kind of sanitation cap over her hair—showed up with some trays on a cart shortly after we'd dressed, and she rolled it in.

"Bless Happiness," she said.

That's supposed to be the greeting on Day Five.

"Bless it," answered my dad, who was doing goofy-looking stretches on the balcony.

Then she left.

"Apples!" chirped my mom, smiling gleefully. "Apples!"

There was a basket in the middle of the cart, you see, with fresh fruit in it beneath a beige napkin.

But when my mother said "Apples!" the napkin was still on—it hadn't been pulled back yet to even show what lay underneath.

And the thing is, apples haven't been around for decades now, since way before I was born. I've browsed them because I look for beautiful objects for collecting—sometimes I have to collect pictures if I don't find things I can hold—and there's an antique painting I love with apples in it. But most kids wouldn't know an apple if it kicked them in the face. The weather conditions that apples need to grow apparently don't happen anymore. The superrich can still grow them indoors, I think, but they're a delicacy you never see unless you're so rich you don't even notice the vast carbon taxes that are charged for eating food that's not on the A list.

Apples were famous fruits once though, in lots of old stories and pictures; an image of one was even on my first interface—some kind of corp logo that's been phased out since then.

"Apples!" said my dad joyfully, doing his usual echo thing.

Sam raised the napkin off the fruit basket and what we

saw was tropical fruit, of course—still a major delicacy—a couple of fresh mangoes like the ones we'd tasted in camp and a sliced pineapple.

"No apples, Mom," said Sam. "Sorry."

"An apple a day keeps the doctor away!" she replied brightly. "These look delicious." And she picked up a mango and bit into it without even peeling the skin off.

"Uh . . ." started Sam.

"This," said my mother, with yellow mango juice dripping down her chin, "is far and away the best apple I've ever had in my life."

Empty of pharms, I would have thought the sight of that dripping chin was slightly gruesome. As it was, I felt like laughing.

"Let me try," said my dad, and she handed it to him.

"Try it, Bobby," she urged.

"Mmm," said my father, chewing. "Far and away."

"Isn't that peel kind of bitter?" asked Sam. "And tough? Here, at least let me peel it for you."

Sam, I could tell, was trying harder than usual to be helpful—probably to expend some of his extra energy on normal things, per our instructions.

"Oh no, the peel is good for you," said my mother. "With vitamins!"

Apparently it didn't occur to her that "good for you" didn't really apply anymore, since she was headed straight for Game Over.

Do not pass go. Do not bother to eat healthy.

Sam looked at me. I shrugged.

"Whatever works," I said. "You know, though, where I come from we call those *mangoes*. Usually."

"Delicious," moaned my mother. My father was chewing and nodding.

I guess they didn't really care what it was. Still, if it was a fantasy they were creating on purpose, the peel-eating was going a bit too far.

Sam and I were ready to bounce off the walls and not too hungry, so once they were done eating their "apples"— which took them forever, chewing that tough mango peel— and some pancakes with syrup, we urged them to come on a walk with us. Accepted walks for Happiness Day are limited to the lavender areas, and there aren't that many of them outdoors, but we really needed to get out of the suite—to get away from the cameras, partly, and just to have something to do. So we persuaded them to come with us to a Japanese garden the hotel sets aside for contracts on Happiness Day.

Sam wanted to take the stairs down ten flights, running (our suite is on the fifth floor). I was like, *Uh, no*, and gave him a warning look.

We got in the elevator.

"Beautiful," said my mother, as the doors closed. She reached out and touched a handrail thing.

"Er, the elevator?" asked Sam.

"Look at this," said my mother. "So smooth!" She was literally caressing the metal handrail. "A smoothness like soap, like satin or honey. How do they get it that way?"

"Machined," answered my father, with a sense of awe in his voice, and reached out to touch it too.

"Um, it's a *handrail*, idiots," said Sam, all punitive.

"Or maybe it's an apple," I muttered.

There were mirrors in the elevator, like there almost always are, and that was where my parents focused next.

"You look old," said my mother to my father.

"You too," he replied, but they were both smiling like this wasn't a negative at all.

"How old *are* you?" asked my mother, staring at his reflection. She reached out and kind of poked his image in the mirror—maybe the lines at the corners of his eyes, or something.

"I'm young," said my father, mildly surprised. "I look older, though."

"How old am I?" asked my mother.

"You're eighty-five," said Sam. "And Dad is ninety-three."

They turned around and stared at him. And then burst out laughing.

Sam and I just watched them in amazement. They were practically doubled over, they were cracking up so hard. When they wound down, the elevator doors were already opening, and they stepped out shaking their heads and wiping tears from their cheeks.

"Sara, darlin'," said my dad affectionately, "you don't look a day over forty." Then he turned to Sam and me. "You jokers."

"Don't pay any attention, they're just babies," said my mom, and then her face changed for a second like something tragic washed over it. Something deeply sad and utterly confused.

But that passed in a flash and her smile came back.

"Ninety-three," said my father, and shook his head as we headed out through the lobby. "That's classic."

And then we were on a gravel path and consulting our map of the resort. With Sam in the lead, we headed to the Japanese garden. It was a very pretty place, with narrow waterways all around in meandering curves and small ornamental bridges over them. There were tall clumps of reeds and hedges manicured into neat shapes. Big birds stalked here and there, big pinkish birds with long beaks and skinny legs, like storks or flamingos or something.

I saw other families, some having picnics on blankets, some wandering and looking. One old person was using a rake to make orderly scratches in an artistic-looking bed of pebbles.

"Fish," said my dad, and pointed down at one of the small canals.

"Do *we* have a fish?" asked my mother in a puzzled voice, turning to me.

"Actually, once we did," I said faintly.

Sure enough, there were big fancy goldfish swimming lazily around down there, spots of white and black on their round bodies. I gazed at them for a while, my mind racing from the pharma. I let it race and stared at the fish. I was thinking, *Away, away, away. Get us away from here.*

I imagined unreal things—magic carpets, giant birds you could sit on that flew you across the sky. I imagined caves and genies and then remembered the tunnels in the black lava. I thought of the future, of me and Sam living in the caldera with turtles and moss-green clothing and probably no mood softeners, not a single one. I wondered if I would have any face access in the camp, if we made it there, and if not how I would live my whole life without it. I'd never been without a face. I felt a sense of longing for my unit at home, which I might never see again.

If I didn't have face I'd have no friends, either—to them it would seem like I'd left them without a word, and when that happened you tended to figure the person had died of a fast-migrating bug.

I wondered how much I would miss the complexes and cities, the largeness of the continent I was born on, where the land seemed to go on forever. I thought of the Hawaiian Islands and the sea level rising around them, and whether we would ever be safe.

"A pagoda!" said my mother, and pointed across at a dark-red gazebo thing with curves on the tips of the roof.

"It must be heaven," said my father.

"The gardens of Kyoto," breathed my mother.

"Or the hanging gardens of Babylon," said my father. "One of the seven great wonders . . ."

". . . of the ancient world," finished my mother.

"Really ancient," said Sam. "I've never even heard of that. What are you talking about?"

"Wind chimes!" enthused my mother, ignoring him.

Sure enough, in one shady area there were a whole lot of wind chimes hanging from the trees, making tinkly sounds as they moved in the breeze. My mom went over there and stood among them, looking up and all around her with wide eyes like a wonder-struck child.

"Bobby! It's Babylon! Have we been to this place before, Bobby?"

"Sara," said my father, and went to stand beside her, taking her hand as she leaned her head onto his shoulder, "we've always been here, darling. We never left. We've always lived in Babylon."

Ψ

We spent a long time in the garden, since my parents were zoned and Sam and I were in no hurry either. We wandered around and looked at things, and tried not to walk too fast or talk too fast either, because Keahi had warned us about that. For a long time we followed the birds around, which were skittish and definitely not robots, and I had to hold Sam back from chasing one, because they couldn't fly— their wings must have been clipped—and when we got too close they did this hilarious awkward run that made us laugh.

But when we finally started to make our way out of the garden and back toward the building my parents were both dreamy and not saying much anymore, just strolling and gazing with their giant-pupiled eyes.

"Happiness is at sunset, right?" I asked Sam.

"Why yes, it is," he said, and gave me a look like maybe I was going to say something I shouldn't. Because the Japanese garden, as he had warned me before, was definitely not a "secure location," like Keahi had put it. "Bless Happiness."

"Yeah, totally bless it," I said.

"It's a really nice day for a Bountiful Passing," said Sam, laying it on pretty thick.

"I'm glad you've finally come around, baby brother," I said, in case a listening device happened to pick us up right then.

"I had to. I mean, just look at them."

We did.

Mom and Dad were up ahead near the Shinto Gate, as the label proclaimed it, that led out of the garden. They were just standing there and kind of, well—making out.

We shot each other these sideways glances, like, are we allowed to say *grotesque?*

"Wow, huh," I said.

"That's really blessed," said Sam. "Isn't it?"

"For sure," I said, though actually it almost made me squirm.

Maybe the corp dope makes it okay to watch your elderly parents suck lips together in public, but I'll tell you this: ours did *not*.

But then we looked at them necking and looked at each other and for some reason, just then, it set us off. We had all that pent-up energy still, and the hysteria spilled out and we were laughing and laughing. We were doubled over, out of control.

And sure enough, as we started to wind down and straighten up from that laughing, there came a corp worker, striding along the path toward us in her beige robe. She wasn't one we'd seen before—maybe she was in charge of the garden or something—but she had a severe hatchet face going on and her lips were tight and wrinkled.

"Is everything all right under here?" she asked in a slightly threatening way.

"Oh yes, sorry—my sister told this old joke," said Sam, and he was kind of waving his hand around, maybe to distract from his small pupils.

"Old joke," I agreed. "Sorry."

"This is a place of tranquilling," she said. "Now, children, please choose a calmer way of being."

"Sure, sure," said Sam. "Yes. Yes, we will."

"We're over it," I said, and we were, we were scared straight, basically. Or as straight as we could be.

But when the woman turned and left—frightening us a bit with a quizzical expression that suggested she was making a note of our behavior and would be keeping a close eye on us—we glanced over at our parents to see if they had noticed how busted we were. And they were *still* making out.

I swear, we almost started laughing again. But we managed to keep our cool, and just walked toward them. As we approached, my mom got distracted by something and stopped the kissing deal, fortunately. She pointed up at the sky.

"Look, honey, look! The trumpeter swans have returned!"

My father shaded his eyes and looked where she was pointing, and then so did we.

I saw nothing up there except the bright, bright sun.

Ψ

For sheer awkwardness and dread, there's not much that compares with the part of Happiness Day leading up to the Glorious/Easeful/Bountiful Passing.

Because our pharms didn't have the passivity of the corp stuff built into them, we weren't all sleepy high like the other survivors must have been—at least the ones I saw wandering and grinning among the fat fish. So we were on a pharmahigh, but we were also restless and there was a pretty major element of anxiety behind the exhilaration.

We had a plan, though. And I think that was what kept us from going more crazy.

After lunch was the most painful time, because that's when we had to all sit around together on the balcony and do the Letter Reading.

The Letter Reading is what it sounds like, the part of Final Week when you have to exchange letters. We'd written the letters, as the corp instructed, before we left home, and now we had to pass them out and read them all together. There were letters from Sam and me to each of our parents, and letters from them to each of us.

The letters had a public section and a private one. The public sections were meant to be read aloud, and the private sections were for reading to ourselves—and keeping secret, if we wanted.

They're also supposed to be keepsakes. So after we wrote

them, we sent them to Jean and she had them printed on fancy papyrus and they had graphics on them too, pictures of us and stuff. We were told to stay positive in the letters, since they were for Happiness Day and not for venting.

Our own letters to Mom and Dad get willed to us, for us to look at later if we want to pull them out and reminisce. That's the idea, anyway. Some people frame the letters and put them up on their walls. I've seen them at survivors' condos.

So we sat out on the balcony, with its view of the cliffwalk and the ocean, and with drinks on small tables at our elbows and flowers the suite cleaners had set up there. My parents read the letters to them first, as the plan recommended. My dad picked mine to start with, unrolling it so the white tassels hung and swayed in the wind.

"*Dear Dad,*" he began, and cleared his throat. "*I try to imagine what it must be like to be you and see the world change as much as you've seen it. I try to imagine being anyone who lived most of their life before the tipping point. I can't. But because of you I keep trying. All my life you've taught me to be interested in what came before, and so I try to browse about history. I try to imagine not being me, being an olden person, Before. And because of you I know that it still matters, even now, what's beautiful. And what isn't. That beauty will always matter. And I love knowing that. You've taught me the world matters, the world and everything that has ever lived in it. Because there's always been beauty. And always will.*"

He looked up from the papyrus then, which trembled a little in his hands.

"Lovely, Nattie," he said.

"Lovely," said my mother.

"Dig it," nodded Sam.

"*Part of me is sorry for Mom and you,*" he went on. "*Because life is so hard with everything you know and remember. But part of me is jealous too. Because of that same thing. Because I can never know or see what you have seen . . .*"

I won't write down my whole letter. Anyone reading this, including you, spacefriend, is probably sick of hearing about my feelings. Point is, my dad got through it without choking up or anything, and then it was my mother's turn to read, and she picked Sam's letter. It didn't start with *Dear Mom*, like I had. Instead, the letter was a list.

"*The park where the old oaks used to grow,*" she began. "*The red swingset after it rained . . .*"

And it went on like that.

The way you used to laugh when I was little and Dad threw me up in the air.

The knot of your hair when you twisted it behind your head to wash dishes.

Your wedding ring too big for your thin finger.

How you danced when Dad put on the olden music.

How you read me bedtime stories, sitting on my bed, and got lost in them and forgot it was my bedtime.

When you crept up behind me and hugged me unexpectedly.

The cross of your legs when you sat on the brown couch and put your feet up.

The tears on your cheeks when you heard about the last penguin.

My mother got to that part and her happy smile wavered. She let the letter fall forward and we could see that it went on and on, a list just on and on down the page.

"Brave girl, Sara," said my father softly. "Brave girl. Keep reading, honey. Go on."

Your always thinking of us before yourself.

Your worry.

Your swearing once when I was little and you cut your hand in the kitchen, then noticing me and saying "Now, that's a mommy word, Sam. A mommy and daddy word."

My dad laughed at that and it lifted my mom's mood a bit. The list continued, and it ended like this:

You trying to tell me the "facts of life" when I knew them already.

All together in the big bed on a weekend morning, when we wouldn't let you sleep in and just wanted to play.

The way you bit your fingernails.

The way you were my mother.

She stopped reading and put the letter down on the table, where my father quickly set a cup on it so the wind wouldn't carry it off.

And then she just sat there, staring straight ahead.

The silence lasted a long time.

Then my father cleared his throat again. "We've raised quite a poet, Sara. Well, two of them! Two poets."

We read my parents' letters to us after that, some mushy stuff, of course, and then some advice on how they wanted us to live the rest of our lives—along with some other stuff about how they knew they had no right to say, and our lives were our own, and things like that.

But what I remember most was how my mom sat there, through all of this, with a faint smile but not saying anything at all, gazing past us at nothing, or maybe out to sea.

Ψ

How they set up Happiness Time itself, at least in our contract, was this: they let the contracts pick the place. It has to be on a certain list of approved spots. (You can't get any more lavender than *this* shit.) There are inside spots and outside spots, which the corp calls—pretty straightforwardly by their standards—Happiness Places. These include the suites, of course, for people who value privacy above all else.

But if you choose an outdoor Place, you have to be okay with not having privacy. Not just anyone can barge in, or anything; the Places are set aside and guarded. But other contracts can be there too, if they want. They don't have enough outside spots for everyone to be separate. You book the spots in advance, of course; the corps are way organized.

And my parents, totally predictably, picked a Place overlooking the ocean.

The method was preapproved, the only method they use at this particular resort. It was Quiet Pharma, pharma you take and don't feel and it just creeps in and puts you to sleep, painless and more or less instant—within a few minutes.

Another thing they don't want is tons of public emoting. So we were on the plan to part company in the suite, that was our last time to see them up close. After that, though, after they left the room, we had to go to an Observing Place—near enough to the Happiness Place that we could see what was going on but not, say, throw ourselves upon them sobbing, making a scene. It was choreographed.

The time got closer and closer, and we were all sitting in the suite's living room listening to preselected music, and my parents were freshly showered—my dad shaved, my mother with her hair brushed to a shine and twisted up on top of her head in this fancy elegant hairdo. They were wearing their Happiness robes, a lot like the beige ones we wore to the therapy sessions but thinner and with this kind of silver braid around the collar.

They seemed to have recovered from the Letter Reading, where to me they'd seemed pretty real and *present*, in corpspeak—they must have trained and worked hard at it—and now they were off the hook and back in full bliss mode. They just sat and smiled and nodded their heads to the music, and alarmingly often they'd get up and hug me or Sam spontaneously, and just stand there hugging us, and we'd hug them back, feeling half-embarrassed and half-impatient and half–something else I can't put into words. I guess that's three halves, but you know what I mean.

And that was even *with* our own happy pills. I can't imagine what it would have been like without them.

Or then, for instance, my mom or dad would say something blissful, like, "Sara! Look how beautiful Nat is. Isn't she *beautiful?* She has your bone structure!" (Not true.) Or, "Sam, Sam, Sam . . . what a smart boy you are . . . what a good boy. A good, good, good, good boy."

He's smart all right but he's never been polite or well-behaved so the word *good* didn't ring true. And there were other words they used like that, words that were generic and positive but didn't seem to really apply to *us*. Not us specifically. A lot of the comments coming out of their mouths seemed to me to be on the totally irrelevant side. Like we could have been two dogs sitting there on our chairs, or two pigs. And they would have said the exact same things.

It was as if, to them, we'd turned into pictures of their kids. As if we, our actual selves, had almost nothing to do with what they were seeing.

Which was probably true, because they were also

back in the loop they'd been in when we rode down to the Japanese garden on the elevator. They would say these nice things to us, and then one of them would look up at the ceiling and go, "Is that a doggy? A doggy face on the ceiling? I miss those little doggies so! Here, doggy! Here, doggy!"

Their dose had plenty of visionpharm in it, that's for sure.

Or there was what they did with the flowers: at one point, about an hour before they were supposed to leave, my father got up from the couch and picked up a vase of those tropical flowers that had bugged me the whole time we were in the suite—the same ones he'd touched when he was remembering the tulips at the hospital I was born in. He picked up the vase and brought it back to the couch and just sat with it on his lap.

My mother reached over and pulled a flower out and held it up so close I was surprised her eyes didn't cross. Then she started picking the petals off till they were all over her lap and on the floor at her feet. Smiling all the time like she was doing the flower a favor. Finally all she had left was the stem. She stared at that for a while, called it *excellent*, and then dropped it too.

Meanwhile, my dad sat there with the full vase on his lap. He said the names of the flowers slowly. "Iris. Iris. Paradise bird, bird of paradise. Look down in them, you can go right in . . . into the bird of paradise. Deeply."

Finally Sam got tired of jiggling his leg and watching, and he got up and snatched the vase away. A little harshly, I thought.

My father just smiled up at him.

After the flower thing, sitting on the couch as we sat in our armchairs, they just gazed at us with their daffy grins on, not saying anything at all but rocking their heads or tapping their feet a little or swaying to the music, and Sam or I would have to actually get up and pretend to be thirsty or say we had to go the waste room or something, just to escape from the totally weird awkwardness. It was stone freaky how they would gaze, smiling, just on and on and on.

In the middle of dealing with this lovey-dovey stare zone we were in, I was getting more and more nervous about what was coming. I was glad we hadn't run into any service corp people so far, I was very relieved about that, but I was also wondering what the plan was, how the people from the camp could ever rescue Mom and Dad at the last minute, whether they'd given up on it, or what the deal was.

I was so anxious that at one point I had to excuse myself and go into my room and count slowly to try to calm myself down. I sat on the bed jiggling my feet like Sam did and trying to get back into the mental space I'd been in before any of it started, with the camp and the escape and that whole outside world I hadn't known till then. Back when I believed the service corps actually meant what they said, even if they were lame. Before I'd heard LaTessa speak in a voice I never knew she had.

I remembered how I had basically trusted my parents' decision and bought into the idea that it was the best for them.

I talked to myself in my head, trying to train myself to be okay with them dying because it was their choice and what they wanted. And maybe it was just selfish of me to want to keep them here—the same thing I used to think about Sam, that he wanted them here for *our* sakes, not theirs. I used to think that was just immature and greedy.

I reminded myself they were pharmadrones now anyway. And what if the pharms they were on had changed them for good? And even if they did somehow survive, which seemed impossible to me, maybe they wouldn't ever be the people they'd been.

Because even contracts who changed their mind at the last minute always ended up signing on again. And maybe that was because they were changed, they were hardwired for Happiness by then.

I sat there arguing with myself in my head. But no matter how much back and forth I did, or how much sense I thought my own arguments made, being okay with their dying was just harder for me now than it had been.

I'd been in the bedroom maybe five or ten minutes when Sam came in. "You better come out. They have to go really soon."

I just looked at him, still jiggling my foot, really strained.

"I know, Nat," he said. "But it's out of our hands now. Don't worry. One way or another, I swear, we'll get through it."

"How can you be so sure?" I asked.

"I have to be."

And in a completely non-Sam way, he reached out his hand. And I took it and shakily stood.

Ψ

They hugged us—the same kind of hugs as before—long and awkward, and then did what they were supposed to. They left.

We stood outside the open suite door and watched their backs disappear as they walked down the hall to the elevators.

And I felt flat empty and lost too, but still somehow I couldn't bring myself to cry. Sam and I went back into the suite and waited until the digital clock numbers were right, according to the plan, and then we left too.

By this time the sunset colors were out, striping the sky pink and orange, and then above the stripes was a billowing vagueness of rounded shapes, all full of the colors leaking in behind them, the purple tinged with pink, the gray with bloodred. You couldn't have asked for a more glorious sky. There was a light breeze, and when we came out onto the deck where we were supposed to watch from, I saw the sun in its low lurk behind some clouds, and boats out on the ocean with their sails reflecting creamy-white over the dark waves.

There was a roof garden on the Observing Deck— palm trees in clay tubs, long tubular plants that looked a little like cacti and bore labels like *False Ocotillos* and *Night-Blooming Cereus*. The palm fronds swished in the wind, and a few stray hummingbirds were divebombing some red hanging feeders.

And there were some corp workers. Including, I noticed right away, LaT.

She was wearing one of her princess robes and moving around gracefully like a high-end waitron, bearing a tray of small drinks. The light sparkled through them, made the liquid inside glow golden and bright.

"This is the first test," said Sam, very low next to me. "When you take your bevvy, don't look at her till you step back with it. Till then just focus on the cup and lifting it, that'll seem pretty natural. Three feet."

I hoped the mikes weren't sensitive.

I saw Xing then, leaning on the rail and peering out, holding a drink of her own. I thought, if I can get next to her I'll feel safer.

Then LaT. was in front of me and I had to struggle to decide where to look.

"Sam, Nat, bless Happiness," she purred.

"Bless it," I said, my voice catching a little in my throat.

"Welcome to Observing . . . a comforting herbal bev?"

"Thanks," said Sam gruffly, and took one.

I couldn't decide if he looked natural or not. I had my eyes on LaT.'s face to see if she studied him closely; in that one glance I didn't see her paying abnormal attention to his eyes, but I wasn't quite sure.

"Nat, over here," came Xing's voice, and so I was able to look up at her as I took my own bevvy off the tray, instead of looking at LaT.

I passed LaT. and walked to Xing at the rail, and we stood there together, my heart beating fast.

"There they are," she said softly, and pointed down.

I told myself I was safe for now, I'd made it past LaT., I could calm down . . . and there was the Happiness Place, near the cliff edge. It was a cluster of white chairs on the green grass, very simple, between some hedges to the left and right, maybe so the Place was hidden from other people on the ground down there.

I'm not so great at measuring distance, but it was close enough so we could recognize them, I figured.

"Here they come," said Xing.

And there were the contracts, a line of them in their robes with their backs to us, winding out of the hotel buildings beneath. I counted twelve in all—six couples.

"My parents are up front," said Xing.

It was the first time it struck me to wonder: Were her parents on some plan too? Were they also supposed to come with us? Or was it too late for all of them?

"My parents are ready," said Xing, in a gentle tone. As though she'd read my mind. "My mom is a hundred and two, and my dad is a hundred and eight."

"They had you so late," I said.

"Yeah, she was sixty-eight. Almost the upper limit."

So that meant Xing was thirty-four. I'd thought she was younger, in her twenties; her skin had no lines at all.

"My parents love the ocean," I said, after a minute.

"Mine too," she replied. "They grew up in a fishing village, on an island. Swamped now. Their whole island was moved, the whole population did a forced relocation back in the early 21st c. My mother used to dive for pearls, when she was a young girl. She was what they used to call a pearl diver."

"Wow." I'd never heard of that but it sounded romantic.

"It was dangerous," she said. "But lucrative, if you were good at it. She was good enough, but mostly she was desperate. Her family was extremely poor, you see."

The contracts were standing in front of their chairs now, in the exact order they'd come out of the hotel. I saw my parents last in line, at the other end of the chairs from Xing's—my mother's hair curled on the top of her head, my father with his upright posture, shoulders back, that always distinguished him. When he was a young man he'd been in the navy, where they taught them to stand straight.

My stomach was nervous. I drained my comfort bevvy, wondering if there was any pharma in it.

Sam was at my other side then, gazing down with us. "So this is what Happiness looks like," he said.

"A lovely evening for it," said Xing. "Look at that light play in the clouds."

And it was true—there were long sunbeams striking down from gaps in the clouds, making lighter patches on the surface of the ocean that glittered against the darker ones.

Then Xing's parents turned around to face the Observing Deck, and both of them looked up at her and raised their hands—sort of a wave, sort of a salute.

Xing smiled at them and blew a kiss. I saw her eyes shining.

Then they turned back around again, and the next couple turned around.

Again, perfectly organized and choreographed. They waved up at the deck too, and a ways along to our right the meathead guy from our early healing session raised his hand and waved back at them. He looked zoned.

And then the next couple, and the next. And finally it came to my parents, and they both turned. But they didn't wave, just looked at us. I could faintly make out the expressions on their faces, though, and they were smiling.

I grabbed Sam's hand and I raised it up, so they could see our arms in an upside-down V. It wasn't planned, it definitely wasn't a V for victory, that's for sure, but it was just what I did.

And they turned away again.

So then it was me and Sam and Xing, I didn't even think of the others, and then those little white chairs and the ocean. The contracts sat down, again in order so it was like a ripple, end to end.

A beige-robed figure appeared—one with black hair, carrying a tray. I couldn't tell who it was. The figure moved from Xing's parents down the line, slowly and with a kind of ceremonial grace, handing them little white packets.

We couldn't see their laps or what their hands were doing, but when the figure walked off that's when they must have opened their packets. And took their Quiet Pharma pills, and relaxed back in their chairs, which had these little headrests on them.

The sun was very low over the sea. I saw my father

turn to the side and kiss my mother on the cheek. And she reached out and took his right hand in her left one.

And then their heads were on the headrests, and they were all very still.

We stayed there at the rail, watching as the sun sank. I kept wondering: *Is this the exact moment they're dying? This moment? Or this one?*

A strange green ray struck up into the sky from the sunset point, just for a second, and was gone.

And then the sun was gone too.

DAY SIX

SEPARATION & GRIEF
Theme of the Day: Missing

I haven't had time to write. It's been nonstop action around here in the Twilight zone.

LaT. led the whole group of us back to our rooms after the Happiness Observing, making the dropoffs one by one at the different suites. It was a quiet procession, almost blasted by silence, you might say, except that—luckily for Sam and me, because it meant we didn't get much unwanted attention—there was one survivor who was sobbing and a mess. Maybe her pharma hadn't taken or something, because the rest of them were zomboid.

Anyway, the girl didn't have any brothers or sisters to help out, like most of them she was an only child, and LaT. had to walk the whole way with her arm around her to keep her from falling. LaTessa doesn't usually touch, it must be against protocol, but she kind of had to in this case because the girl was like a human puddle. LaT. held her with a mixture of delicacy and what I personally suspected was revulsion.

The puddlegirl's suite was on a floor above ours so we had the benefit of a distracted LaTessa all the way home. She barely even nodded at us when we got up to our door. We went into the suite, where we had one hour of Personal

Time on the plan before we were supposed to meet in the Twilight Lounge for dinner and an evening healing. I leaned back against the door after I closed it and let out a long breath. I didn't see any of my parents' stuff around, which was a relief, but also alarming. It was like someone had come and cleaned it out, because I was pretty sure they'd had a few things sitting around. But I didn't have the heart to go into their bedroom yet.

We went out onto the balcony, and I hid Sam from anyone who could be watching from the outside by blocking his body with my own and chattering as he checked the light fixtures and corners and railing for bugs. When he decided the area must be clean he turned to me.

"So here's what you do next. We're separating for a while. You take the things you can't stand to leave behind and stuff them in your shoulder bag—no extra clothes or anything. Change out of that robe into the loosest, darkest clothes you have. Then go to the waste room—give it five minutes after we finish talking—and wait there."

"But—what happened down there? What about Mom and Dad? Are they—"

"We have to wait and see, Nat. I don't know."

"We have to take on faith someone's trying to help them? We have to just hope that wasn't them really, truly *dying?*"

He stared me down.

"Are you heartless?" I burst out. "They're our *parents!*"

His face got stony and his mouth twisted like it does when he's really upset and trying to hide it. "We're taking care of ourselves now, Nat. This is us. *Living.* As they'd want us to—their *real* selves anyway. And we don't have any time to waste. So just—do what I told you to!"

I stared back at him, furious.

But a couple of minutes later I *did* do what he'd told me to—though I was still angry at him, my face still prickling with heat. I stuffed this journal into the bag, and my collection and the goodbye letters, and a babyish, tiny stuffed animal I've had since I was a kid and still keep with me. A mouse.

I know it's juvenile, but it was the only thing I had from my old life. I've had it forever and it reminds me of my earliest memories—the one house we ever lived in before our condos, before separate houses disappeared. The worn mouse has a particular smell of oldness—not a bad smell but just a really specific one. And the smell reminds me vaguely but nicely of that house. It was an olden-times house, one of the last remaining on a big complex, with two others like it right nearby; it had a porch swing and faded, flowery curtains, these creaky boards on the floor, and bushes in front that made the old porch smell like lilacs.

Then they bulldozed it under the new housing rules, and we moved into a complex.

Anyway, I stuffed my possessions into my bag and shoved it all under my shirt. I couldn't allow it to show up on the cameras as I walked down the hall.

From the living room, I called out to Sam that I was headed to the waste room and would be back in a minute.

I was amped still from the meds, I realized, as well as being really pissed at him, so I was actually glad to be able to expend some of that excess adrenalin.

Does it have to be the waste room? was what I was thinking. I would have preferred to rappel down a wall or something.

But I took what I could get.

Ψ

Once I was in there, and saw it was empty except for me, I started looking around. The waste room didn't have windows, only these vents high up, and I knew the hall outside was covered with surveillance cameras, so I was confused about how I was supposed to get out of there undetected.

I barely had time to do anything, though, before the door opened and someone stepped in. Not Keahi—I was kind of disappointed, I admit—but his friend from the night before.

"Didn't the hall cameras catch you?" I asked.

"Don't worry about that," he said. "Come over here. You're not going to like this, I warn you. But it's necessary. Here."

And he walked straight past me to the far back corner of the room and clicked open a wall panel, which fell forward from the ground. There was an opening behind there—about three feet by two feet or so.

Unfortunately, it was the waste chute.

There was a smell coming out of it, not of waste exactly but of waste covered with a perfume that helped disguise it. The combination was nauseating.

"You're kidding me," I said.

"I'm not. Listen: I can't come with you, I have another role to play. So do what I say. At the bottom you'll be in a waste compost room. Put this over your nose and mouth."

He took a white mask out of the pocket of his robe and handed it to me.

"The fumes can be overwhelming. Wear that while you're in there. Go out the door and along the path to your right. Right, not left. The first door you see. Out that door, you'll see a sign that says, *Employee Transport*. Follow it. You'll see a row of big recycling bins. Hide behind there until your guide shows up. It could be minutes or hours. Just stay put. Got it?"

I repeated it back to him and he nodded at the chute door.

"It's safe? The—the fall, I mean?" Because we were on the fifth floor.

"Safe as we could make it," he said. "There's a full bin beneath. You'll drop into straw and feces."

Nice.

"One other thing. These chutes aren't soundproofed well. So as you fall, whatever you do—*don't scream*."

I couldn't go without asking him one more question. "Listen. Um, I need to know . . ." I began.

"Yeah?"

"My—my parents. Do you know? Did they—are

they really—" And I couldn't say it. Even then. *Dead.*

He looked at me steadily and then put a hand on my shoulder. "You have to be okay on your own, Natalie."

My stomach sank. I tried to blink back tears.

"And if you want to live, you have to go *now.*"

Every bone in my body shrieked out against it; I still felt confused, partly terrified and partly desolate. But I put on the mask and held my breath out of pure fear and then he grasped my arm to guide me. And I stumbled in.

I must have done it more awkwardly than I should have, because I didn't fall straight, I bumped against the side of the chute a couple of times as I fell, and it was all so quick all I knew was adrenalin and the pain of bumps and scrapes as I plummeted.

But I didn't make a sound.

I'm still proud of that.

Ψ

I didn't even notice the smell at first, I just lay there stunned and thought about the throbbing pain in my hip and the searing pain in my elbow. I felt like my whole skin was a bruise. And into the confusion of the pain was mixed confusion over my parents—my parents who, now, were confirmed gone.

But no bones seemed to be broken, and I hadn't hit my face on anything.

I pulled myself up after a while, dizzy and sore and disoriented. I was in a kind of square bin, with walls almost as high as I am tall. The room was dim, the walls of the bin I'd fallen into seemed high, but I climbed out of it with a little effort, my feet slipping and churning in the straw and the waste, and then stood on the clay floor and lifted my arm to look at my elbow. It was bleeding hard from a big gash and the blood was dripping down my arm and all over my hand and onto the floor, even, which couldn't be good, so I grabbed some dirty straw from the bin and tried to sop it up. Well, it was more of a scraping than a sopping. But better than nothing.

I had no cloth to wrap my elbow in except the mask, so I took that off and was hit by a terrible stench and just held it to the cut as I jogged out the door. Luckily the directions weren't hard to follow; it was more about whether I ran into anyone, because there was no way, now, I could pass myself off as a normal obedient survivor. Covered in straw and waste.

But I made it to the building door, which was closed and said, *Emergency Exit Only Alarm Will Sound*, and that stopped me for a good minute while I pondered if that was actually true or if they'd been able to disconnect it. And finally I took my chances and pushed on the bar, and it opened silently.

Silently for me, that is. Somewhere else, on the speakers of some monitor, I knew it might be shrieking hysterically.

That pleasant thought powered me as I ran along the gravel outside, probably looking like a 20th c. Halloween monster with hay and dung hanging off me like dirty hair. I saw the row of recycling containers, which were these big metal bins, and I ducked behind them, basically into a thick hedge with waxy leaves and bright flowers. I pushed myself along between the bins and the hedge so I was further in, and then hunched there, shivering.

I was wet as well as filthy—damp all over, and the blood from my elbow had soaked through the mask, which was useless for stopping it anymore. So I threw the mask into the bin in front of me and rummaged in my bag for something else to stop it, but all I had was the bag itself and my ancient stuffed mouse. I used the cloth of the bag.

Above me the sky was dark, the stars were out, and I had nothing to do but hold the bag against my elbow, wait for the blood to stop, and think about the fact that it would be easy to find me here, if you were a service corp worker. It wasn't the smartest hiding place.

At some point the blood stopped flowing and was more like seeping to the scraped, raw surface of the flesh, and though the pain was almost worse at that point the blood wasn't much of a problem itself anymore so I took the pressure off. I sat down on the ground under a gap in the hedge and picked straw off my clothes to pass the time, counting my aches and pains. Elbow, hip, knee, ankle.

Then I counted the ways in which I was mad at Sam for his coldness about our parents. Then I counted the ways I'd failed as an older sister. Finally I got done with counting.

I didn't have a handface, of course, so I don't know how long it was but it seemed like forever before anyone arrived.

It was Keahi.

I was so relieved to see him I didn't even have time to remember I was smelling and looking grotesque.

"Where's Sam?" I asked.

"His plan's on track," he said, and I tried to read his expression but couldn't; Sam was coming, I told myself. Sam would be there.

Keahi was rushed but focused, his actions compact and neat. He stripped off his beige robe and underneath it he had on his camo gear. "Stash this in your bag for me, okay?" he said. "I'll need it again. Now let's book."

I knew I shouldn't have been thinking like this, that it's kind of selfish, but he was so efficient in that moment that I felt I could have been anyone, that I was nothing special to him. And I bundled the robe into my blood-wet bag and scrambled to follow him through the dark. We had no flashlight to guide us, because that would be too easy to spot, I guess, if anyone cared to look, so I just followed right behind him through all this bushy vegetation, with nothing to guide me but his narrow back and wide shoulders, which I could barely make out sometimes. He went fast and my body was starting to ache more and more from that fall, I felt like one giant bruise, but I gritted my teeth and tried not to grunt or moan.

Once or twice when the twinges were extra bad or I panicked, not being able to see him close enough, I did beg him to slow down—but either he didn't hear me or he *did* hear me and the answer was no.

It went on and on, like the waiting had before that,

but worse because it was so hard, till it seemed like hours that I'd been following him with my last vestige of energy, and then the last one after that, when I already felt tapped out. It was always uphill, it was always through trees, we were slapped by slick leaves and branches and scrambling in slippery mud. I was sweating and panting, out of breath and bone tired all through me.

Then at a certain point there was no more vegetation, and around us it was even darker but airier, and I knew we were in a lava tube.

Up ahead was a light, dim but real.

We went toward it, slogging, dragging. At least I was; Keahi was still moving fast.

There were more lights, strung up along the tunnel wall. And there were people.

There was Xing. And Keahi's mother.

I practically fell into their arms.

Ψ

They gave me the bad news a bit later: Sam wasn't there.

And not only that.

I heard the story lying on a cot in the camp, while Aviva, the baby-guarding lady, sewed up the cut in my elbow and some other cuts I turned out to have. One was on my head, under my hair, and she had to shave some of the hair off to sew the scalp together. The blood from that one had run down the back of my neck, though I hadn't noticed it, and soaked my shirt. There was another cut I hadn't noticed on one of my bottom ribs. She sewed that one up too and then put ointment and a bandage on it.

The stitches actually hurt a lot and I didn't hear everything that was said to me while I was clenching my teeth and trying to ignore the pain of the needle. But I got the gist.

What happened was, the plan for Sam had gone wrong. He did what he was supposed to do, it wasn't his fault at all, but the corp caught him.

One of the cameras Keahi and his friends had disabled set off a backup alarm it wasn't supposed to. That is, the backup had been disabled too, or the connection to it anyway, but the central computer fixed the connection faster than they thought it would. So in the middle of Sam's breakout attempt it switched back on and there he was in his full digital glory—perfectly visible to the guys watching the screens in the guardroom.

Not only Sam was caught but also Keahi's friend, the one who made me jump down the waste chute.

So while I was lying there on the cot, the people from the camp blew up one of the lava tubes, the one that led most directly to the resort and which, if they tried hard enough, the service employees could maybe have got to us through. The rebels had certain key parts of the tunnels rigged with explosives the whole time, Aviva told me, in case they had to do just that: cut off access on short notice.

We heard the low rumble and we felt the vibration.

"But then how can we get to Sam?" I asked her, panicked. "How will we get him out?"

"It'll be harder now," she admitted.

Ψ

They must have moved me while I was fast asleep and dead to the world, because in the morning I woke up alone in a small tent, lying on a thin bedroll. I sat up and inspected myself, the bandages stuck onto my skin beneath some clothes I didn't recognize, a pair of camo pants and a dark tank top. I touched the back of my head gingerly, the bandage over the cut up there.

And then I remembered Sam.

And my mother. And my father.

I looked around for my shoulder bag, suddenly needing to know I had this journal and my collection and my old, bedraggled mouse. The bag was still with me, luckily, crumpled near the bedroll, and I leaned over and pulled my stuff out, the journal and the pouch housing the best of my collection. And the mouse and my parents' letters.

I just sat on the bedroll for a while clutching those things and feeling alone. Not only alone but completely out of place, a mistake, something shaken loose from where it was supposed to be and dropped in a corner, forgotten.

Everything was black or shades of gray, like the inside of my tent, which had a kind of dim gray light filtering through the cloth. Outside could have been anything, with only that flat grayness showing through.

And I still smelled really bad, I noticed. I hadn't bathed—how could they take baths or showers here? I'd probably never be clean again. I smelled like the sickly sweet perfume they used on the compost, and behind that of pee and moldy dung. So here I was, sitting cross-legged and slouching in a gray tent, patchy with crusted blood and filth and sporting a shaved-bald patch on my head and without anyone in the world who was mine or loved me. All I had were the pouch with my few collected items, some pieces of bound write-fiber with cheesy sayings and messy writing on them, and a sad little stuffed mouse missing its tail and both ears.

You couldn't even tell the thing *was* a mouse anymore, I realized. It looked like a fist-sized ball of lint.

Sam had to be even worse off than me, I thought next, and then . . . my poor parents . . .

I thought: *They wanted to be gone.*

I thought: *They insisted.*

But it didn't make me feel better.

More slowly than you'd think, maybe, I also realized the amped-up feeling was gone, that I was empty of all my happy pharms and the adrenaline that had been driving Sam and me.

In all ways, I was flying solo.

I wondered how many years it had been since I was completely flat like that. I wondered if this was depression; I'd never been depressed before, only sad. It was hard to see an upside.

Almost impossible, actually.

The people here—the people at the camp—hadn't said we *couldn't* go get Sam, though, I reminded myself.

They'd just said it would be more difficult with the tunnel blocked. But they hadn't said they were giving up.

Not yet.

I sat there pathetically for what felt like a long time until finally there was nothing to do but get up, so I opened the tent flap and wandered out into camp.

It was a bustle of activity.

I wandered through the people, who were striding back and forth smartly, all seeming to have tasks, all knowing what they were doing. I alone was lost, meandering slowly among those fast and purposeful humans with no particular goal, just looking around, taking it in—and at the same time, in my flatness, feeling pretty indifferent to everything.

They buzzed past me, some pushing wheelbarrows, some carrying loops of cable or other equipment. I kept being impressed by their industriousness, and I realized as I watched that I hadn't been around momentum much in my life. It was as if my parents and Sam and I had waited in rooms for years. We'd just waited out our lives in a bunch of rooms, not doing much except watching—watching the news on face, watching commercials, watching tutorials, occasionally gaming or chatting, but mostly watching. We'd sat in some rooms and watched some screens.

And now here were people doing something. Doing a lot of things.

As though their actions mattered.

Plus they were all new people, which normally is exciting to me—realmeets with strangers, or people who used to be strangers and now might possibly be friends.

But this time, as I considered in a stunned, background kind of way how wasted my life must have been up to then, I was a solid wall of misery. No joy rose in me to greet the sight of them.

One or two glanced in my direction as I stumbled through them, but no one stopped to say anything and I had a strong feeling of being an intruder.

I hoped the rushing around wasn't because of Sam and me—that we alone hadn't caused all this and disrupted them. But I was afraid it was. There was the blown-up lava tube, after all, and the fact that one of their own people was trapped with Sam, in the grips of corp guys like the man-mountain Rory. I wondered if any of the people around here hated me. They had a right to: they didn't even know me, but now they were in danger because of me and my family.

For the first time it occurred to me to wonder why they'd bothered. They didn't even know us, yet they'd taken risks for us—risks that, now that I thought about it, didn't make sense unless there was something we had for them. Something more than just the will to live—something other people didn't have to offer them.

My ribs hurt, and my head and elbow. Everything throbbed all over.

Some of the people, I saw then, were pushing trees around. I swear—they had these potted trees in giant planters with wheels on the bottoms of them. I mean these were big trees, not little saplings or anything, they had to weigh thousands of kilos. And groups of boys and men and the occasional woman were pushing them from out of the forest around us into the clearing, rolling them on their platforms.

I looked up and saw the trees were blocking us, from up above. I stood staring up. It was like they were filling in the clearing where the tents and the Quonset and the other shacks were with these portable trees. The trees had broad canopies, they were all tall with slender trunks compared to the wide vegetation on top of them. That had to make them relatively light—easier to move for how much cover they gave. I was pleased that I saw it clearly. They were camouflage trees.

"In case of flyovers," came a voice.

I looked down and there was Xing.

I was almost as relieved to see her as I had been the night before, when she was standing under the faint light at the end of the tunnel. I'd almost forgotten she was there, what with feeling so abject about my family. My flatness didn't exactly lift at the sight of her, but I felt a bit less lost—slightly more rooted in the ground beneath me.

Unlike the giant potted trees.

She was dressed in camo, like me, only she had a jacket on too, an army-green thing with a lot of pockets. She smiled at me. "How're you feeling?"

"Not great," I said weakly.

"If you mean the depression, don't worry," she explained. "It's withdrawal from the pills we had you on. Sucks, coming off them. But it'll get better. You'll see."

That was a relief. But it was hard to believe, the way I felt. Like nothing would ever get better.

"All this . . ." I said. "Is it our fault? Did we do this?"

She stepped up close, slung an arm around my shoulders, and squeezed gently. "Don't worry. They were prepared. They have good defense strategies. We've moved to Plan B, that's all."

"Plan B," I repeated.

"Come on," she said. "Let's get a little food into you. And water. Water's important here. Living outdoors, you have to remember to drink."

I hadn't noticed before, but suddenly I was practically aching with thirst.

She led me through all the moving people, through the trees they were wheeling around and arranging. We got to a little structure with a roof over it and a pipe; she turned a handle on that pipe and water poured out of its tap into a bucket. There were cups on a small shelf in the structure, little cups of some light metal, and she filled one for me and handed it over. I drank the whole thing in a quick bunch of long gulps, despite the absence of fruit flavor we've always had in our water, which I only realized after I swallowed. At home they put in fruit smells and flavors on a certain schedule as a code, to let us know the water was okay to drink. It meant the corporates were all in sync on keeping waterborne bugs out of the supply. Here, I thought, no one was testing it at *all*, or more like, *we* were testing it—drinking it right out of the ground!

That's where it came from, she told me. Right out of the ground.

Drinking that water was like licking mud.

And yet here I was, doing it.

And even though I could taste something in it that I thought must be the metal of the cup—it reminded me of the taste of blood, that iron tinge—it was still the most thirst-quenching water I've ever had.

"If you want to get clean," she told me, "you can do that too, as long as you make it superquick. I'll show you."

She led me into the jungle a little ways, along a path, and I saw a wooden fence and behind it a bag hanging from a tree, a big, long bag.

"You stand on the grill here, see? There's a basin underneath so the water gets captured and recycled. You pull on this cord, and the water comes out of the showerbag. It's solar-heated so you don't freeze. Soap's there; washcloths and drywipes are there," and she gestured at a rack a couple of feet back.

She looked down at a nanoface on her wrist.

"I'll give you three minutes," she continued. "You can get the smell off, if you scrub hard. But try not to get your bandages wet. We don't have time for the full tour today, everything is in flux and we can't get your wardrobe from laundry yet so you'll have to put on those same clothes. But at least they didn't go through the waste chute with you."

"Plus other people won't have to smell the compost," I said.

She smiled and left me there, to shrug off the camo clothes and stand under lukewarm water falling out of this bag in the trees. Beneath my feet were bamboo slats covering a hole the water poured into. Or dripped, more like. I have to say that water didn't pour, it more trickled reluctantly. I felt like someone was splashing me from above or possibly just spitting on me. I tried not to think of spit. *Warm rain*, I told myself, *it falleth like a gentle rain from heaven*, though I have no idea where the thought came from.

I had to really scrub to make the dirt come off.

It felt extra weird to be naked outdoors, where anyone might see me if they peeked around the fence or crept out of the jungle behind us. It was like naked-plus. Hypernaked.

But even though it was rushed and furtive, it was still really nice to get the stink of the waste-composting bin off my skin. It made a big difference. And standing there, half-shivering in the open air with light shifting on the leaves around me, I felt like collecting the moment. Just like I'd tried with the opera singer and the beautiful song she sang, the second after it was done. I closed my eyes and tried to capture it, to keep forevermore. This outside light, the leaves, the water hitting my bare skin. I shivered in it and felt raw and new. I felt I had to be easier to hurt here, like this, than I had ever been in our complex. Anyone could see me, anyone could suddenly appear.

But at the same time I was stronger. I was somehow *more*.

It's incredibly hard to collect pieces of time. And yet I can't help feeling it's worthwhile—that if I can learn how to do that, I can learn how to do anything.

Before I had time to think or process any more than that—the quick relief of not having that compost stench on me; a few seconds of dappled light in the trees—Xing was calling my name. She was telling me to throw my clothes on and come out, so I dried off in a hurry. We had to be moving on, she said, it was time for us to join in. It was time for me to become part of them.

Ψ

Well, friend, whatever Plan B was supposed to have been, I will never find out.

Because right after my shower, it turned out we had to move to Plan C.

I was jogging down to Xing on the path from the shower when she looked down at her wristface, and I saw it was blinking a bright green color.

"Oh no," she said. "Oh *no*. Come on—quickly!"

The blinking green was a silent alarm, I'd learn later. She beckoned for me to follow her and we rushed between the potted trees—where everyone else was rushing too, streaming in the same direction. We happened to have started out pretty near the destination—that big Quonset hut—and so we got a space inside. Xing pulled me through the door into the crowd, which was gathered in front of all their tech.

There was a lot of it; I was surprised. There were whole banks of portable faces, power cells, all that. And on the far wall of the hut, inside, there was a wallscreen. It showed a swirl, a huge, dark-red swirl rotating over a map of the Pacific.

I knew it without needing to have it explained, because I'd seen the image in my tutorial emergency procedure lessons. It was the worst category of storm there is: a Cat Six.

And it was headed for a row of blobs I knew was actually a chain of islands, the bottom one bigger than any of the others—i.e., Hawaii. Us.

The whole place was packed with people, but instead of the noise of nervous whispers or chatter there was a total respectful hush. A woman stood up on a platform at the front—Keahi's mother, Kate. Two men stood behind her, one of them whispering into a headset.

"We're in Storm Mode," she said curtly. "This could be the worst one yet. It has that potential. Word is, most of Samoa's gone, with one retreat colony surviving on Mt. Silisili. That's *one colony* out of twenty. The surge is enormous, hundreds of feet, and wind speed is new tornado force. We need everyone headed to Deep High Station at top speed. Task protocol is Total Evac. We pull together, we do what we have to. We're capable of it and we won't fail each other."

I glanced sideways and saw people nodding, their faces trusting her, and I was glad. I was glad of their confidence. Their confidence was almost leaking into me.

Until I thought of my brother again.

"Check your wristfaces every ten minutes," said Kate, finishing. "Go."

People were already moving, surging back out of the Quonset, and we moved with them as the crowd flowed out the door, we didn't have a choice, and I grabbed Xing's sleeve. Even though she's a person with calm expressions as a rule, she looked agitated and strained.

"Xing!" I whispered. "What about Sam?"

"Total Evac means we have to drop all nonessential business," she replied. "All but the tasks we've been assigned. You don't have any tasks yet because you're new but I've been in planning sessions before this, on face, so I do have some. You need to stay with me, Nat. Without your own facc you're not safe anywhere else. You'll get one soon but not yet. So that's your job here. Stay close. I have my tasks, and you have me."

She headed across the clearing, back toward the tent area where I'd slept, and I hurried along beside her.

"But Xing, we're in between mountains here. We're not on the beach or anything," I pestered, trying desperately to understand. "Not like—not like Sam is. I don't get it, why do we have to move?"

"We don't ask. They have the scenarios worked out," said Xing. "That's number one. My guess is, the size of the tsunami is still a risk to us. We're not as high here as you'd think. Close to sea level, in parts of the valley. It's hard to predict the size of the wall of water when it hits. There's also rainfall flooding even if we're not swamped. And number two is wind speed. We're fairly well protected but tornado-grade winds can still get in, they whip up along the lava formations and riverbeds . . . we have to save our charges. We have to be as safe as we can. My task is eggs. You can help me."

I followed, I didn't ask anything more right then, and I

did what I was told, but the whole time I was thinking of Sam, in the hotel perched right on the edge of the ocean. I wondered how high those cliff walls were—not more than a hundred feet or so, I guessed, maybe a hundred and fifty where we'd walked down to set the tiny balsa boats on the sea with the candles in them.

I thought of the tsunami footage I'd seen from Indonesia and other places, the footage of when the enormous waves hit, before and during and after. First the water fell back from the beaches, almost seemed to be sucked back—the tide went way, way out and the water looked almost gone. I'd seen old footage of kids playing there, kids playing on a beach with the water receded. Just sucked back so the whole beach looked empty.

And then the huge wall of water approaching.

And the kids, a minute later, just gone.

As if they'd never been.

Ψ

When Xing said eggs, she meant turtle eggs. We had to lift them out of the artificial sand dunes where they were buried and pack them into lined baskets.

The adult turtles themselves paid no attention to us while being loaded onto carts by burly guys who seemed to know what they were doing. It took four of these guys to move each turtle, though, and they were straining and heaving as they lifted them—some of the turtles were as big as tables.

Xing said the turtles didn't guard their eggs anyway, they just ignored them—unlike some of the nearly extinct birds the camp also tended, which would come screeching and flapping at your face and even attack with beak and claws if you went near their nests.

But the turtles, Xing explained to me as we loaded up eggs as quickly and carefully as we could, were hands-off parents. In golden days, when there were lots of them, they just left their eggs on beaches and swam away again—hundreds and thousands of miles away, in fact—which was one reason they were easy to drive extinct. Hungry people would come collect the eggs after the turtles swam away, to either eat or sell them.

She was telling me this and I was thinking of Sam. I was thinking of the kids playing on the beach, of the turtles that left their eggs, just trusting to the world that nothing bad would happen to them.

But you couldn't trust the world.

Not anymore.

I thought of Sam, and how I was all he had now.

And I had left him on the beach.

I wouldn't be here except for him. I'd be in the resort right now, grieving obediently, taking my pharms and saying my affirmations.

I wasn't sure how that made me feel.

But at the front of my mind was the stark fact that I didn't know how to get to him. I didn't have the faintest idea. For all intents and purposes I was lost. I didn't have my bearings on the island; I didn't know where I was and

I didn't know where he was in relation to me. Were they evacuating the hotel? Where to? Did they have a safe place for all those hundreds of contracts and other guests, in case of a tsunami?

I had to ask. I knew there was a storm looming and I had to do what I was told, but I couldn't let it go. So while we carried the baskets out of the camp—walking as carefully as we could but still moving at a pretty good clip, through this path in the jungle that Xing seemed to know better than I thought she would—I started bugging her again with questions I wasn't supposed to ask.

"Xing, I know what we're doing is important. I know it's not in the same—that it's more than just about one person, like me or Sam or anyone. I do. But he's my brother and I'm just—I'm so worried. Being right on the beach—when the wave comes—how are they going to save them from the tsunami? The people at the hotel? There are so many! Where will they all go? And how'll they get there in such a short time?"

She didn't say anything for a while. She was bustling ahead of me, and there were more people in front of her, carrying metal cases I thought maybe were full of tech, or power equipment, or something. The cases looked heavy.

"My guess," she finally said softly, and I had to move closer, right up behind her, to hear her better, "is they're not going anywhere at all."

"What?" I wasn't sure I'd heard her right. I had to keep myself from hitting the baskets against the branches sticking in close to us. "What did you say?"

"I'm not a hundred percent certain. But I'm about ninety-nine. Saving lives isn't what they do at Twilight. Is it?"

"No . . ." I said hesitantly.

"My guess is there's a pecking order in emergencies. The choppers and the safe zone likely go to the service managers—the higher up, the more likely they are to get a seat. That'd be my guess. Nat, the resort capacity is something like two thousand. That's two thousand guests and maybe eight hundred staff. And from what I saw on the helipads, I think the place has a total of three choppers."

"So what—so you mean . . ."

Someone said something behind us, barked out an order though I didn't hear what it was, and we all stood back to let them pass. It was a line of people carrying babies in carriers strapped to their chests and backs. The babies seemed to be sleeping—just sleeping as they were carried.

Those tiny humanoids were perfectly able to sleep, even as they were marched at top speed along that rugged path.

The last in the line was Aviva, and she smiled at me quickly as she went past, one baby hanging on the front of her and another in back. They looked so funny with their bouncing, froggy little legs drooping out of the packets they were sitting in. The chubby legs, with the limp feet hanging from them, jiggled in the walking rhythm of the grown-ups carrying them.

I was distracted from my worry for a second. Small people are comical. I found myself hoping that I would get to be with them more, get to know them, even. They were a good kind of mystery; there was something about them

I'd never seen anywhere else. They looked at you and knew nothing about you, but they seemed to know something.

"What I'm guessing," said Xing, when the babies and their keepers were vanishing up ahead and we could start walking again, "is most of the employees, the low-down ones like our friend LaTessa for instance, and the regular guests? My guess is they're sacrifice."

Ψ

I walked the rest of the way trying not to freak out or cry, not even able to wipe the tears of confusion from my eyes when they spilled out because my hands were holding the baskets. I'd been so mad at Sam last time I saw him, I'd blamed him for my parents dying—completely unfair, I knew that, and now he was in danger. Not only in danger—he was going to be hit by a tsunami. And it was my fault because I was older, and I was supposed to take care of him, and I hadn't even succeeded for one goddamn *hour* after my parents died. I'd failed him right away. I'd failed him completely.

My parents would despise me if they knew. And they would be right to.

I shouldn't have left without him. I should never have let us be separated.

Ψ

It turned out we weren't going to Deep High Station yet,

or High Deep Station, whatever it's called, because we had more tasks to do. Once we got to an opening in the mountainside—it was another lava tube entrance, not one I remembered seeing before—we handed the egg baskets over to some old women waiting there, who Xing said were biologists, in charge of the breeding, and we turned around and headed back the way we'd come.

It was easier to talk on the way back down, without the burden of the eggs. Xing led me along a different path so we wouldn't get in the way of people coming up the first one. The downward path was wider, though still muddy and interrupted by tree roots, and we didn't have baskets to protect so we could walk side by side.

By this time, though, the trees around us were starting to move in the wind, and we could hear the rustling of dry fronds and the sweep of leafy branches against each other like a sighing high above. The sky, when I tipped back my head and could see a piece of it through the leaves, was heavy, with dark banks of clouds rolling across. The air felt even wetter than usual, full of warm, moist particles though rain wasn't actually falling.

"I can't believe they don't have an evac plan for the people at the hotel," I persisted—bugging Xing, I guess. "How can they just leave them? I mean, if they do that and the storm hits and people get drowned—won't facemedia find out? Won't they get in major trouble? Bad PR and the law and stuff?"

"There's a lot you don't know yet," said Xing, "about the service corps and their cohorts in other sectors. But these aren't people who, in a tornado, would worry much about evacuating hotels. They wouldn't think twice."

"Sam said something I didn't understand, something that made even LaTessa look shocked," I began, after a minute. "The other day, in the healing session, when he was on those meds? The truth drugs or whatever they were? He said something about *quotas*. Right before we faked the sickness and I dosed him with those tranks he gave me. I knew it was something he shouldn't say, just from how her face looked, but I didn't get what he meant at all. Do you know what he meant?"

She glanced down at her wristface, which must have been hard to read while she was walking.

It was blinking orange now, I saw, not the green from before. But there was the pond ahead, with its sand mounds and its eggs.

"Less than two hours before we have to be secure," she murmured, more to herself than me. "We may have to abandon the last load of eggs. I hope not. But we may."

We started gathering them up and laying them gently in our baskets; we hefted the baskets onto our hips.

I caught her eye as we turned to start up the trail again.

"Xing. Do you know what he meant?" I repeated.

She sighed and shook her head, then ducked past me. I followed at her heels, struggling to balance my basket.

"I'm not sure you're ready for that," she said.

"But Sam was? He's younger than I am, Xing, he's only fourteen!"

"Well," she said slowly, "look, Nat, if I had it my way he wouldn't know either. It's messed with him a little, frankly. But you can't do much to stop a gifted hackerkid from learning what he wants to know. Or even what he doesn't know he *doesn't* want to know."

"Uh, you're kind of losing me," I said, a bit impatient.

She took a deep breath. "Here goes. The deal is, the service corps are tasked with population reduction. That's their whole reason for being. Their official mission. So it's not just that older people in the First are *ready* to go, Nat. That's propaganda. It's all prop—pharms and prop. Because they're *made* ready. They're prepped with a tailored pharma diet over many months. The old-age 'vitamins.' Buying the contract is a part of that; it's not the first thing that happens. They only buy once they're already sucked in. By making the system look and function like a service, the corps can meet their reduction quotas *and* collect revenues in the process. That way what private monies still exist are shifting to the corporates. In the First—the gated communities—they take people's money and their lives at the same time. A neat deal; they get carbon credits when they make their quotas, and they trade those to get even richer. It's an enormous racket."

I slacked off in my walking a bit, just processing and kind of dazed. Thinking, my parents were so smart—how could they fall for that? And thinking of all the other people who did.

Basically, everyone.

Or almost.

"But that's not the worst news," Xing went on quietly. "That's just the tip of the iceberg."

"So tell me what the rest of the iceberg looks like," I begged. "*Under* the water. You have to tell me, Xing."

"The First has it easy, though the targets for contracts are certainly getting younger all the time. It used to be ninety, now they're moving to eighty-plus. Soon it'll be seventy-five. Then seventy . . ."

"And?"

"And in the poor parts, which is a carbon nightmare, the corps have much, much higher reduction quotas. The targets are pegged to what particular regions can sustain, carbon-wise. So certain types of forested areas in the poor parts tend to have lower quotas than certain arid ones, for instance, you understand what I'm saying? In areas where poors are more offset by carbon storage, natural or manmade, they're not being taken out as fast. The corp scientists work up the equations and they're the ones who determine the quotas, in collusion with corporate management. In the Resist—the resistance, in case you haven't heard that before—we call it Death Math."

"Death Math," I repeated.

"In the poor parts there's no money to be made off dying people. Because no one has money except the corporates there—regular folks have nothing. So the corps don't care if the people they take out are young or old. There, they don't bother to ask for anyone's permission. There *are* no contracts there, because there don't have to be."

I stopped still, dead still, staring at her and gaping. "But that's—but murder's illegal."

"Only for you and me."

I didn't say anything—I couldn't.

"Remember the guys in the boat on the way over?" she asked. "The Indonesian guys in uniform, who didn't talk to anyone?"

I nodded. I'd had a bad feeling about them.

"There are some of them on every boat, pretty much," she said. "Those were corp mercenaries. They get transported all over the world to do the corp dirty work at the ground level. They're like indentured soldiers. And there are many of them—some operate the drones, others do infantry work. But they, and the corporate bosses, have killed more people than the bugs ever did. In fact, the corps greatly exaggerated the bug risks, to keep people under control."

I don't know exactly what happened, but I lost my focus in the shock of that and fumbled, and my basket jittered in my arms and tipped. I righted it, panicked, but not before one precious egg fell out and shattered on a rock in the path.

Xing and I stopped and looked down at it, and just then, when I was feeling flabbergasted and sick to my stomach, we heard a loud whirring overhead and looked away from the broken egg and up into the tree canopy. It was a helicopter noise. At first we couldn't see anything, then a black dragonfly shape passed between the green blurs of the vegetation, hard to follow through the foliage but unmistakable.

And then another one. And one more.

"They're headed inland to safety," she said. "Yep. That'll be them. Probably the first wave. Later they'll catch a ride on a corp ship, somewhere between here and the mainland. Sorry, but we'll have to talk more later."

I was feeling cold suddenly, cold in the sweaty heat of the jungle.

"But *Sam*," I said. "What can I do to help him, Xing? What can I do?"

"There's no time to rescue anyone but ourselves. Your brother's resourceful. And he's not all alone. Look, Nat. Being scared stiff for him won't help him and it could hurt you. And those who depend on you. I need you to focus, okay?"

"Okay," I said, but it was weak. The sound of the choppers was fading away. It was like a wish—out of reach now and gone.

"He's free now, Nat. I know he wouldn't have it any other way. And you know too."

Free? I thought. It's a word I don't really understand, except for in the phrase *free death*. It means unmanaged, I get that, but all I could think of when she said it was the other word in that phrase. *Free death. Free = death.*

I nodded.

"We've got to pick up our pace." Xing patted my arm. "But no running downhill on this path, okay? We can't afford an injury. Too high a risk of ankle sprain or other slippage, given the incline and the lack of traction in this wet soil. So let's walk as fast as we can without losing our footing. Grab onto a sturdy branch whenever you need to."

We did pick up the pace—we rushed. It was hard to talk at all after that. I didn't think about the quotas or the poors just then, I pushed it all to the back of my mind.

Denial is a highly effective strategy, as my father used to say when he was still himself, and only half-joking.

All I could think was, *Sam, Sam, Sam, my baby brother,* as the trees whipped around overhead and my feet moved over the muddy ground and I stared down at them.

Sam. Forgive me.

Ψ

By the time we picked up the very last eggs the turtles themselves were all gone. I wondered how the men were managing to push those big carts along the narrow, muddy paths in the jungle, but as we passed through the camp again I was amazed how much had already been moved. By then big drops of warm rain were starting to fall and I was wearing a membrane-thin, clear raincoat Xing pulled out of her gear for me; she must have only had one because she let herself get wet, and she wouldn't take it back.

The Quonset still stood there, and a couple of other permanent-type structures like the cute little painted shack where the babies had been, but in just a couple of hours most of the tents had already been pulled up, and the solar panel arrays were gone, and the cooking equipment and the chairs and tables and just about everything else that wasn't sunk into the ground on posts or actually growing there.

I saw that some of the potted trees set up to camouflage the camp had already been knocked over by the rising wind. They were lying across the clearing, forlorn and bedraggled, soil spilled around the bottoms of their trunks, their branches spread out over the ground. And I wondered, if the grove of fruit trees was destroyed, and the vegetable gardens, how would the camp feed itself? Did they get all their food from right here? Did they bring anything in? They had to bring in components for pharma and tech.

I realized I didn't know how it worked yet, how alone the camp was or what its ties were to other rebel camps in other places across the sea. How many of them were there? Of us?

Kate had said something about Samoans, about twenty camps being destroyed. Were there a handful of others, or were there hundreds?

The rain was coming down harder as we struggled up the hill again with our last baskets, making a steady, almost deafening sound in the trees, and there was no way you could hear anyone talking. The sky had turned almost black. There was a purple hue to some of the clouds, though, a purple tinged with sickly yellow, like giant bruises.

I'd never been anywhere near a Cat Six. The worst storm I'd ever lived near was a Five, and it didn't hit us directly, only some people on the coast nearby, and afterward we hosted some refugees at our home.

It was before we lived in the complex we live in now—I mean, used to live in before the Final Week—and we had a bigger place back then, with an extra bedroom. The refugees slept there for the months they stayed with us—

two whole families, seven people in all. Four parents and three kids, a little older than we were.

I remember them well because of how sad they were, the parents more than the kids, because people they knew had drowned. They tried to put a brave face on it and they tried to find work and pitch in, but after a while, when they couldn't find work or bring in any money, the condo seemed really full and we didn't have quite enough food for them and eventually they had to leave. We never heard from them after that except for one message from the boy of the smaller family, which he sent to Sam—a face message on a social site. He said they were in Canada, he and his father, in some reforestation camp where life was hard, almost like slave labor, and that his mother wasn't with them anymore because she had died of a new disease.

Sam cried when he showed that message to me. The mother had liked to read to him. He was about ten then, I think. Soon after that he began really learning about interface, hacking corporate prop and browsing rebel sites and getting really interested in how the world worked.

Anyway, I thought about Sam crying as Xing and I trucked up the hill—I didn't like thinking of that but I couldn't help it. The trail was harder going now because of the rain. Water was pouring down the edges of the trodden part of it, collecting in gullies like little brown streams, turbulent and fast-moving. Those got deeper and faster until the force of the water washed parts of the path away, and sometimes we had to get off it and bushwhack through the trees because the path itself was too slippery.

The path seemed to draw water toward it, and you had to move out of its way.

I got scraped on top of the bruises I already had, and once I slipped and tore the skin off one knee beneath my camo pants, but I kept on going and didn't mention it—I knew it was minor compared to what we were dealing with, even though it hurt constantly and the pain nagged at me. There were people behind us and ahead of us, and sometimes the ones behind would pass because I was so slow. They were stronger, the rebels, from living out where they did. I admired their toughness—it was a kind of good all to itself, a kind of integrity that seemed to shine out of them and be worthy of envy.

I wondered if I would lose my softness over time and grow muscles and abilities, learn how to tie knots or fix tech or grow vegetables—if I'd become like them, if I kept living here.

If I kept living.

Because it was a Cat Six, roaring toward us across the purple-black sky.

They didn't even have Sixes before the last century. The worst storm category they had before the Greenland ice-sheet melt was Fives, and even those were extremely rare. They had to invent a whole new system for classifying storms, in fact, and throw away the old one. Sixes, at their greatest extent, can be the size of a country. They can take out entire coastlines. I've browsed about Sixes that turned a thousand miles of lived-on shoreline into oil-slicked mudflats, Sixes that caused nuclear plant meltdowns and left radiation plumes firing into the sky like poisonous fountains for years after the rain and wind had died down. Some of the most notorious Sixes have carried half a million people out to sea.

And here we were, on a fairly small island in the middle of the ocean. I told myself to face facts, that this was extremely dangerous. Maybe we wouldn't make it, in the end, and I should be like a heroine on face, looking death squarely in the eye.

We will survive, I said to myself instead. At least for me, it didn't work to dream of being a dead hero. I talked to myself about life. I said these mantras in my head, things with a rhythm that let me keep marching. *We will survive. We will survive. One foot and then the next.*

I thought of space, all around us and on and on until the end of the universe, or past the end of the universe to whatever's beyond that. And how the Earth must seem so small, from way out there; the storms must look almost pretty, if you're seeing them from beyond the stratosphere. Anything can look beautiful from far enough away.

Like on a wallscreen, where vast landscapes are neat and contained and nothing but a nice picture.

Rotate, rotate. Swirl, swirl.

Ψ

We made it into the lava tube, Xing and I and some stragglers with wheelbarrows and some baby goats they herded in at the tail end, just before the full force of the storm hit. The goats smelled unlike anything I've ever smelled before. I don't even have words for it. They really have a stench to them. No offense to those dudes; they were cute in a way, but it was more important that they stank. I'm sure I could get used to it—they say you can get used to any smells if you live with them long enough, that people live in dung heaps and don't notice it, etc. Xing told me the older goats are even worse.

The only thing I'd ever smelled before that even faintly reminded me of the goatstench was at a schoolmeet once where we got to go to an olden farm, a historical reconstruction of when real animals (other than fish in fish farms) were raised to be eaten. Those schoolmeets only happened once a year, so I always remembered them—a whole group of us together not on face but in the flesh. I was young then and couldn't stop staring at the exhibit of chickens, these funny weirdos strutting around like they were mega-important. I remember how strong it all smelled, how unlike life in the complex, and I remember wondering if olden farmers used to wear nose plugs.

Still, it wasn't anywhere close to the goatstink.

We wouldn't feel the storm's force ourselves, exactly, because we would keep on walking for hours, up and up and up—sometimes on stairs built into the lava tube, where it was narrow and steep, and sometimes just winding through the dark with only a few stray lights to guide us, bobbing and winking ahead, so that I often felt half-blind and stumbled into Xing's heels.

I had plenty of time to mull over what she'd told me—

how all over the world the corps were murdering innocent people, how they were making war on them, just mowing them down by the hundreds of thousands to slash the planet's carbon footprint. Something lodged in me as I walked, a kind of solid grief that felt like it changed the contours of my bones.

This was the most important thing I had ever learned, I realized.

In a way, it was the *only* thing I'd ever learned.

Ψ

When we finally got where we were going, we still didn't feel the storm. We could hear it as a faint rush, though, through these small holes somewhere in the system that let in oxygen from the outside. And somehow we could sense it, or at least I could, as though my whole body was paused, waiting for an impact.

And that was how it would be for more than a day, as it turned out. With only the sounds of the wind and the rain, the sound of a massive but muffled roaring, we would pass the storm tucked away in a vast, dark cave, a lava cave whose black walls were not flat but bulging and wrinkled. It was a cave lit with all kinds of lamps the camp people had brought in over time, old-fashioned lamps that ran on gas, lamps that had batteries, solar lamps, lamps that were candles, lamps you powered by winding—all these different kinds of light, white and yellow and orange and red, some bright and others dim.

We clustered there, sitting or kneeling on the folded and bumpy lava floor, some people lying on blankets, others perched on crates or folding chairs they'd carried up with them. There were hundreds of people in that cavern. Later I'd learn that the camp had numbered more than four hundred, before the storm.

The giant sea turtles weren't in there; they'd stayed down lower, in another holding area that wasn't inside the mountain at all but at some other protected location, and the same with the other animals, I guess. Only the baby goats had come into the tunnels with us, because they were small and good climbers and didn't mind narrow spaces, I was told. Luckily for me—because otherwise I would have had to smell the goatstink the whole time—they hadn't come the whole way up either. They were being kept in a smaller cavern, down lower than ours was.

Keahi and some of the other animal specialists had stayed down there looking after them, along with the turtle biologists who were taking care of those eggs.

Xing introduced me to a few of the people, some of the younger ones and some of the older ones too. They were all shapes and colors but one thing struck me about them that was different from most of the people I'd met in the past: they had a glow of sun to them, a shine to their skin that must have been from spending most of their time outside, instead of inside the walls of a complex. There was no wasted flesh on them—I mean we don't have fat people since the 21st c. anyway, food rations and footprint taxes and that, but plenty of us aren't muscular, we aren't fit because we're immobilized, using our faces, most of the time. But none of the rebels were like that. Every piece of them seemed useful and solid.

I was glad to meet them because it made me feel less alone, though I was also worried and half of my mind was on the ragged green slopes of the island outside us, the wind that had to be raging through the trees, the vast wall of water that might be approaching, might have crashed on the shores already, might already have swept away my little brother.

And those tiny glittering hummingbirds, I thought— the ones that buzzed around us at the resort, diving and sucking at red and pink flowers with their needles of beaks. Where was the shelter for them?

Every so often one of the babies would cry a little and then be rocked to sleep again, or walked around and jiggled or given a drink. A couple of them were bigger and could already walk, after a fashion, and they would totter around from person to person, clutching onto people's knees and seeking attention. I put on one of the white masks and played with one of them for a while—weird since it doesn't know how to talk. Him, I guess. Not it. But I really liked him and I wondered what he thought about me. Did they think about other people at all? I didn't know.

He was a starer and a drooler, just looked at me for long periods out of those glassy round eyes while water dripped from his gaping lower lip. Those messy habits, which in a grown-up person would make you think of mental challenge, were apparently quite normal.

People were murmuring low conversations with each

other, some shared out the snacks they'd brought or passed around water canteens. We rode out a lot of the storm like that, waiting, sleeping, and talking, since there was nothing else to do. For me it wasn't bad because I met people, something I've always loved and never did that often in the flesh—at least, not until this trip. Some of them told me a bit about themselves and I answered questions about myself, though most of them had more to tell, I thought, and I felt flat boring by comparison.

Lots had hard jobs in the camp or dangerous histories, they'd lived in bug ghettos or worked in places where there weren't too many food deliveries and the water was teeming with parasites. A sad-seeming guy, who wasn't that much older than I am, had lost a whole city. He'd lived in a place I hadn't even heard of, though the name sounded Indian, where one summer night people began to get a sickness whose major sign was blood leaking out through the pores in their skin. It happened fast, he said, the blood seemed almost to turn to water, a pinkish color, and more *soak* out of them than drip, as though they were sponges. He didn't say more than that except to tell me he'd walked among the dead until there was nothing to do but leave and no one left to stop him.

He'd come alone from there, over the ocean in a ship, because he'd been an apprentice in the corp merchant marines and knew how to steer them. He'd ended up on the Big Island, and was lucky enough to find the camp. He brought his ship to them, he said. They hid it from aerial surveillance, and they had it still.

I liked meeting the people from the camp; I worked on memorizing their names, telling myself I was collecting them because that might help me to remember. I know you can't collect people, of course. But some of their stories lodged in me like heavy stones—ominous promises of more bad news to come, news that would pull me down.

By and by it seemed like a good time for me to talk to Xing again, because I was still wondering why Sam and I had been invited—who'd made the first contact, why we were worthy of risk in the first place. I got to speak with her while we were both on baby duty, passing a very small, squish-faced one back and forth and trying to stop it from crying by bouncing it up and down and feeding it a bottle, with Xing showing me how and singing to it in a soft voice now and then. She said babies were not her specialty, not at all. They were tough, she said. Harder than turtles for sure. But she'd held a couple of them in her time and she didn't mind stepping in when she was needed.

"I'm wondering," I said, "why me, Xing? Why *us?* I know you need new people and all that. But there have to be other people who want to get out. Where did you all come from, the rebels? How did you end up here?"

"Some of us are natives," explained Xing. "The camp began that way, with native Hawaiians. But every community needs immigrants, or it dies the death of inbreeding. Not just genetic but—well, call it *of the spirit.* We've known that and we've tried to keep our community alive and changing. Many people have come to us through Twilight Island itself. I recruited in the First, you see, since that was my own background, and over the years a number of families used their Final Week as an opportunity to join. It's why some of them—though just a few among hundreds of thousands—selected the Big Island."

"So of all the survivors and contracts staying there right now . . . I mean, why was it me and Sam you picked? Was it—was it his hacking? Him being so good at tech?"

Because that was my fear, that was what was eating at me: that Sam was the one they'd really wanted, and they'd only brought me along because he asked them to. And now what if they didn't have Sam at all, only me, and I wasn't good for anything? I was soft and weak and I didn't know shit.

"We believed Sam's skills would be valuable to us," said Xing carefully.

My heart sank, because I'd been right and I so much hadn't wanted to be.

"Those skills are what put us in touch in the first place, but not why we recruited," Xing went on. "The First is full of hackerkids. It's not the talent; it's how you use it. I was on a rogue listserve with Sam, one of the ones that changes locations constantly so it doesn't get shut down too fast. Standard recruitment strategy—as long as I lived in the First, doing my work as a psych counselor, it was my job to find new recruits and bring them in. I conducted most of my research on face because it's far and above the most efficient way. What attracted me to Sam, what made me pursue a correspondence with him, was personality. That's what everyone looks for, in the end. We need talents, but more than that we need friends. I liked the soul of your family."

"The soul—?"

"There was Sam himself, of course. I loved his attitude and it's always good to have another techie onboard. And there was you, with your collecting—art is being lost these days, and we look for artists. We always do. We desperately want to bring art back."

"O-oh," I said haltingly. *Art.* Believe it or not, I hadn't ever thought of my collection like that.

It made me feel a strange lift of hope.

"But there were also your parents. Kids tend to underrate the value of those. Yours in particular: they had a history as rebels themselves, you know. Before they gave it up."

"I know. They were the last of the treehugs," I said, not without pride. "I—I always thought that was cool of them. It had to be hard to stand up for—for things that couldn't stand up for themselves. And really hard to lose."

Xing peered at me quizzically, over the bundle of baby she was hefting onto her shoulder. "Your mother was more than just any treehug. Once upon a time, she was one of the greatest. The most fearless. She was a revolutionary."

"A *what?*"

"Her specialty was explosives. I got from Sam that you two hadn't been told. Yes. That's how she lost the fingers on her hand. Those fingers got blown off."

I think, right at that moment, my mouth must have been gaping open as far as the drooling babies'.

"Explosives?" I didn't know whether to laugh or accuse her of lying. But somehow I couldn't do either.

"She was a chemist by training, you know that part, but the pharma job she held down for so long was a cover, while she was an activist, and just an income, after she retired. What she made best was bombs. Along with your father, who was one of the people working with her, she blew up stuff. Not people, you understand—never people, nothing alive, she was very moral that way. She took down installations. Corp properties, strategic sites—weapons and drug warehouses, communications centers. She fought the corporates."

My mother had never fought anyone, was what I'd thought. Except when she yelled at my dad and they got going. But that was over things like taking too long in the waste room. It was halfway funny, most of the time.

It wasn't bomb material. Bombs and my mother didn't go together.

But neither did bombs and Xing—Xing talking in admiring tones about rebels with explosions as she jiggled a drooling big-eye and seemed to be patting its butt repeatedly.

"In the end she got disillusioned, you see, and went into retirement. She'd always loved the natural world, she did everything in the name of animals and landscapes and the people who valued them. Even her operations were named after animals—Marten, Wolf, Lynx. Her monkey-wrenches, as the treehugs used to say. The end of her career came after a series of extinctions, when the last of the captive animal populations died out in the zoo pandemics. The word went out she'd collapsed, she'd said she was stopping the fight forever. And that . . . well, that was what happened."

I watched some people huddled in a corner, passing around a jug and pouring liquid from it into their canteens. People could look so regular, I thought—so *average* on the outside. But who knew what was inside them? Who knew what they'd been in the past, or would be in the future on some distant horizon?

"What was amazing was that she never got caught. I mean that was sheerly amazing. The corporates never found out her real name or her codes. They never knew what she looked like. They never had her DNA. The DNA she'd put on record when she went to work for the pharmacorps, for instance—after she gave up, and her only goal was to bring up you guys—belonged to someone else entirely. No one ever knew how she did it. But she was so good at disappearing that they were never able to grab her and torture her, as some people feared they would. Despite her injury, which should have made her stand out in the most obvious way possible . . ."

I remembered how strictly, how carefully she'd always put on her attachment to go to work—the rubbery prosthesis she called her *fake fingers*.

"Somehow she managed to disappear," said Xing, with a kind of reverence. "She flew the rest of her life under the radar so she could raise the two of you safely. Your mother was a hero to many."

The rest of her life.

I don't remember what I said after that—it must have been something inane, because all I cared about was what she'd said to *me*. They were the best words I'd ever been given—purely collectible. My mother a hero. And then the fact that I'd never known it made it a complicated thing, and I felt tears coming and a tearing, acute pull of wanting to change the past.

The most hopeless want of all.

"That's why we had to risk trying to bring you in. Because we believed in *all* of you," said Xing softly.

The next moment my loss came back full force and it made me sadder than I'd been before, to think that my mother was lost not only to these people who had believed in her, like Xing, but to Sam and me. And we hadn't even known how brave she was.

Or really, if I'm being honest, that she was brave at all. I thought of her as my mother. I barely thought of her outside that.

And now I was mad at myself because of it.

I wandered among the people for a while but found I didn't want to talk much anymore, just tended to smile weakly. Words weren't really flowing for me. After a while I kind of accepted that for once I wasn't feeling social. I sat down with my knees drawn up, leaning back against the wall and thinking; finally I lay down, wondering about my mother, shunting ideas and regrets back and forth in my head. First I was elated at the new picture I had of her, then I was crushed that she was gone, then I was torn up that she'd hidden her rebel past from us for all our lives. Next I was telling myself she'd pretty much had to, if she wanted us all to stay together.

And alive.

Eventually I dozed off, sleeping fitfully on my thin mat. As the storm battled on late into night and then stretched into the early hours of day—or so I was told, because time passing was a half-dream in the cave—most of the others fell in and out of sleep too. I'd turn on my side and watch one or another of them, sometimes exhausted, sometimes alert. Or I'd get tired of looking at faces and just watch the lamplight flickering on the walls. There was a timeless quality in there, a strange mood that combined anxiety and relief—anxiety over those who weren't with us and over our uncertain future, relief that we still seemed to have one.

Through the whole storm that place felt secure. I remember marveling at that, at any place that could make people feel safe during a Cat Six. We were surrounded by the most comforting walls I'd ever known. They weren't the flimsy, temporary walls that humans built but thick and abiding. They were the warm body of a mountain—and a living mountain, because Deep High Station was under the volcano.

DAY SEVEN
ACCEPTING & GRATITUDE
Theme of the Day: Recovery

The noise of the wind finally dwindled and died down, and we started to get impatient and restless. Where before the walls had felt like shelter, now they were starting to feel suffocating.

It seemed like way too long till the scouts were finally given the signal to go out. When at last they were dispatched, they went jogging off down the tunnel carrying portable tech, small satellite dishes, and facesets to check the weather systems. You can't get face signals in the volcano—you can't know anything about the outside world in there. It's just too thickly insulated, Xing told me.

But if we ever had to retreat here for longer, she said, we might be able to. It would mean work, and where the rebels put their work effort is carefully chosen, Xing explained. The holes that were drilled for oxygen—the system of ventilation already installed in the mountain—were a first phase of a something called Project Safe House. There's still a lot more planning that has to go into it, though, a lot of engineering and a lot of energy, but it will probably get done sometime in the future. There are geologists in the Resist, she said, who believe that certain places inside the mountain are safer than outside—that new eruptions of magma would be less likely to touch us there.

I had a chance to talk to Kate while we were waiting for the scouts to come back with their report. Xing was helping with the babies and with one person who'd been hurt in the evac, an old man with an injured foot. Kate must have seen me sitting alone and decided to be nice to me; she sat down beside me and inspected my injuries, taking the bandage off my head wound and checking to make sure that it wasn't infected, then moving down to the bandage on my side.

Because she wasn't the kind of person who was content to do a single thing at once, she also told me more about the camp.

And about the rest of the world.

While she was looking at my injuries, and trying to distract me from the soreness while she patted more disinfectant onto the stitches, she talked on and on in her matter-of-fact voice. And a realization dawned on me: I'd always lived in the kind of cave we were huddled in now. In a way I'd always been sheltered like that, always had a thick roof over my head and no signals from the outside.

Because I hadn't *tried* to hear those sounds. I'd never worked at it, not like Sam had. I'd done my collecting; I'd only wanted to look at things that were beautiful.

I hadn't wanted to look at the opposite.

Kate said the corps were mostly trying to get rid of people—as fast as they could, because it was people who were the biggest carbon footprint, and the corps wanted to make the world livable again.

And of course, she said, there was nothing wrong with wanting fewer people to live on Earth. "Everyone knows there are too many of our species, by orders of magnitude. But the answer isn't Death Math. Now, the corps aren't doing their kills because they think it's right; they simply don't care what's right. They just want a stable world back, and they want it for themselves. They think they can groom it back to being their playground again—and mind you, dear, our world being a playground for all the powerful corps is exactly what got us into this mess in the first place. For them, Death Math is the fastest way back."

The Resist, she said, believed in livability too, just not through Death Math, and for the poors as well as the First. Only by not having many babies and by raising the ones that were abandoned or targeted.

She added that there was a powerful movement in the corps that didn't believe the last tipping point was irreversible. They believed if we took people out now the globe could recover more quickly, and then they could have it for themselves. But Resist scientists said it would take hundreds of years no matter what, and all we could do was reduce our numbers slowly, live simply, try to rebuild a better culture, and wait.

In the Resist they believe in science and philosophy, she said, literature and art and even some kinds of the softer godbeliefs, as long as the beliefs are open to anyone.

Corps mostly believe in math. And not math in the best sense, but math only as it served them.

"So Sam had these lists of numbers I found," I said. "In

his room. Some of them were really big numbers, hundreds of thousands . . ."

"You know what those were, now, don't you?" she asked softly, and closed up my last bandage.

"They were numbers of people killed, weren't they?"

She didn't nod because she didn't have to; she just went on talking. She hadn't seen Sam's lists but he'd mentioned them. Those numbers, she told me, were whole populations taken out by corp-army actions. Because bombs had a big footprint, they mostly used sneakier weapons, like gases and chemicals that killed people but left buildings intact. Sometimes they poisoned water supplies, if they knew the water supply would recover. There were poisons that had a shelf life, she said, poisons that disappeared from the water over time, so that a few months or years after they did their work the water was safe to drink again.

Then Kate rose to her feet. She told me not to give up. She told me the Resist was all over the world, with spies in corporate, even, inside the corporate machine, who gave us information.

"In the end," she went on, and leaned forward to pat my shoulder, "in the end we will win. But it may not be in my lifetime, Nat. Or even in yours, possibly. Our task is to keep going. To remember that we, and those babies, deserve a second chance—we do, and so does everything else in creation."

A scout came back in then and whispered in her ear, and she stood up and announced to all of us that the storm had officially passed.

And we could go outside again.

Ψ

We had to move out slowly, along the tunnel, and it was a frustrating couple of hours, wanting desperately to be outside and see what the island looked like but having to move steadily downward through the lava tube in this orderly fashion. And because it was dark in there except for our lamps, it was like it was night still, and no time had passed.

Or maybe all time had passed, and the world was simply gone.

It felt unreal.

And when, after two or three hours of careful walking, I finally emerged behind others into the light of day, my eyes seemed newly blind. I'd been away from sunlight for less than twenty-four hours but my eyes had already forgotten how to look at it.

A great brightness fell on us, as we stood there on the side of the mountain. The whiteness struck me and before I could see anything out of it—I was tearing up and blinking—I could feel and smell. We moved along this kind of lava shelf on the mountainside, where there was space for us to stand. The air was warm and wet but seemed so expansive around me, so alive and moving compared to the closeness and stillness of the cave. It was delicious, full of the smell of rain and earth and leaves and of the salt breeze off the sea.

Still, fear moved up through me, tingling, from the

soles of my feet to the tips of my fingers, and I shivered.

As I stood there blinking, the white light faded and resolved into a picture. We were on the mountainside and the sky was bright blue and clear. It had been a fast, vast storm, and now it was definitely gone. I knew something had been destroyed, I knew that things had been lost down there, things and people, but it somehow seemed to me that this was the most beautiful place I'd ever been. It was the freshest, best-smelling air I'd ever breathed.

Here I was loose, here I was open to the world. It was the lightest I'd felt in my whole life: anything in the world was possible.

Maybe this was what it would feel like, I thought, living and dying unmanaged.

Beneath our feet on the lava shelf the jungle spread out, a sparkling emerald green, water reflecting off leaves. There were dents in it, I saw, flattened holes here and there in the canopy where you could tell a bunch of trees must have fallen. There were hills and jagged lava outcroppings, there were clearings that must have once been farmland, orchard rows of fruit trees in the distance, and over us in the blue there were just a few small clouds, white and gray and even purple on their edges.

All that remained of the Six.

The Six that might just have killed my baby brother, I thought then, and my exhilaration caved in and practically turned inside out. Here I was, soaring, with a weird, frightening feeling of newness. Of liberty, maybe, as I'd imagined it. And where was he?

We had a view all the way to the ocean, though it was harder to see what was there, since it was far away. I remembered when Sam and I had climbed the lower slopes of the volcano together, how we'd looked back and been able to see the white structures of the hotel—a clear view. But we were much farther away here, I guess, and up higher in elevation . . .

I shaded my eyes from the brightness above and peered in what I thought was the hotel's direction, but couldn't really see past the trees.

"Here, look," said someone beside me.

It was Keahi. He'd been in the shelter with the goats so I hadn't seen him at all during the storm, and I felt another skip of euphoria when I peered at his face again, its clean and handsome lines, the eyes and the set of his mouth that always looked like he knew something I didn't and it might be just slightly funny.

He stood close to me and I felt the warmth of his side through my clothes—more, I think, than I'd feel someone else's.

"It's not going to be easy," he said, "but you need to look through these." And he lifted these teched-out specs so I could see through them. They had small screens inside.

But my hands were shaking as I held them so Keahi put his hands over mine, standing behind me. It felt right to have him there. I wanted to relax back against him, but I was too shy for that, so I just looked through the specs again.

On the small screens, which came together into one as

I looked, there was a dab of white. I looked harder, trying to make out its shape.

"I'll zoom for you," said Keahi in my ear.

And the picture got bigger and nearer.

Keahi let me hold the specs myself and dropped his arms so they were around me—almost holding me up, I think now.

It was the hotel all right. But it also wasn't anymore. Just a shell, torn into pieces with big struts and beams sticking out in a jumble. There were fallen walls and empty holes in the ones that hadn't collapsed; pieces of the buildings looked like a giant claw had dropped down and scooped into them.

I let the specs fall and just stood there with my throat closed up. I couldn't say anything.

Sam. Sam.

And the others. I knew there were others. But I could only think of my own brother.

Keahi dropped his arms from me and turned me to face him. "Nat, it's going to be okay. You're strong."

"Listen, we can't stay here," said Xing from a few feet away, and I saw people were moving downward quickly, into the path in the trees, hiking back down the mountain. "We're visible in the clear and we can't risk it. We need to get under the tree cover. Come on."

Ψ

Sure enough, as we weaved our way through the jungle to

find out what was left of the camp—me trying uselessly to get my head around the mangled remains of those huge hotel buildings and what they must mean—the black dragonflies whirred overhead again, headed out to sea.

They were leaving the island entirely. Nothing left for them here, now that the resort was a ruin.

"They'll be going to rendezvous with a ship, most likely," said Keahi.

He was walking right behind me, and Xing was in front.

"They can't make it all the way to the mainland. Not with the small size of those helicopter fuel tanks. They're probably meeting a corp marine transport of some kind, a big one that wasn't swallowed up by the Six."

I was thinking I couldn't imagine what it would be like to be one of the guys in those choppers—one of the guys who'd left a whole resort full of people to fall under the waves.

But then I thought, *But I left Sam. And where is he now? Where's my brother? He trusted me. He trusted all of you too.*

And maybe I was just like the corporates at Twilight, only they had two thousand people to kill.

And I'd only had one.

Keahi must have read my mind—maybe he had ESP. Or maybe I had said my thoughts aloud.

"It's not the same at all. Don't beat yourself up. They built this system. They built a hotel without evac capacity and they made big, big money off of it. They did their Death Math and yesterday they were just following the equation like they always do. Innocents died under their watch—innocents always do. And there was nothing you could have done to stop it."

I noticed, as we walked on in silence, that I wasn't as down as the day before, that I was still scared for Sam, I was full of all of this new knowledge I hadn't really understood yet, my mind muddled with anger and grief and the confusion of my new unmanaged life—the strange, scary looseness of being at large in the world.

But I didn't have the flat depressive feeling I'd had when I was coming off the pharma, and I was so glad of that one part that I could have yelled.

My mind was clear as the sky I'd looked up at when we came out of the cave. I felt like I could take on things, like I wanted to live a new way, and it filled me with a kind of excitement and determination.

I felt as if maybe, for the first time in my life, I was going to really *do* something. Something my parents, once upon a time, could have admired.

Ψ

But when we came off the mountain path and got down into the camp, my heart sank.

It was like a bog or a marsh or something. There were ponds in some of the lower places where the tents had been, all the potted trees everywhere were down and flattened on the ground, and some of the big trees actually growing around the clearing were down too. The mess of the downed trees was everywhere, some of them floating in the pools of muddy water.

The Quonset was just a frame now, all the sides ripped off and flapping in the breeze. It was like the skeleton of a great beast, a massive, empty rib cage like they have in face museums.

I thought the place was wrecked and I stood there beside Keahi, just gazing out at the water and the collapsed edges of the forest.

Then Kate moved past us, carrying a loop of cable over one shoulder and smiling. "Not bad!" she said. "We can fix this, Nat. Don't worry. We just need some elbow grease."

I had no idea what elbow grease was; it sounded disgusting. But she was smiling, so it couldn't be that bad, I guessed.

And then the best thing happened.

Out of the ruined Quonset stepped Keahi's friend from the resort, the one who'd helped me escape.

Behind him was Sam.

I couldn't help it, I shrieked. And ran up to him and threw my arms around him.

When I stepped back, I saw he wasn't looking that great, he had a black eye and a cut on his lip. And there were deep bruises and more cuts on his wrists, like he'd been bound.

But he was alive. And right then, that was the same thing as perfect.

Xing came over, and Keahi, and we were all standing around grinning and talking fast and asking too many questions. Sam spoke in a kind of subdued voice, and I thought he looked older—what he had seen, I guess, or what he knew had happened.

The storm was what had saved them, he explained quietly. Because the storm had diverted all the corp's attention. The storm had taken out everything, all those people vacating, he said—it must have. But it had saved him.

Yet even before he told the story, he said, right now he needed to talk to Kate privately. He and Keahi's friend, whose name was Mano, needed to talk to Kate right away.

So they went off to the side and huddled. I was curious and stood there waiting, watching their faces to try to figure out what they were talking about.

Then Kate went away for a while to talk to some other people in the camp, and then she was back, and nodded. And Sam and Mano went into the jungle again, and when they came back they weren't alone.

Behind them was a group of hotel refugees.

The only people, Sam told me later, who had survived, as far as he knew.

I didn't recognize any of them at first, they were so bowed-over and wretched. Their clothes hung in rags and they were shivering and holding themselves protectively, their arms folded, their shoulders bent. Some of them didn't even have shoes. But as they filed into the clearing—I think there were eighteen in all—I finally picked out two I actually knew. There was the meathead guy from our survivor group, one of his arms in a sling that must have been made out of his torn-up shirt, because he was bare-chested. He looked shell-shocked. And at the very end of the line, limping, there was a shivering, thin woman, her long yellow hair matted and tangled, with nothing on but a once-beige bathrobe, now dark brown with mud, and a pair of tattered slippers.

It was LaT.

"The rest of them are just guests. She's the only corp staff," said Sam. He was beside me now. I hadn't even noticed he was there, what with staring at them.

"Hey, I'm surprised you didn't bring Rory," I said, making a weird and lame attempt at humor. I must have been nervous, and it was a shock to see her there, since she was what we were escaping from.

I was also thinking how exposed the camp would be to bugs, with these new people here—the more people, the more vectors. That was what they always taught us on healthface. Even before we were old enough to read on face we had to recite it, practically in our cradles: *Hug strangers, bug dangers.* Then I reminded myself of what Xing had said: the bug danger wasn't as big as they always told us it was.

Still, I wondered if Kate would let them stay.

"At first we didn't have a choice, we *had* to let LaTessa come," said Sam. "She clung to us, tagging along. We were just running and soaked and scared and the winds were coming up and it was chaos. And then we hid out in this little hut she knew about, a ways back from the hotel, this little hut made of stone that was really old and built more solidly, into a hillside. Back toward the snorkeltank where we went on the fieldtrip. She helped. She actually led us there."

"LaT. saved you?"

"She pretty much did. And we talked a little, during the storm. You should hear where she came from. Her whole family was wiped out, she was starving for a while and she had a bad sickness that almost killed her, and when she got better she tried a lot of things before she took the corp job. Things that were way worse, for her. Things that can . . ." He shook his head as though he didn't know what to say, and then moved on. "But she's tough and she survived. In the end, you know, she was just making a living the best way she could. She's not so bad since she dropped that corp act."

He sounded sad, and I thought again how much older his voice was. He was way past fourteen.

"You did good." I reached out and squeezed his arm. "You're here! I'm so proud of you. I'm—I'm so happy. I was really scared."

"Not as scared as I was," he said.

"And I'm sorry I was so harsh to you about—what happened. To Mom and Dad. I felt so bad later—"

"No, there's nothing you should say sorry for. Don't sweat it, Nat. I just knew we didn't have time to talk. Or even think. It was life or death for us too."

We watched as Kate and Xing handed out water and blankets to the refugees and then led them back into the trees to rest. Before long, someone was going around giving them shots.

Apparently they were staying.

Ψ

For hours after that, as the sun crossed the bright blue sky, we worked on fixing up the camp.

The adults and other experienced people did the most complicated stuff—the work to connect hoses to drain the water out, for instance, or get the frame of the Quonset draped so it was protected, or hook up the face and weather tech again. Sam and I and even some of the refugees, the ones who weren't still collapsed from fatigue in sleeping bags under the trees, did the grunt work. We went wherever we were told—we carried tent poles from place to place and set up tents, piled soil into planters to try to save some of the potted trees, collected fruit that had fallen in the orchard so that it could be salvaged.

I was psyched—we were getting real things done and the camp was coming back to life. I felt useful. We would jog across the clearing with the stuff we were carrying and yell out questions and comments, me and Xing and Sam and Keahi and Mano—we were getting to know each other as we worked.

I'd never worked with other people in the flesh like this. Not really. We had momentum, like some kind of dance.

All of a sudden I was exhilarated.

This was what life was like, I thought, among the people, outside the complex, apart from my face—in the open air! This was what it would be like to spend my time with actual human beings around me.

But as I was kneeling in the orchard with Sam, the knees of my pants muddy and soaking wet, piling mangoes into a crate and laughing at something he said, I heard that sound again.

It wasn't a good sound.

It was the *chop-chop-chop* of the black dragonflies.

Ψ

We gathered under the trees—they regularly held drills to practice for flyovers, so everyone but Sam and me and the storm refugees knew what to do. We copied what they did as best we could.

The problem was, the storm had knocked out a lot of the camo so the camp's exposure was way worse than it would have been a day before. We shrank back into the trees so we were surrounding a clearing that mostly looked empty, but we probably hadn't gone fast enough, Keahi said—our usual sentries weren't posted because they were on cleanup and animal care and various other storm-related duties, and the tech that would normally have warned them of a flyover was still being set up.

And so the choppers went overhead, and the noise of them dopplered away, *chop-chop-chop,* and you could almost be relieved, if you were me.

But just when it seemed to be fading, it whirred closer again. This time, as they came over, I saw things sticking out of the doors of the chopper on both sides, pointing down.

Then the choppers were past, again.

"So what was *that*?" I asked Sam.

Keahi, who had been beside him, dashed off then and was zigzagging through the trees and people toward Kate, who was talking to the guys in headsets that seemed to be her right-hand men, or whatever.

"I think they were zooming in," said Sam. "They were surveilling, trying to figure out if there are people alive here."

Off to my right I saw Kate was telling Keahi something, and he nodded, and then I noticed some other guys were splitting off into these positions along the jungle edge, hunkered down beside boulders, one of them right near us. It was Mano kneeling there, at our boulder, and then the boulder itself was being pushed—it must have been hollow or something because otherwise it would have been too heavy to move.

Mano pushed it aside and there beneath it, stuck into a hole in the ground, was what looked like a kind of big telescope to me, a long thing like a pipe on a tripod.

"It's probably some kind of anti-aircraft gun," said Sam. "Projectile-firing thing. They're old-fashioned wartime weapons with terrible footprints. It must only be for severe emergencies."

The *chop-chop-chop* got louder again and this time the helicopters came in from another direction, swept up the length of the camp instead of flying across it. They were on the other side of the clearing from us, luckily, moving along from the right to the left, and the middle one dropped something into the trees. I saw pink clouds rising, clouds of pink billowing out over the trees.

"Oh no. Shit, *shit*," said Sam. "That must be a nerve agent. A gas, Nat! Shit! They must be doing a sweep. They want to make sure no one's left. If they drop it on this side we're—"

And then we all had to fall onto the ground and cover our heads—that was what people were yelling at us to do, though I couldn't hear them, actually, I just did what they did. I heard these loud explosions, one-two-three. The noise was so loud I couldn't hear anything after that because it had been so close to my ears. Everything was quiet and I was afraid I was deaf, but then the deafness passed and sound came back again.

I glanced up and saw one of the helicopters burst into flames. It wavered to and fro and crashed into the trees. And then the second one was turning around and around, out of control, making me a little queasy even to watch it, until it swung out of sight and a few seconds later we heard the crash from that too, though we didn't see any flames. Right away some of the people from the camp headed over to where it had gone down.

But the third one was too swift or smart, I guess, and it swerved up and away, higher and higher and out toward the sea until it was a dot, and then just like that, incredibly fast, it was gone.

Ψ

They held a meeting after that—they blocked off the sites of the crashes because those areas were dangerous. Of course no one went near where the pink clouds had been; the gas lingered awhile, Sam found out, and if you came into contact with it the effects were horrifying. Shaking and convulsions, and after that you died. Your throat closed and you couldn't breathe.

So we stayed in safe places and the elders went into their meeting.

I asked Xing why they just dropped them in the trees, and she said they'd probably thought we were hiding there, and they would have come back and gas-bombed the side where we actually were hiding, next. It was pure luck they hadn't chosen our side *first*. That gave us time to retaliate. And now the problem was the remaining helicopter, and the report it would take back to the corps.

That report had already been sent in, she said.

And they knew we were organized and even armed, so we'd have to leave and find a new camp. Up till today, Xing told me, they hadn't known there was Resist here at all. But now they did.

It was probably going to be a high priority for them, dealing with us, because they didn't like it when their choppers got shot down. They didn't like it one bit.

So all the work we'd done to restore the camp after the Six was for nothing, because now we had to leave again.

And this time we couldn't ever come back.

I felt torn up at first, hearing that, because I'd been picturing living in *this* place, this beautiful valley with its fruit trees and greenery. I already felt something for it—I'd already been relying on the idea that it was my home now.

The good news was, they'd planned in case of this, and there was another site already picked out, a backup location. We shouldn't be too alarmed, said Xing, it wasn't bad, they'd tended it for a while.

But we'd still have a lot to do. We'd have to race against the clock.

Until the black dragonfly came back.

Ψ

The elders didn't take long—everything happened fast here. There's never been time to waste, at least not since I arrived.

They mapped the way to the backup site and everyone was assigned tasks. Mano gave Sam and me our own wristfaces and a brief tutorial on how to use them—just the basic functions, he said, what the colored alarms meant, and how to send and receive messages.

Sam was in charge of the refugees until the relocation was finished, because they knew him and they had spent the storm together so there was a level of trust. I'd help Sam out, for now. Our job was just to take direction from Xing and move the refugees.

And so we left again, even though it was late. The sun was already going down so we were carrying flashlights or wearing headlamps, and we were all tired. The site that we were moving to, Xing told me, was just four miles away, not up the mountain, luckily, but kind of around its base to a small canyon. It was a place the rebels already used for certain purposes, where the turtles had been moved to and guarded in the storm, for instance, because it was too hard to move them into the volcano. There were already some structures there, so we weren't completely breaking new ground, she told me. We weren't going to start all the way at zero.

I found myself walking beside LaTessa for a while, or trudging wearily more than walking, I should say (and we were the lucky ones because we weren't carrying heavy equipment, just some packs on our backs that had been handed out to us—heavy enough for a recovering wuss like me). She'd been given some clothes and boots and she had washed most of the mud off her face; her hair was tied back with a piece of twine, though it was so dirty you couldn't see the usual light-golden sheen.

It was the first time we'd been near each other since she showed up at the camp. It was hella awkward and I didn't have a clue what to say. Above us the sky had reached that deep indigo blue it can get when twilight is intense, and the stars were beginning to come out. On both sides of the trail there were trees, and ahead of us marched the other refugees, with Sam at the front of the group. We were close to the end of everyone from the camp; behind us there were only some slow-moving guys carrying a hurt person on a stretcher.

"So," said LaT. finally, and cleared her throat. Her voice,

I have to say, sounded lower and rougher, like the whole time in the healing sessions she'd been using some kind of falsetto. "Breaking the ice here. Things have changed. I'm not working for corps anymore. So you don't have to pretend to listen to me anymore."

"Man. It's weird to hear you talk normally," I said.

She shrugged.

"I guess you got used to being that person?" I asked.

"What I got used to was eating three squares a day." She cleared her throat again and this time she actually spat. Not at me, just on the ground beside her. It was gross and all that, but coming from a former Aryan Barbie, it was okay with me. "For that I would have done way worse than talk horseshit and dress up like a vestal virgin. I *have* done worse. You better believe it."

"Sam said you had a hard life before you got that job."

"I had the life most people have," she said, annoyed. "Hunger and being sick and weak and doing whatever you gotta do to get through the day with all your digits intact."

"You didn't live in the First?"

"First, shee-yit," said LaTessa. "The First isn't a *place*, kid. It's just a way of living when you have money. The First is just wealth."

"But I mean, you didn't live in one of the complexes."

"You got that right."

"Where—where did you live?"

"Anywhere. Everywhere. The streets, the tent cities, the ghettoes. I had what most people have, which is nothing. The life you knew is barely real, kid. You lived on a stage set. Trust me: you didn't know the world one bit. Picture a doll's house, painted pastel pink, in the corner of a stinking toxic dump the size of the world. Well, you and your brother lived in that dollhouse. And the windows and doors were sealed shut."

I opened my mouth to say something, but no words came out.

"And that," she said sharply, "is what your parents knew that you didn't, and why they wanted to die."

I felt defensive for a second, but the feeling faded quickly. She might have been right, I knew, but it pissed me off that she brought up my parents. She who, until the Six came along, had happily, falsely been in the business of killing them.

"I get it," I said tightly.

"You should consider maybe they were right. Because pretty soon now the last dollhouse is going to fall." She sounded angrier by the minute.

"I got it, LaTessa," I snapped. "Okay? You don't have to yell at me."

We walked in silence.

"Sorry," she said after a while.

"It's okay," I said back. But I pushed the words out like they were bags of rocks.

"Look, I know it's not your fault. Not any of ours."

"Yeah. Well. Thanks, I guess."

"And after all," she said, and switched to her honeyed voice, "why worry? *The world is just a sunset-time glorious nowness of being.*"

We could have laughed.
But we couldn't.

Ψ

We got to the new camp in pitch darkness.

We were so beaten into exhaustion by then, all we did was help set up the tents. We didn't look around, we didn't get a feel for where we were; we just did what we were told in a state of fatigue, staked in the tents and then raised them, with help from Xing. Sam and I were sharing one. We drank some water from the canteens being passed around and each ate a food bar they gave out, these protein bars made of who knows what—tasteless except for the cinnamon they flavored them with. They weren't wrapped in fiber like I'm used to: Xing pulled them out of a homemade-looking sack. Inside it the bars were in a big pile, crumbling and smelling of something like old fruit. I'm going to have to get used to eating food that's not safe from germs.

I'm going to have to get used to not being safe myself.

After we ate the tasteless bars we pulled our sleeping bags up over our shoulders, burrowed in, and fell right asleep.

Ψ

The color of the bruise around his eye had changed—that was the first thing I noticed when Sam shook me awake in the morning. It was yellowish now, where it had been purple and red before.

I also noticed he needed to brush his teeth. And I definitely needed to brush mine.

But that was a small relief, actually, because it meant life had something regular about it again. Even if that one regular aspect had to be morning breath.

I sat up in my sleeping bag and rubbed my eyes and saw he had the door flap folded back and outside there were legs walking past, in both directions, and part of another tent the same dull color as our own, and everywhere low bushes with shiny, big leaves. I could hear the sounds of people talking and laughing.

They seemed to feel safer here.

"Come on," Sam said. "It's late, I tried to let you sleep in but then I got impatient."

It reminded me of Wintermas morning when we were little—how he wouldn't let me sleep because he was too excited about what his gift might be. So I figured he'd been up for a while and asked him where I could wash my face and rinse my mouth out. Was there water? A bucket or anything?

He said there was actually a hose, hooked up to a spigot—there was a whole pipe system made out of pieces of bamboo. He pointed out the tent opening.

"I'll go with you," he said, and we wriggled out of the tent together, still in our clothes from the day before. We found a jug of minty water there and a cup to use, which we had to rinse out afterward, and even a pile of clean washcloths. I was amazed and glad.

When I felt less mealy, my face wet and fresh from the cold water, I waited for Sam to finish and glanced around.

The tents were clustered in a disorganized way, and there were people rushing everywhere, already hard at work. I couldn't see much of the new camp itself, only the tents and the green trees around us, but I heard something: water rushing. There had to be a stream nearby.

To our right rose the mountain, so close you couldn't see up to anywhere near the peak—just the side rising away, with more trees on it and a couple of those gray tongues of lava above.

"This used to be the husbandry camp," said Sam. "I just went over a map of it on Xing's handface, I know all about what they do here. But I haven't seen the best part yet. Come on!"

He'd figured out directions already; with me following him we wended our way toward the stream. It turned out to be a sparkling, churning brook, not too wide but deep and dark in places, with lots of miniature waterfalls where clear water was rushing between stones and lava outcrops. There was a trail beside it and we walked along it and up through some trees, where we emerged to a flatter place with fences.

The canyon spread out a little more into a valley, though the flank of the mountain was still close to us on our right. There were the turtles, in a sandy enclosure, and beyond them some livestock—goats and sheep and some chickens.

"Let's go this way," said Sam.

We moved between the rails of the fences to a tented area. It wasn't small, regular tents but an overhead awning kind of thing that stretched back to the mountainside.

There were more enclosures there, and ponds and food stations that looked more or less permanent—they definitely hadn't been thrown up overnight.

"There," said Sam, and pointed.

And in the enclosure nearest us I saw a huge lizard the size of an alligator, and then another one, curled up asleep. I wasn't sure it was an alligator, its head wasn't quite right for that, I thought, but I had no idea what it was.

"Komodo dragon," explained Sam. "Supposed to be extinct, like the turtles. They're from Malaysia or Indonesia—I'm not sure. One of the chaos centers."

"A dragon," I said, marveling. "I didn't know those were *ever* real. Does it breathe fire?"

"It's not that kind of dragon. And here, follow me."

We walked to the next enclosure, and there were big white birds with long skinny legs, black faces, and caps on the tops of their heads where the feathers were bright red. Sam's face lit up when he saw them.

"Look," and he pointed to a sign on the enclosure, which was actually a clipboard with some markings on it. *Whooping Cranes*, it said at the top.

"That's cool," I said uncertainly.

"These are amazing! Once they were almost gone! There were like ten of them in the world, or something. And they brought them back! Of course, they can't live here forever. They need to fly. One day the dream is to let them back into the wild. When . . . when the wild is there again."

I looked at the great white birds. They were a puzzle—graceful and kind of absurd at once, skinny necks and heads on top of a big swell of white body.

"These enclosures go on," he said. "They go on and on, around the base of the mountain. And each of them has a tunnel network, with inside habitat underneath in case of eruption and lava flow. Manmade, not lava tubes."

"You're kidding." The scale of it was starting to dawn on me—what it must take to feed these creatures and keep them alive. To have brought them here in the first place. The skill and dedication of the rebels.

Just then Keahi came out of one of the enclosures, carrying a bucket of what looked like grain. He gave me a slow smile. "Let me show you guys." He put the bucket down to take me by one arm. The arm, right then, felt like the center of my body. "Look at these," he said, and he led me past a couple of other bird areas to a muddy enclosure with a big pool of water in it. There we saw these funny animals, large and dark and leathery and covered in mud, with soft square snouts and short, squat legs. "Pygmy hippos."

The three of us walked along for a while, looking at those animals. There were plenty of things I'd never heard of: spider monkeys that were really smart—their enclosure was full of trees—and anteaters and hairy piglike creatures called peccaries and sections of small cages that had snakes and mice and even bugs and caterpillars in them. *American Burying Beetle*, said one label, and there were these huge black-and-red beetles in there, really dramatic looking.

"We should go back," said Sam, after a while, and Keahi squeezed my arm almost imperceptibly.

I peered down and noticed my new wristface was blinking—a blue light, which wasn't an emergency-type alarm but just told us it was time for a meeting.

"This way," said Keahi, "it's faster along the stream."

So we turned away from the animal enclosures—I was reluctant, because there was still a lot to see—and headed downhill a bit, walking along the creek again.

Ψ

Instead of Kate leading the meeting this time it was an old man. He was standing up on a box and he wore a mike, so everyone could hear him, but it was hard to see him from where I was standing.

His name was Rone. He was a coleader with Kate and his job was logistics, for those of us who didn't already know him. He'd been in the army a long time ago, and in the army that had been his specialty. And he was going to direct the establishment of the new HQ.

First off, he said, they needed to bless the camp. And say goodbye to the old one. Xing was next to me and she whispered they always did that when they had to move, it was part of the ritual. They'd been at the old camp for six years; before that it had been mostly a fruit orchard, which they had planted and tended.

That time, she explained, they'd moved not because

any helicopters came and not because of a high-cat storm but mostly for convenience. They wanted to be closer to both the resort, where their recruits often came from, and a secret, sheltered port they used.

The port was where the boats came in—the boats that carried the babies.

"The name of the new camp shall be Athens, after the ancient Greek city of democracy," said Rone. "And now for the blessing."

That sounded a little corpspeak to me, it reminded me of *Bless Happiness*, and I looked around and saw LaTessa, who was standing on Xing's other side. I was shocked for a second: she'd cut off her princess hair. It was chopped off in a messy way all around her head, making her look like a boy. But she was standing proudly with her shoulders thrown back and I could see what Sam had said, that she had a toughness to her, and I guessed she wasn't vain and had cut her hair to be practical.

I felt a bit different about her then, maybe a little admiring.

Rone sang a poetic song, which *didn't* sound like corpspeak, and everyone in the camp seemed to know it because they sang it along with him. It was a religious poem, Xing whispered to me, a poem from the Christian godbelief, but some nights there were blessings from Buddhist systems or Jewish or Hindu or even Earth godbeliefs, with tree nymphs and that kind of ancient thing. *"All things bright and beautiful, all creatures great and small, all things wise and wonderful, the Lord God made them all,"* they sang.

After the blessing things got less ceremonial and down to brass tacks, as Rone put it. He detailed the process for setting up the camp, what the priorities were, and the order we had to do things in. We were each part of a work group, and Sam and I and LaTessa were all in Xing's, which reported to Keahi.

We worked the whole day after that, until we were exhausted all over again. I won't tell all the things we did—I don't think I'll have much time to keep a journal for a while, and there are only a few pages left in this booklet even though I've written everything so tiny. But they were things like moving the tents into a pattern they mapped out for us, helping to set up cooking and eating areas and also the composting systems—toilets and otherwise.

Let's just say ours isn't the work group with the most glamorous tasks. But one really good thing is, I'm also going to have two spaces of time each day—one in the morning and one in the afternoon—with no tasks at all. And during that time I'll be able to do my collections. There's going to be a special shelter, the man named Rone told me, where I can show the items I collect, and other people will also put things there.

He said it will be an important place, "a place that honors the beautiful," is what he told me, and my collections can be there too.

Ψ

When it came time for the evening meal we all stopped

working and gathered at the tables. Normally we would be eating the evening meal in shifts, I guess, since there are almost five hundred of us. But this was a special occasion because we were inaugurating the camp so we packed the tables fuller than usual. Off to one side, an older boy sat on a tree stump and played a weird instrument Xing said was an accordion, which pumped open and closed. The music was haunting and festive by turns, depending on what he playcd, and gave an air of ceremony to the proceedings.

It was cool to sit at a table I'd helped put up, to know how all its parts fitted together as I sat there. We'd brought all the boards for the tables from the old camp; even the screws that joined the parts together had been carefully labeled and packed and pulled out again when we arrived. Not even a nail went to waste in the camp. I liked how everything had value; I liked how careful people were with what other people had made.

In the middle of our table's long boards, the cooks' helpers set out baskets of bread and huge bowls of soup, steaming into the cooling air. Each of us had our own plate to eat off—actually not a plate but a rectangular slab of bamboo with a handle on one end. They called it a *trencher*. Sam and I were told we had to carve our initials in the side of our own trenchers, with a special design we invent to stand for ourselves. That way we'd always know whose was whose. Everyone has her own trencher and bowl and utensils, and we have to wash them after every meal and keep track of them and all that.

We served ourselves pieces of bread and ladled the

thick soup into our bowls. I wondered how they'd baked the bread—was there an oven set up already? I hadn't seen the kitchen area yet at all; a lot of the workings of the camp were still a mystery to me.

I picked up a spoon but Sam elbowed me. "Wait," he hissed. "We always have to wait for the food blessing. They usually sing it too."

Yet before the food blessing Xing stood up and spoke.

"Arriving here," she began, "to work and live with you is the culmination of many years of work for me. And so many years of anticipation."

She said she'd never expected a Cat Six to welcome her to the island and the camp, but that was the world we lived in—the only thing that wasn't surprising was that there was one surprise after another.

Then she asked Sam and me to stand. She told everyone who we were, and who our parents had been. When she finished speaking—it was like a eulogy for them—everyone clapped; it started with just a few people but soon everyone joined in, and people stood up and pushed the benches back so that some of them even fell over behind them.

All the people in the whole camp were clapping for my mother and father and for what once, long ago, they must have done.

Ψ

After dinner, when the dusk had settled into dark, we washed our trenchers and bowls where Xing showed us, in a basin beneath a tap, and set them to drip dry on a big rack woven together with what looked like rope and vines.

Xing went off in the direction of Kate's tent and Sam and LaTessa and I sat by the brook listening to the water and talking a bit. Or sorry, not LaTessa—that was her corporate label, I guess, not her real name at all, but I'm still getting used to it. Her real name's Fred. I kid you not. It's short for Frederica, the name she was born with. She says she was always a tomboy growing up—though she's very pretty, she only dressed all girly at the resort because it was her job to—and no one has ever called her Frederica, they just always called her Fred.

The camp doesn't do old-fashioned campfires too often, for obvious security and carbon-footprint reasons, but we do have some orangey-red solar lights we stick into the ground that are hard for planes and other surveillance equipment to pick up on. They don't have much of a footprint, as fuelfires would; they don't give off any heat, either, that I can tell. All they do is cast a gentle light on the underbrush, on the contours of tree trunks and the sides of tents.

In the distance the accordion had been retired but there was still music, this time from someone's tent—a sad song played on a string instrument. It was the evensong, Fred said—she'd once lived in a camp, briefly. Every night we would have evensong, music to thank the sun and praise the onset of the cool and healing night. It floated out onto the air and for a second I had the weird feeling it was taking me with it, that I was as fluid and light as the notes themselves, as movable and changing as waves of sound.

I felt a tap on my shoulder and jumped a bit.

It was Kate standing there, a flashlight in her hand. "I'd like to show you something."

We followed her through the camp and into a tunnel. There were no lights turned on inside—maybe this tunnel hadn't been wired yet, I don't know—so all we had was the spots of her flashlight and our headlamps bobbing in front of us. It was a wide hallway, and pretty flat underfoot, by lava-tube standards. A couple of twists and turns, and then there was enough light to see by coming from the room it opened into, so we switched off our lamps.

There were rows of narrow beds there, with curtains hanging beside them. The cloth of the curtains looked oddly familiar, and then I got it: they were made of the off-white, waffled cotton robes from the resort, the same ones we'd worn for healing and therapy sessions. They'd been cut up and stitched together.

I remarked on the recycled robes and Kate smiled, seeming pleased that I'd noticed the detail.

"This is our infirmary," she said. "It's where you'll come if you get a bug or break a leg. Though I have to warn you, you might find yourself sharing the space with a sick bird or a big lizard. It's happened before. We treat some of the animals here too."

We smiled politely. I was thinking, great, they have a place for health care, but is it really worth forging through darkness for? Could it not have waited till morning?

"We have three doctors," she went on, still walking

ahead of us between the rows of beds, "and then there are Aviva and four other nurses with good training. They work in shifts, so at any given time there's usually just one doctor and two nurses on duty."

The curtains could be pulled around the beds for privacy. Mostly no one was in them right now—we could tell because the curtains around empty beds were open—though I recognized the man with the hurt leg from the cave.

Back and back we went, to a curtain at the rear. Kate pulled it in toward the wall.

And there she was.

Our mother.

At first I thought she was dead and Kate had brought us her body—her eyes were closed and she was pale and completely unmoving.

I felt a shock that wasn't that far from anger, a kind of fierce impulse. Then I saw a bag of liquid hanging off a stand beside her, and the bag fed into a needle in her arm.

My stomach lurched and my hand flew up to my mouth. "How'd you do it? We thought—I was told—"

But I wasn't even listening to what Kate said, I was in a kind of panicky buzz. I leaned in close, I wanted to do something for her but had no idea what that might be.

Sam just stood beside me, gazing. He did appear almost happy, though, I thought in passing. For once.

"And our—our dad?" he asked.

I already knew in the pit of my stomach. For our father there hadn't been a save at the eleventh hour. It was clear from the empty bed beside her.

I didn't even look up at Kate, I really couldn't, just stared down at my mom's face. The cheekbones my dad had claimed I got from her.

"I'm sorry," said Kate.

"How did it go down?" asked Sam, trying to cover his disappointment.

"The Happiness Attendants had to induce comas in both of them, so they could meet the death tests. And he wasn't—he just wasn't able to pull through on his. As you know, he was almost a decade older than your mother. His system wasn't as resilient. He couldn't come back from it."

"Is she—she's still in a coma, then?" I asked.

"A medicated sleep. It'll be a long time till she can see or hear you."

I moved closer to my mother, after a minute of standing there rooted to the ground. It was almost like I was noticing everything *but* her—the red clay of the floor, with its uneven, raised patches, the lever on the side of the cot that would lift up the head part.

I leaned in close over her and touched her cheek and then laid my own cheek against hers.

It was warm.

Somehow that made her real, suddenly. I was tongue-tied and didn't know what to do or say; there was heat in my face, heat rushing through me.

"It will take time," said Kate. "You'll have to be very patient and just go on with your lives for a while, as though she isn't here at all. Because she's not, really—not right now. We have to bring her out of it slowly. And then her brain will need retraining, she'll need to be weaned off all the sunset pharms she was on. The pathways in her brain were literally reshaped by those drugs, and they'll have to be reshaped again. She may have to relearn some skills—relearn who she really is, in a way."

Sam and I both stood next to the cot, awkward, staring down at our mother's face, which was so pale white it almost looked blue. Underneath the thin blanket, her body seemed straight and formal, with the toes sticking up at the bottom. She might have been an ancient mummy or a lying-down statue of a saint.

"Kate," said Sam solemnly, "I don't know how we'll ever make it up to you. Well, I mean we can't."

"We can't," I whispered, with no breath behind the words.

And I remembered how my father had echoed all the time in his last days, those last days of not being himself. I remembered his song about the chariot of fire, and what he'd said about wanting the dinosaurs to come back.

I remembered him standing over the ocean and wishing it was still full of life.

"You will," said Kate.

Tears sprang into my eyes. In his own way our father had been so hopeful, I thought, even though he despaired. You could be full of hope and sadness at the same time, I thought. And I wanted to collect that feeling—how hope and sadness could live in one person.

We'd survived, the three of us. We'd gotten here.

And he was gone.

I outright cried then and wasn't even embarrassed. In fact I was almost proud. I stood there crying for my dad.

Ψ

When I was done with the emoting that used to mortify me, I realized Kate wasn't beside me anymore. She'd disappeared like smoke while I wasn't looking. Sam was wandering slowly around the room, staring at the pieces of equipment they had and talking to a couple of other patients who were there.

It was odd to look at my mom lying there and think of her the way Kate and Xing said she was, a hero first, admired by rebels, and then a disillusioned person who retreated, gave up, and went home and had us because she couldn't keep fighting.

Or maybe it hadn't happened in that order. I don't know.

And finally, of course, she hadn't been able to handle what the world was anymore. She turned into a victim, I'd been assuming, of service corps and other corporates whose downfall she'd once spent so much energy, and even some fingers, fighting for.

It was weird to consider walking away from the ideas I'd once had about her. Maybe she wasn't a hero *or* a victim. Maybe she was a person who first believed in something, and then just didn't anymore.

I wondered: what if it was less *what* you believed in that made the difference in your life than whether you believed at all?

Maybe belief is what makes the world glow.

After a while Sam found his way back to the bedside, where I was still gazing down at her eyes and mouth and cheeks—inert and lifeless-seeming as only a shut-down face can be, a small machine with no power. (I think I may have mouthed the words silently, like a crazy booze migrant. *Machine with no power.*) But Sam wasn't looking at me, and I snapped out of my trance finally.

"When she wakes up," he asked, "what do you think she'll say?"

I peered up and around us—at the ceilings, which were a dark-gray, sometimes dark-brown color, and stippled with lavacicles jutting down in irregular peaks and points. In a long row beside the cots, the bedside lamps were all perfectly round and gave off a phosphorescent blue light.

This was her new home, I thought—after the condo she said goodbye to for always. *Goodbye, everything.* After the hotel room with its fakeness and bright tropical flowers. After the small boats with the candles in them burning down to nothing, sailing away.

Now there was this room of silent beds laid out in rows under the thickness of magma. Like a tomb in a pyramid.

And she was one of the lucky ones.

My mind wandered to the ruins of the resort, to which I'd already heard them planning an expedition. They were going to look for salvage we could use. There was too much there, potentially, for them to waste the chance. It was the one good thing to come of the storm, I'd heard Rone say to someone else—the fact that there would be useful objects in the rubble, important building blocks for Athens. There could be tech, there could be furniture, appliances and hardware, wires and pipes of all kinds, even minor items like drywipes and blankets. And of course food and clothing.

All kinds of objects it might have taken us years to make or get on our own.

I wondered if I would have to go with the salvage team; I didn't want to, but I would if they asked me. What would we see there, in the ruins—people's bodies?

There'd have to be some bodies, after a storm like that. Not all of them would have been washed out to sea. I hoped my father's had, though. I hoped the ocean he loved had taken him back again.

And the kids, the kids that had been there. There hadn't been many, but still—there was a lot I didn't want to see, in those ruins.

But maybe, I thought, that was the price of living unmanaged. You had to be willing to look at what you didn't want to see.

I thought of the animals in their pens outside, the birds with crowns, the ancient prehistoric turtles that moved their heads like defective robots, these tufted anteater things with their long snaky tongues. There was the stream that ran through Athens, the trees growing away and away down the foothills and into the valleys in their bright-green splendor. A few hours' walk away there was the spray of the ocean's waves as they crashed against the rocks and the mist that rose up.

This would be an unmanaged life. From now on, we had the others but we didn't have our pills. And I was less scared than I had been before, and more excited. I didn't believe pharma was bad all by itself—it was medicine, some of it, and I knew it could help us when we needed it. But it had been used against us, I saw that clearly now, and what we didn't need it for was to face the world every day.

Sam had been right. I'd been flat for some time, no pharms at all, and more and more the separate parts of the world shone at their edges.

My spirits were lifting.

The best part of it all was the rawness of life without pharms—how exposed I was to the things that might happen but, in exchange, how much more this felt like living.

"Maybe not right away, but in the long run," I said, "I think she'll be glad. That we didn't let her go. Don't you?"

We stood there looking down at her—at the moons of her closed eyes, her poor claw of a hand lying on top of the blanket. She *didn't* look her age, I thought: she and my father had been right, when we were all in the elevator and they were laughing hysterically. She still had a kind of beauty to her, even if it was, at the moment, like the beauty of stone.

One day maybe the stone will move again.

"I bet she'll see the world in a new light," said Sam.

After that we went out from under the mountain and left our mother to her long sleep.

P.S.: My Final Bulletin to the Capsule

I guess you already know, my astronaut friend, we never made it into space.

We took a step or two, though. Some guys in white went dancing on the moon—my lots-of-greats-grandmother watched them on a television from her crib, shaking a rattle as they made their giant leaps.

And later robot probes were sent to Jupiter.

But in person we never got beyond our own backyard in this huge spiral galaxy. As it turned out, we never took a spin around the planets in airships with round windows. We never headed for the stars.

We did it in books and vids and games, though. We did it in our dreams. It may be for pretend, but that doesn't mean that out there in the universe there *isn't* somebody watching. There are too many worlds, too many galaxies, too many stars for us to be alone. Somewhere there must be other homes.

These days I have this place to think about, this Earth and how to save it. But I still like to think about the faraway neighbors we must have. Sure, maybe they look a little bit different from me. Like you, spacegirl or spaceboy—maybe *you* even look different from how I pictured you at first, my cosmonaut.

Maybe you're not so similar to me. Maybe you're not young, not what I already know as beautiful.

Maybe you're not even, technically, human.

The important thing is that you're a friend, and like me, like all of us, you're traveling. You're making your way past all the things you had to leave behind—you're passing unknown planets and unfamiliar asteroid belts, shimmering clouds of interstellar dust. You move across the diamond-and-black velvet of space and stars toward a strange and beautiful new country.

If you could see me, you would smile and wave—and at my brother too. You're someone we'd both be glad to know, even if we've never known anyone like you before.

One day I'll copy this journal into a face and send my words into the infinite ether. And one day you may find these words and take the time to read them.

The only thing left to say is this: My astronaut friend, I still believe in you.

So please, believe in me too. Believe in *us*, won't you? We made our mistakes, fell when our wings melted. But we did other things too. We saw that the world we'd been given was beautiful, we tried to understand that beauty. Some people even gave their lives for what they believed was true, and a few of those sacrifices were made into stories and legends.

But far more of people's sacrifices went unheard of, passing unnoticed into the dark.

I know we can be worthy of what we were born into, I *know* we can do better. I swear, we'll never stop trying, we'll never ever give up. We'll hope and hope and be brave, right through the end of time.

LYDIA MILLET is the author of eight novels for adults as well as a story collection *Love in Infant Monkeys* (2009), which was a finalist for the Pulitzer Prize. Her first book for middle-grade readers, *The Fires Beneath the Sea,* was named one of *Kirkus'* Best Children's Books of 2011, and, along with the second in the series, *The Shimmers in the Night* (2012), was a Junior Library Guild selection. *Pills and Starships* is her first book for young adults.